It's everything but *business as usual.*

INK

A Love Story on 7th and Main

Emmie Elliot hadn't expected to come back to Metlin, California. She definitely didn't expect to stay. She returned to her childhood home with a mission: sell the building that housed her grandmother's bookstore and move on with her life.

But life doesn't always go according to plan.

To reopen her grandmother's bookshop, Emmie will need a hook. She'll need a strategy. She'll need an... Ox?

Miles Oxford doesn't have much interest in quiet bookstore owners. He's a tattoo artist without a space to work, and the last thing he wants is to get involved with anyone after his last disaster of a relationship. Work and pleasure don't mix for Ox, but since he doesn't have any interest in the cute girl with the bold business proposal, he should be safe from any awkward complications, right?

She sells ink. He tattoos it. Unusual? Yes. But a bookshop/tattoo studio might be the ticket for both Emmie and Ox to find success on their own terms. As long as they keep their attention focused on business.

Just on business.

"...a wonderful and engrossing story of seizing chances even when they are not what you originally planned."
—RT Book Reviews

INK

A LOVE STORY ON 7TH AND MAIN

ELIZABETH HUNTER

INK: A Love Story on 7th and Main
Copyright © 2017
by Elizabeth Hunter
ISBN: 978-1-941674284

This is a work of fiction. Names, characters, places, and incidents are the products of the author's imagination or are used fictitiously. Any resemblance to actual persons, living or dead, business establishments, events, or locales is entirely coincidental.

Cover: Damonza
Editing: Anne Victory
Formatting: Elizabeth Hunter

PRAISE FOR ELIZABETH HUNTER

Elizabeth Hunter's books are delicious and addicting, like the best kind of chocolate. She hooked me from the first page, and her stories just keep getting better and better. Paranormal romance fans won't want to miss this exciting author!

THEA HARRISON, NYT BESTSELLING AUTHOR

Developing compelling and unforgettable characters is a real Hunter strength as she proves yet again with Kyra and Leo. Another amazing novel by a master storyteller!

RT MAGAZINE

This book more than lived up to the expectations I had, in fact it blew them out of the water.

THIS LITERARY LIFE

A towering work of romantic fantasy that will captivate the reader's mind and delight their heart. Elizabeth Hunter's ability to construct such a sumptuous narrative time and time again is nothing short of amazing.

THE READER EATER

For bookworms and artists,
farmers and ranchers,
mechanics and chefs,
and everyone who dreams.

CHAPTER ONE

EMMIE ELLIOT LASTED three breaths in the old bookshop, her measured exhalations stirring dust motes that danced in the afternoon light streaming in from the large display windows that looked over Main Street. She backed out the front door and turned her back on Metlin Books, staring at the lazy midday traffic driving south on 7th Avenue. Then she bent over, braced her hands on her knees, and let her auburn hair fall, shielding her face from the afternoon sun.

Daisy walked out of the corner shop and came to stand beside her. "What's going on? You're even paler than usual."

"I can't do it."

"Can't do what?"

Emmie straightened. "I can't sell the shop."

Daisy's eyes went wide. "I thought you and your gran—"

"Yeah." Emmie took a deep breath, clearing the dust from her lungs. "I know."

What are you doing, Emmie?

She had no idea.

She'd spent her whole life trying to get away from this town. The bookstore was her grandmother's. Sure, she'd grown up in it, and sure, she worked in a bookstore in San Francisco, but that was just temporary. She was just doing that until something happened. Something bigger. More important. More... something.

Emmie was twenty-seven and still waiting for something big to happen. She had a job she tolerated, an apartment she loved. No husband, no boyfriend, a mother she barely spoke to. She didn't even have a cat.

Her assets in the world consisted of a newish car, a very small inheritance from her grandma Betsy, a circle of carefully chosen friends, and a three-unit retail building on the corner of Main Street and 7th Avenue, right in the heart of Metlin, a sleepy town in the middle of Central California.

She and her grandmother had talked about it a year ago, when they knew the cancer wasn't going into remission. Emmie was supposed to sell the building and use the proceeds as a nest egg for...

They'd never really talked about that part.

"What's going on, Em? What are you thinking?" Daisy frowned and twisted a lock of dark wavy hair back in the bun on top of her head. It was afternoon, but she was still wearing her apron from baking that morning. With her tan skin, dark eyes, and retro apron, Daisy looked like an updated Latina June Cleaver if you didn't notice the tattoos at her wrists.

Her friend Tayla had offered to accompany her from San Francisco, but Emmie had refused. Emmie was taking a full two weeks off work from Bay City Books, but Tayla worked at a big accounting firm and couldn't afford to take the time off. She'd never been to Metlin and had no desire to visit. Tayla was a city girl to her bones.

It's fine, Emmie had told her. *It's not like I have any reason to stay. My mom cleaned out my grandma's apartment. I'll visit Daisy and Spider, sign papers to put the place on the market, and leave.*

Emmie straightened her button-down blouse and played with

the buttons on the sleeve of her cardigan. She wasn't dressed for Metlin; she was dressed for an upscale bookshop in Union Square. If anyone from her childhood were to pass by, they would have a hard time putting Emmie's sleek hair and tidy, professional appearance together with the rumpled girl who'd spent most of her life hiding behind a book.

She didn't belong in Metlin anymore. She never had. She'd always wanted a bigger life. A more important life around people who liked music and art and travel, not farmers and mechanics and ranchers.

Daisy said, "I know you must have sentimental attachment to the building, but I'm not sure you realize—"

"How bad it was?" Emmie picked at a thread on one of her buttons, twisting it between her thumb and forefinger. "I know how bad it was. Grandma was completely up-front with me."

Emmie had no illusions about the state of Metlin Books. The shop was barely hanging on. The only thing her grandma'd had going for her was that she owned the building, the apartment above it, and rented to two successful neighbors, a family hardware business and Café Maya, Daisy's restaurant.

She walked over and sat on the cast-iron bench in front of the bookstore windows, kicking at the doggie water dish chained to the bench. The dish that had remained dry since her grandmother had passed six months before. "Bookstores are not a good bet."

"Not generally, no."

"She told me not to be noble." Emmie eyed the water dish again. Then she took the water bottle out of her purse and dumped the contents in the bowl. "We had a plan. Sell the shop with provisions for you and Ethan—"

"Leave me and Ethan out of it," Daisy said. "I loved your grandma, but I think I can speak for Ethan—"

"Speak for me how?" Ethan Vasquez, owner of Main Street Hardware, set down the A-frame sign advertising daily deals and walked toward Daisy and Emmie. "Em, you all right?"

Daisy kept talking. "We both loved Betsy, but this is your life and inheritance, so don't worry about us."

"What's going on?" Ethan and Daisy hovered over her.

Daisy straightened. "Emmie's not sure about selling the shop."

"Great!"

"No," Daisy said. "Not great. This was not the plan."

And all of Emmie's friends knew how much Emmie liked a plan. She was famous for them. Emmie would plan a night out three days in advance and email a detailed schedule to everyone "so they were on the same page." She didn't do spontaneous. The idea of returning to Metlin permanently was giving her heart palpitations.

You're waiting, a little voice in her head whispered. *What are you waiting for?*

Ethan crossed his arms over his barrel chest and let out a long breath. "You know I can't be unbiased on this one."

"So stay out of it."

"I *am* staying out of it." He scratched his beard thoughtfully. "That's why I'm reminding her I can't be unbiased."

Emmie looked up and took a deep breath. "Don't be unbiased. I want your opinion."

"A new owner is likely to kick me and Dad out," he said. "Just when I'm turning things around. You know that. Our shop is huge, and space on Main Street is at a premium these days. A new owner would likely split our store in half and make double what we're paying now. So of course I want you to stay." He crouched down. "Metlin's different, Emmie. It's not the same town you left."

"That I can agree with," Daisy said.

"And I know the store needs work," Ethan continued, "but me and my dad would help you out. Anything you need. We're free labor after all the favors Betsy did for us over the years. You know that, right?"

Ethan's big brown eyes pleaded with her. Emmie looked past him to the new paint on his store, the fresh awning, the racks of vegetable starts for backyard gardens. Main Street Hardware had been flailing until Ethan came back from college four years ago and revamped his family business.

Now, instead of depending on the dwindling business of the retirement crowd, Main Street Hardware appealed to young do-it-yourselfers in their late twenties like Ethan and his buddies who were buying the old Craftsman cottages south of downtown and fixing them up. Ethan led workshops on container gardening, and his dad taught plasterwork and hardwood-floor-refinishing courses.

Beyond the hardware store, Café Maya bustled with midday customers. It was a narrow café and bakery started by Daisy's grandmother Maya, who'd come from Oaxaca and started the restaurant with determination and a treasure trove of recipes. Daisy's mother had modernized the menu, and Daisy had added a bakery. Café Maya was a Metlin institution and business had remained solid.

Beyond Emmie's building, stretching west, sat the rest of downtown. Sitting at the base of the Sierra Nevada mountains, Metlin had never been big enough to attract attention from any of the big chains. It had only ever had one bookstore, Metlin Books. And for as long as anyone could remember, it had been run by the Elliot family. Emmie's great-grandfather had bought the building and started a book and toy store. Eventually the toys left and her grandmother had focused on the books. Emmie's mom, despite her bookish roots, had never been a reader and lived an itinerant life as a working musician. She was happy, but Metlin wasn't her home.

But for Emmie—growing up in the fishbowl of Metlin—the bookshop had been her home, her refuge, and the gateway to a much larger world.

"I have an apartment in San Francisco," she said quietly. "Friends. A life. A job."

Ethan asked, "Aren't you working in a bookstore up there?"

"Yeah."

He frowned. "But you *own* a bookstore here. Why on earth would you live in San Francisco, pay God knows what in rent, and get paid to work at someone else's business when you could own your own business here doing exactly the same thing?"

Daisy said, "Back off."

"She knows I'm right." He stood and pointed at Emmie. "You know I'm right."

Emmie's stayed silent. She didn't deal with confrontation well, but Ethan wasn't entirely wrong. How many times had she tried to change something at the bookstore she worked at in the city, only to be told "that wasn't the way things were done" at Bay City Books?

Still, she hesitated. "I manage a store. I don't know if I could run a business. My grandma wasn't like your dad. She didn't give me a lot of responsibility in the shop. I know nothing about book-keeping or—"

"You'd figure it out," he said. "You're one of the smartest people I know. You helped me with my place when I was drowning."

She shrugged. "You would have come up with those ideas on your own with enough time."

"I doubt it. You have a great brain for marketing. You know what people like now. How to put everything online. How to find the right customers."

Daisy shook her head. "Books are a tough business, Ethan. I know exactly how much Betsy was making with this place, and rent from your place and my café was the only thing paying her bills. Competing with online retailers—"

"Can't be any tougher than competing with the megamart hardware stores," Ethan said. "Emmie knows—"

"Emmie knows"—Emmie stood and cut them both off—"she needs to spend some time thinking about this."

Daisy's mouth fought off a smile. "Emmie also knows she

needs to stop talking in third person, right? Because it's obnoxious."

"Whatever you do," Ethan said, "don't talk to Asshole Adrian until you've made up your mind."

Emmie frowned. "Adrian? Adrian from high school?"

"Yeah, Adrian Saroyan. He's in real estate now. And he's an asshole."

Daisy tried to shove Ethan away. "Ignore him. You know he never liked Adrian."

"Nobody likes Adrian." Ethan let Daisy shove him. "You were the only one who liked him, Em."

"Me and the female half of my high school class." Emmie watched Daisy—a foot shorter than Ethan—shove the big man back to his shop.

Ethan repositioned his sign. "He's a dipshit and an asshole."

Daisy said, "He stole your girlfriend; that's the only reason you hate him."

"That's not the only reason," Ethan muttered. "Just one of them."

Emmie left them bickering and walked back into the bookshop. She stood in the mosaic-tiled entryway and examined it with critical eyes.

Pros: She owned it, free and clear. It had a recognizable name and a good location. It was a beautiful space with huge built-in shelves and custom woodwork her giant bookstore in San Francisco tried to imitate but never really could. Metlin Books had history. Charm. And a two-bedroom apartment over the shop. If she lived here, she would have no commute and no rent.

Cons: Profits under her grandmother had been pretty much zero. The only real income was from renting the rest of the building, and that just paid the bills. The bookshop was a ton of work with a very small profit margin. She'd be solely responsible for it. There would be no vacation days accrued. No retirement plan. No one else paying the bills. No one to call in sick to.

But it's mine.

Yes, it was. Emmie walked around the shop, rifling through the stacks of used books her grandmother had collected. Most of the new inventory was so old she could never sell it at cover price. She'd be starting over.

Betsy had stocked lots of romances, but nothing modern. There was a nice stack of vintage Harlequins she might be able to sell online to a collector. She needed far more new names. Romance ran bookstores. She'd have to get an updated selection and figure out how to buy from self-published authors who made up so many of the new writers these days. It was something she'd pushed for at Bay City, but the owners were complete snobs about self-publishing.

The shop had a good mystery section, but it leaned toward cozies. Her grandmother hadn't cared for thrillers or any dark psychology.

Hardly any literary fiction or poetry, but in Metlin that was probably a safe call.

Nonfiction was in dire need of updating. Judging from the traffic at Ethan's store, gardening manuals and idea books would probably sell well, as would interior design and home-improvement stuff.

With growing tourist traffic from the national park, local history and outdoor guides could be a winner.

Emmie wandered across the shop and looked out the windows just as a trio of motorcycles revved their engines at the intersection of 7th and Main. Emmie watched two guys in an animated discussion in front of the custom-car-upholstery shop and listened to the buzz of music and voices from Ice House Brews that sat catty-corner to Metlin Books at the intersection. Directly across from her on Main was Bombshell Tattoos. Beyond it, a specialty cigar and smoking club. A couple with vividly dyed hair and heavy ink left the tattoo shop hand in hand and walked past the T-shirt shop on Main headed toward Top Shelf Comics and Games.

What books would that couple read? How about the guys in front of the car shop? Graphic novels? Steampunk? Auto history?

Emmie watched from behind her windows as a trio of women dragged a giant mirror from one of the antique shops farther down 7th, laughing as they tried to fit it in the back of a battered pickup truck. Decorating books. DIY manuals.

Across the street, a graffiti-style mural decorated the front of an art-supply store next to an auto-body shop. Art history books? Political science?

Ethan was right. Metlin was changing. The industrial and the traditional were colliding and creating something odd and new and more than a little cool. And Emmie realized the bookshop— her bookshop—was sitting right in the middle of it all.

Maybe she hadn't belonged in the old Metlin, but times changed. Towns changed. People changed.

This was not in the plan, her logical side said.

Maybe the plan needs to change.

Emmie pulled out her phone. Her finger shook as she touched Tayla's number and waited for her best friend to pick up.

"Hey!" she answered. "Did you get everything signed? How's Daisy?"

Emmie took a deep breath, stirring the dust again. "I have an idea. And it might be crazy or it might be amazing."

"If it's a really good idea, it'll be both. And it might also involve handcuffs or Silly String."

She blinked. "Silly String?"

"Do you really want to know? You sound weird."

"I didn't sign any papers to sell the shop."

"Okay...?"

"I think you should quit your job, move down to Metlin with me, and help me reopen the bookshop."

Tayla didn't say a word.

Emmie squeezed her eyes shut. "I know it sounds nuts, but you can have free rent."

Her best friend remained silent.

"Tayla, please say something."

"Maybe it's because I caught one of the senior partners staring at my boobs *again* today, but I am actually considering this."

Emmie tried not to jump up and down with excitement.

"That's not a yes. Or a no," Tayla said. "But... maybe?"

"I'll take maybe."

"Tell you what, it's Friday. I'll catch the train tomorrow morning," Tayla said. "I can't guarantee anything, but I want to see this hick town you claim to hate but now suddenly want me to move to."

"I'll meet you at the station."

"Is this a result of valley fever?" Tayla asked. "I've read about that, you know."

"I don't have valley fever."

"Isn't that something someone with valley fever would say?"

Emmie squeezed her eyes shut. "Tayla, I can't explain it. I just think it might be awesome. Or nuts. But you know how you were getting on my case last month for always being cautious and never taking chances?"

"Yep."

"This..." Emmie turned around in the empty shop. "This is a chance."

CHAPTER TWO

SHE STARED at the pictures of shiny espresso machines. "The cheap ones are over three thousand dollars. Forget it. This is a crazy idea."

Tayla flipped the catalog shut. "You're not buying a commercial espresso machine. You'll get a nice pot or a single-serve thing and a suggested donation box. Otherwise you need a food-service license, and you don't want to get into that mess. You don't want to sell coffee, you want to sell books."

Daisy was measuring the tape they'd put on the floor and making notes on a Post-it. "I think my aunt has a couch this size she's trying to get rid of. It'll need to be re-covered, but I can help with that. You might even want to do a slipcover so you can change it out seasonally."

Tayla pointed at Daisy. "Great idea."

Emmie nodded. "Presentation is everything. Getting people in the door is the first step."

"I've seen the windows you did at Bay City." Tayla McKinnon spun in the middle of the room, her pink-striped skirt flaring as she turned. She'd dyed her brown hair platinum blond and had a very "Marilyn" look going at the moment with her fair complexion and bright red lips. "And this is a much cooler space with better foot traffic. You have a talent for windows. If you translate that to the displays here, you're going to attract a lot of customers."

"I'd need to build some kind of platform to elevate the display area."

Daisy said, "Ethan and his dad could help with that. They offered, remember?"

Emmie took deep breaths and tried to calm her racing heart.

This wasn't insane. This was good business. This wasn't a lark, this was a solid plan.

Tayla had spent all morning at the shop, looking over the accounts with Daisy. Then she and Emmie had roughed out a budget that increased the rent a reasonable amount for both Café Maya and the hardware store, giving Emmie an increased operating budget for reopening the bookstore. If Emmie sold her car and some of her furniture in San Francisco, she'd have a chunk of money for some initial start-up costs to freshen up the store and buy some new inventory. Since Emmie would be living over the shop, she wouldn't need her car to commute.

Of course, that left her stranded in Metlin.

Completely.

Utterly.

Stranded.

"There's always the train," Emmie said under her breath.

"What?" Tayla looked away from the windows.

"Nothing!" Emmie walked over to Daisy and held down the end of the tape measure. "What about here?"

"Big floor pillows would work until you can find some chairs that don't break the bank. I could help you make some bean bags. Weren't you talking about doing a children's story hour?"

"One of the best ways to get new people in," Emmie said. "Story hour at Bay City is always a hit. You sell kids' books and a lot of paperbacks to the parents."

"Got it."

Emmie perched on the desk her grandmother had used as a sales counter and watched the foot traffic on Main Street. "I think the key in Metlin is creating a community. This town has a ton of young families. Story hour might rope the kids in, but if we give parents a cool place to hang out, they'll come back."

"Would you restart the book club?"

"She only had one?" Emmie asked. "Bay City has three. There's a YA club, a romance club, and a literary fiction club. They also did a special book-to-film thing every time there was a big movie opening that was based on a book."

"That's a great idea," Tayla said. "Looking at online retailers, the highest-ranked books definitely seem to be the ones that get film or TV adaptations."

"A YA club would be fun," Daisy said. "You're pretty close to the high school. If you did something after school, I bet you'd get a lot of kids looking for a place to hang out."

"One thing you definitely have is space." Daisy cast her eyes at the mostly empty 7th Avenue side of the store. "What's the plan for over there?"

"Grandma always talked about putting tables over there, doing homework clubs or craft days or something, but she never followed through."

"What about another renter?"

Tayla had taken out her yellow legal pad. "Another renter means more income. You could definitely use that."

"I don't know." Emmie took a deep breath and blew it out. "I hate the idea of putting up a wall here, but there is a separate entrance on 7th Avenue, so I guess—"

"Not a wall. Just do a divider of some kind," Daisy said. "Or a combination business where you share space. You could cross-promote that way. Maybe a craft store. The yarn shop went out of business. You could do Yarn and Yarns, crafting and bookshop." Daisy giggled. "Okay, that's pretty bad."

Tayla walked over to stand next to them as they looked at the space. "A café is the obvious choice, but besides Café Maya, there's more than a few already open on Main Street. Opening another wouldn't fill a current gap in the neighborhood."

"Yeah, don't cut into my business," Daisy growled. "I don't want to have to get rough."

"Ha ha." Emmie tapped her foot. "I don't want food service here. Coffee is one thing—that's pretty low labor—but a café is a lot more work. What about a boutique?"

"What kind of boutique?" Tayla asked.

"I have no idea."

"A bar?" Daisy said. "Books and bars kind of go together, right?"

"I researched liquor licenses in Metlin when I was coming down on the train," Tayla said. "It's not the easiest process."

"And then you have the food-service thing again," Emmie said. "No, if I'm going to have another business, it should be retail. What goes with books?"

"Wine."

"Knitting."

"Chocolate."

"Cats!"

Emmie turned to both of them. "You're not helpful."

Just then a voice drew Emmie's attention from outside. Someone on the street was shouting loud enough to make it through the thick windows of the bookshop.

"It's drama girl," Emmie said.

Daisy glanced outside. "Not again."

Tayla and Emmie walked over to the windows and stared at the scene unfolding on the other side of Main Street. A muscular Caucasian man with intricate black tattoos had his arms crossed over his chest while a petite white woman with flame-red hair and a figure-hugging dress wagged her finger at him. Every now and then, Emmie could hear the man's low voice, but she couldn't make it out. The redhead, on the other hand, was clear.

"Every time, Ox. Those bitches come in and you—"

He cut her off with a waved hand and an inaudible comeback.

"I don't care!"

Daisy stood beside them. "I swear this happens every week. Every. Single. Week it's something new. She just needs to break up with him. Or he does with her."

Emmie had noticed them both before. She didn't recognize either from high school, but the town had grown, and lots of new people had moved in. Some people her age were familiar from high school, but an equal number were transplants or had grown up in smaller farming towns around the growing city.

The woman was hard to miss. She was beautiful and glamorous and usually dressed in skinny jeans and halter tops that made her look like a rock star. The guy... Well, he was equally hard to miss. A strong jaw and a killer smile. She'd noticed the smile because it was rare but made his piercing expression more human. She'd seen him walking across the street to Maya's shop more than once. He held doors and talked to old ladies. She didn't know who he was, but in the week she'd been working at the shop, he'd become Emmie's favorite scenery on Main Street.

"Who are they?" Tayla asked. Her eyes were wide and she was smiling. "Give me all the dirt."

"Ginger and Ox. Miles Oxford. I went to school with his sister, and his mom was friends with Betsy, Em. He grew up outside town. Ranching family. Ginger owns Bombshell and he's a tattoo artist at her shop. They've been on and off for a year and a half or so? But look at him. He's a good-looking guy, right? The girls love coming to him for ink, and it drives Ginger nuts. Which is stupid, you know? I mean, if I got crazy every time Spider put a butterfly on a college girl's butt, they'd have to lock me up."

"And we wouldn't be friends," Emmie said. "Which would be tragic."

Daisy laughed. "Your butterflies aren't on your butt."

Emmie felt her face heat up.

"Wait," Tayla said. "You have a tattoo? When did you get a tattoo? How did I not know this?"

Daisy said, "You've never seen her tattoo? It's huge."

"Little Miss Cardigan over there?" Tayla asked. "I don't think I've even seen her bare arms. She's notoriously modest."

"You act like it's a bad thing," Emmie said.

"Her tattoo is beautiful," Daisy said. "Spider's been working—"

"Not important right now." Emmie leaned closer to the glass. Whatever heat had been flaring between Ginger and Ox had morphed into heat of a different kind because she was leaning into his chest and their lips were locked together. Emmie felt a spike of jealousy.

Why couldn't she find a guy who kissed her like that?

"They are *hot*," Tayla said. "Smoking. I'd let him ink my butt too."

And the tattoo artist would probably thank her. Tayla was a full-figured knockout who drew men like magnets. She wasn't only a bookkeeper but a minor celebrity on social media where she ran a plus-sized-fashion blog. She had confidence that Emmie couldn't match and way better fashion sense. Emmie only dressed decently when Tayla picked her clothes.

Daisy nodded knowingly. "You can tell he's a good kisser."

The man knows how to take his time. Emmie couldn't stop the small sigh.

Just then his head lifted and turned toward the bookshop, locking eyes on the three faces in the window. Daisy waved. Tayla blew a kiss. Emmie whirled away and walked back to the counter.

"Can we keep talking about the shop instead of my hot neighbors?"

Tayla pursed her lips. "You think he's hot?"

"Of course I do. I'm not blind." Emmie flipped open the coffee supply catalog again and flipped through pages of machines she couldn't afford.

"What do you mean, of course? He is so not your type."

Daisy said, "I'd have to agree. You usually go for the scruffy hipster-type with tweed jackets and bow ties."

"Bow ties are cool," Emmie said. "And Metlin is too hot for tweed most of the year. And isn't having a type narrow-minded? Can we talk about coffee *please?*"

Daisy planted herself on the bar stool by the register. "We are returning to this conversation at a later date. For now, let's decide what other business you can put on the other side. I vote craft shop. The yarn selection at Tompkins is abysmal since Trudy took over. She's clearly not a knitter."

Tayla said, "You really are the retro homebody, Donna Reed–type you present yourself as, aren't you?"

"I'll have you know my vegetable garden kicks ass," Daisy said. "And I will make you weep with my baked goods."

Emmie added, "Ask her about her skimpy-apron collection sometime."

Daisy glared, but she was too tiny and adorable to be threatening. "I knew I shouldn't have let you and Spider drink together."

"Bad girl, Emmie," Tayla said with a smile. "This hometown version I'm getting to know is fun. City Emmie is all business and sweatpants and early nights in. Metlin Emmie owns a pair of jeans."

Emmie shot her a rueful smile. "If I'm going to be in Metlin, I can wear jeans."

"Now we just need to get you a pair that fits," Tayla said.

Emmie tapped her notepad. "I think the craft shop is a good idea, but I want to keep an open mind. We shouldn't rush into anything. For now I think I'll put a play area over there for kids at story time. A children's boutique might be a good idea too. Does downtown have one of those yet?"

Daisy shook her head. "No, and it's not a bad idea, but you'd have to find someone—"

The bell over the door cut her off and a tall, lanky black man with a goatee and a pair of horn-rimmed glasses walked in. His wide smile brought a wave of recognition to Emmie.

"Jeremy?"

"I heard you were back," he said, opening his arms. "I could hardly believe it when Daisy told me."

Emmie ran over and hugged him. Jeremy Allen was one of the few boys who hadn't made her hide in high school. He'd been gawky, shy, and extraordinarily kind. She pulled back and looked up at the much taller man in front of her. "You got taller."

He smiled wider. "Just a little."

"And way handsome." She tapped the tightly curled hair on his chin. "This looks cool."

A hint of pink touched the top of Jeremy's cheeks. "I think I remember you teasing me about the beard a few times."

"Did I? I was a fool. Clearly you were ahead of the curve." Emmie pulled back and waved Tayla over. "Tayla, this is one of the few people I liked in high school. I was under the impression that he'd fled town like me, so this is a surprise. Jeremy, this is my best friend from San Francisco, Tayla McKinnon."

"Miss Tayla." Jeremy held out his hand and his eyes lit up as they swept over her. "I am charmed."

Tayla took his hand and looked him up and down. "As am I. Where was Emmie hiding you?"

"I could ask her the same thing."

The flirt is strong with this pair. Emmie tried not to roll her eyes. Jeremy had been shy, but he'd always loved the girls. Clearly he'd grown into his natural charm.

"Hey!" Daisy kicked his foot. "I'm here too."

"And you are still as wonderful as when I saw you this morning." Jeremy leaned over and kissed the top of Daisy's head. "Did you make my pie?"

Daisy rolled her eyes. "Jeremy opened up the comic and

gaming shop across the street last year, and ever since he's come in for coffee and a cinnamon bun in the morning, then put in his pie request for the day."

Emmie asked, "Does that work?"

Jeremy turned and batted his lashes at Daisy. "Is there a blueberry cream pie waiting for me?"

Daisy smiled ruefully. "Yes."

Jeremy turned back to Emmie. "It works."

"I only take your requests because you have good taste."

"Wrong." Jeremy shot a smile back to Tayla. "I have *great* taste."

Tayla raised an eyebrow at Emmie. "Oh, he's good."

"He's definitely improved his technique over the years. This is not high school Jeremy." She gestured around the shop. "I'd offer you a place to sit, but we don't have one yet."

"Are you reopening the bookstore?" Jeremy leaned against a wall. "I'm not gonna lie, I've missed it."

"I'm going to give it a shot," Emmie said. "Your shop is comics and games, right?"

"More games than comics, but we do carry some graphic novels and some of the more popular stuff, especially if there's a gaming tie-in, so we might have some overlap, but not much."

"Geek chic?" Tayla asked.

Jeremy shot her a broad smile. "I was a geek way before it was chic. It's a good climate for comics and games right now. Lots more people from the college are staying in town because the job market is good and housing is still pretty affordable if you're looking for fixer-uppers. Lots more people commuting online to the Bay Area and LA too. I sell games, but I do tournaments and host club stuff too. That brings a lot of people in."

"I heard you were in LA."

"I was until my pop got sick," Jeremy said. "You know how that is."

"How's he doing?"

Jeremy shrugged. "He's a cranky old bastard because he's got to use a walker since he broke his hip, but other than that, he's in good shape. I'm living on the second floor of his place over on Ash. You taking over the apartment here?"

"Yeah. Your parents?"

"Still up in the mountains. They love it even with the snow in the winter. I love it when there isn't any snow and I can climb."

Emmie said, "Jeremy's mom and dad bought this cool old cabin on the lake when we were in high school and fixed it up over the years. Now they live there full time."

"Living off my labor," Jeremy said to Tayla. "But I do have visiting rights. You'll have to come up for the boat parade at Christmas. It's beautiful."

"Am I invited too?" Emmie asked.

"If you bring your cute friends."

"Just my cute friends?" Emmie asked.

Jeremy walked over to her. "I have not met a woman in the world who wasn't cute as sin in her own way, Em." He gave her a sideways hug. "I gotta get back to work. I am happy as hell you're moving back to Metlin. Come over anytime. I'd love to show you the shop."

"It's a relief to see you," she said, hugging him back. "I was sure everyone other than Daisy and Spider would be gone."

Jeremy smiled and walked to the door. "Towns change. People do too. Glad you're giving us a chance." He opened the door, then nodded at Tayla and Daisy. "Ladies."

"Nice to meet you," Tayla said.

"You know the pleasure was mine."

Tayla winked. "I know."

"Brother." Daisy rolled her eyes. "Jeremy, I'll set aside a couple of pieces of the blueberry cream for you and your pop."

He blew her a kiss before he shut the door behind him.

Tayla went to the register and started tapping a pencil on the wooden counter. "I have to say, this town gets more attractive every day."

CHAPTER THREE

IT WAS Sunday and the whole of downtown Metlin was quiet as Emmie boxed up books in the back office. She heard the bell over the door ring. "Tayla? I'm back in the office. Do you think we could sell this vintage pregnancy manual that recommends women stick to wine and beer instead of hard alcohol? Or would we end up getting sued?"

"Uh... it's not Tayla." The deep voice echoed in the near-empty shop.

Emmie immediately went on alert, grabbing the thick ring of keys sitting next to her. Metlin was a safe town, but you could never be too careful. "Who's there?"

"It's Adrian Saroyan. I'm a realtor, and Daisy Villalobos—"

"Adrian?" Emmie's eyes went wide.

"Hi. Yeah... uh, Emmie?"

"Gimme a sec!" Adrian Saroyan was in her shop? She looked down at her clothes. Dirty jeans with a book T-shirt and a cardigan. Of course. Her I LIKE BIG BOOKS AND I CANNOT LIE T-shirt had large patches of dust on it and the cardigan had a ripped pocket. She was a mess. Emmie stood and tried to tuck her flat hair back into something that wasn't a messy bun, but...

Yeah, it was just gonna be a messy bun.

She walked down the hall and turned the corner just as Adrian was walking farther into the shop. They nearly ran into each other. Emmie put a hand on her chest, letting out a small gasp and probably smearing even more dust over her already dirty shirt.

"Oh! Hey. Hi," she said. "I was just cleaning. In the back."

"I'm sorry to interrupt." Adrian Saroyan, former high school soccer star and nerd-girl fantasy had aged well.

Because of course he had.

"Is now a good time to talk," he continued over her silence, "or should I make an appointment?"

"It's fine. I'm fine. You're fine. I mean, you're fine to come and talk to me now. At this time. It's a good time for me." Emmie cleared her throat and sneezed, nearly at the same time. Her hand still over her mouth, she realized that shaking the hand Adrian held out was a very, very bad idea.

"Are you okay?" He frowned at her.

"I'm just going to..." She motioned to the back. "Bathroom. Hands. Give me a second."

"Okay, no problem." He was smiling.

Of course he was smiling. He was gorgeous, and she was still a walking disaster.

Emmie quickly walked to the bathroom down the hall, washed her hands, and wiped the smudge of dirt from between her eyes. Poorly timed the sneeze/cough might have been, but at least she had time to compose herself.

Adrian Saroyan was one of those boys that Emmie hadn't wanted to like in high school. He was too handsome and too popular and too smart. Everyone loved him, so Emmie wanted to hate him out of sheer spite.

Except...

She didn't. Not even a little. He was a smart, decent guy. He volunteered at the homeless shelter before it was a thing to put on social media. He helped his grandma out at the family pizza place.

He drove a black vintage Mustang instead of a boring white pickup like all the other boys.

Adrian was just... cool.

And every girl had a crush on him. And every guy wanted to be his friend. Adrian was even nice to Jeremy when Jeremy was unpopular. They were neighbors, and Adrian often gave Jeremy rides to school.

A tiny part of Emmie had hoped that Adrian Saroyan would have aged badly. Just a little. Maybe lost some hair or gotten a weird scar or something that would have made him slightly more approachable.

But as she walked out to meet him and he smiled, Emmie realized...

He'd gotten better looking with age.

The nerve of the man.

She plastered on her "talking with customers or vendors" smile and held out her hand. "Hygiene achieved. Nice to see you, Adrian. How have you been?"

"I've been great." His eyes lit up. "It's so nice to see you. I'd heard you came back to town occasionally, but I thought it was a Metlin urban legend."

Emmie laughed. "Right."

"I was very sorry to hear about your grandmother. She'll be missed."

Emmie's smile fell. "Thanks. And yeah, she's already missed."

"My grandfather passed a few years ago, and it's still hard to remember that I can't just call him up anymore."

The professional facade she'd been holding cracked a little. "I know what you mean."

Adrian's smile fell. "And then seeing my mom lose her dad... Yeah, it's been rough."

Why was he so nice? It made it impossible for her to keep her guard up, and she really didn't want to act like a nervous teenage girl around him. She mustered her polite smile again. "So are you randomly visiting old classmates on Sunday mornings now?"

"Old friends." His face lifted. "I'd say I was visiting old friends. It's nice to see familiar faces. How's San Francisco?"

Did Adrian Saroyan consider Emmie a friend in high school? That was... interesting. "San Francisco is cold and damp of course. Isn't it always?" She laughed. "But my friend Tayla is down this weekend visiting, so I lured one of the nicest parts of the city down south."

"Oh." His smile faltered. "So when are you planning to head back?"

Ohhhh, right. Ethan had mentioned Adrian was buying most of Main Street.

Emmie kept her smile plastered on. "It doesn't look like I will be. I was working in book retail in San Francisco, but I'm..." How would Tayla put it? "I'm currently exploring the opportunities for a similar business here in Metlin."

Adrian's eyes went wide. "You're going to reopen the bookstore?"

"Probably yes."

"Really?"

Emmie's eyes narrowed. "I'm not sure why you seem so surprised. Metlin Books has been in this location for over eighty years. I own the building. I've been working in someone else's bookstore for years. I grew up in a bookstore."

"Doesn't everyone buy books online now?"

Emmie kept her polite smile plastered on. "Is that how you bought your last book?"

Adrian seemed flustered. "I... Probably. I think my mom—"

"Oh, you don't buy books?" Well, that did it. There was nothing more unattractive than someone who didn't read. Any and all nerves fled. "Well, since I'm an avid reader who's also connected with the online book community through social media and I've been working in retail for over five years now, I probably just have a better finger on the pulse of the market. It's actually a great time to open an independent bookstore."

Emmie was bullshitting. It was never a great time to open a bookstore. But damn if Adrian was going to see that.

Adrian's face was all business now. "I respect your ambition, but forgive me if I don't agree with you. Urban demographic research has proven what businesses succeed and fail in communities with Metlin's demographics, and bookstores are not on the succeed list. I'd love to help you sell this place or find more suitable renters for the building when you get serious." He put a business card on the desk and gave her the charming smile again. "But it was nice to see you, Emmie. Good luck."

"Thanks." That card was going in the trash as soon as he stepped out the door.

"I really mean that. I hope you succeed. I'm probably just too much of a realist."

If that wasn't a humble-brag, Emmie didn't know what was. *Too much of a realist.* Please. She left the card on the counter and held out a hand. "Nice to see you. Enjoy your Sunday. I really need to get back to work."

Adrian shook her hand. "Of course. I hope you'll consider what I'm offering. You wouldn't have to sell the building if you didn't want, but I could find you tenants that would really make the most of the property. My property management company is starting to receive more and more attention from midlevel national retailers."

Translation: I'd love to chop your building up into small pieces and try to lure Banana Gap Outfitters to Metlin.

No, thank you.

Emmie turned and left him at the desk. She heard the bell ring a few seconds later.

Ethan was right. Adrian Saroyan was a dipshit. *Urban demographic research.* It wasn't that she didn't believe in research, but research didn't understand everything. There were too many factors at play in bookselling.

You could have the best plan on paper a bank had ever seen and still fail. You could fly by the seat of your pants and succeed. It was the same with books. Did it make her nervous? Hell yes. But the more people doubted her, the more perverse confidence she gained.

Maybe bookshops were like books. The "it book" that a big publisher was pushing hard could land like a stone when it reached actual reader hands while a small press or independent release took off into the stratosphere. Emmie's personal theory was that book lovers were contrary by nature and hated being predictable. Since she was already a book lover, she could think like her customers and thus had a better chance of succeeding.

It might be wishful thinking, but for now she was going with it.

———

EMMIE WAS BACK in the store on Monday, still attacking the glamorous job of cleaning the bookshelves and boxing up paperbacks she'd never be able to sell. Her grandmother had been an idealistic book lover and never wanted to throw a book away, convinced that every book published had the perfect owner and it was her job to find it. She also accepted any trade-ins, no matter how dated, a practice that Emmie was going to stop immediately. Used books were a great market, but only if you kept stock that people actually wanted to buy.

She sneezed again, but this time she was prepared. That morning Emmie had left her contacts at home and stocked up on tissues. She'd be eternally grateful when the shop was clean and less dusty. The air was wreaking havoc on her allergies.

Emmie was halfway through the used middle grade fiction and deep in fifth grade nostalgia, so the raised voices on Main Street hardly registered. Her neighbors must have been fighting again. She'd been privy to another shouting match between them the night before. The bar next to the tattoo shop was blaring music; Ox and Ginger were yelling.

Emmie had liked the music. The shouting, not so much. But like any good bookworm, she was pretty good at blocking out the world when she had a book—this time stacks of them—in her hands. She was ignoring the ruckus until the bell over the door rang, heavy footsteps thumped into the shop, and a booming voice yelled, "Hey! Is anyone here?"

She stood slowly, clutching a stack of *Island of the Blue Dolphins* in front of her as she leaned around the bookshelf. Her eyes went wide when she saw him.

Miles Oxford stood in the middle of the bookshop, looking angry and sweaty. Seeing him indoors, it was obvious why the nickname "Ox" had stuck. The man was huge. His chest and shoulders were barely covered by a white undershirt, and worn jeans hung off his hips. He was nearly as tall as her front door, which meant he was well over six feet tall. He had a buzz cut and a furious expression. Emmie was tempted to hide, but she was too baffled as to why the man had walked into her store.

Ox spotted her behind the bookshelves. "Hey! Do you have a box?"

Emmie blinked. That was either the rudest or the most confusing greeting she'd ever heard. "Excuse me?"

"A box! A cardboard box. Like a packing box? I've seen you moving stuff in and out of here the past couple of days with your friends, so I thought you might have one."

"Yeah, I think—"

Something thunked against Emmie's window. She ran out from behind the bookshelves to see Ginger throwing clothes at her bookshop. A pair of jeans slid down in a pile, joining some T-shirts that were scattered on the sidewalk.

Emmie could hear the woman screaming through the windows. "Are you fucking her too?"

Ox turned and walked out the door. "Are you insane? Cut this shit out, Yvette!"

Whaaaat had this man brought into her shop? Emmie wanted to shut the door on him and lock it, but Ox was too fast for her. He was back inside before she could cross the room. Should she call the police? The fire department? Ethan's dad? Everyone listened to Mr. Vasquez.

"I'll take care of this," Ox growled. "Sorry."

"I thought her name was Ginger." It was probably the stupidest response to the situation, but what could Emmie do? The woman was throwing jeans at her store window, and she was pretty sure they were button fly. "Tell her if she breaks any windows, she's paying for them. These are custom-sized and they're not cheap."

Ox shot Emmie half a smile before he went back into the fray, grabbing Ginger by the wrist and dragging her back across the street where a crowd was gathering in front of the tattoo shop. "Cut it out. You're kicking me out? Fine. That girl has nothing to do with it. You want to piss off your neighbors *and* your customers?"

The door was open, so Emmie could hear Ginger scream back at him. "You're a lying sack of shit!"

"You think that because you lie to everyone, but I'm not you."

She punched his arm as they walked, but her fist looked like it bounced off the man's massive shoulder. "You're out of Bombshell! Do you hear me? Out! Your chair is mine."

"I'm devastated."

"And you better get all your shit out of my apartment, do you hear me?"

"You've thrown most of it out the window already."

Emmie quietly grabbed two packing boxes from behind the counter and set them by the door. The man had enough to deal with from the looks of it. She could give him some boxes.

CHAPTER FOUR

"WHAT THE HELL, YVETTE?" Ox bent down, trying in vain to keep their argument at least a little bit private. "We've been over for *months*. You haven't let me in your bedroom since June. We have been roommates and you know it. You jerk me around and create all these scenes? This is the last straw. I'm done."

"Don't call me Yvette! And *don't* pretend like you've been going without," she hissed. "I know exactly what your appetite is."

"I do not cheat on my girlfriends." And he'd had blue balls for months because of it. Ginger would wind him up, turn him on, and then piss him off. He didn't know what she got out of it, but he was finished trying to figure it out. She was a bad habit. One he'd been needing to break for months.

"I am not your girlfriend."

"Yeah, yeah." Ox stood straight. "Bullshit relationship definitions and all that. We've been living together for a year. Get the fuck over yourself. I didn't cheat on you. Frankly, being your man is too exhausting. I don't have time for anything but you and work."

"And your precious mommy, don't forget about—"

"Are you talking shit about my mom?" Ox bent down and got

29

in Ginger's face. He'd had it with the drama. "My mother? Who tried to treat you like a part of my life until you pissed her off one too many times? You do not talk shit about my mom, Yvette."

"Stop calling me Yvette." Her beautiful mouth was twisted and mean. "I should never have told you that."

"Don't worry. After today, I'm going to forget *all* your names."

She smirked. "You wish."

Ox folded his arms over his chest. At any moment, she was going to bat her eyes and remind him of those times over a year ago when she'd been hilarious and fun and easy to laugh with. That Ginger had lasted as long as it had taken him to move in. Though it had been her suggestion they share the apartment over the shop when the lease on his apartment had been up, she'd changed completely once they were in the same space.

She let a touch of hurt creep into her eyes. "Ox—"

"Don't. I'm done. I'm fucking done. We are not right for each other. I admire the hell out of your talent, and I hope you get your shit together and figure out whatever hang-ups are messing with your head, but I do not want to be in a relationship of any kind with you. I don't want to work for you. I don't want to *know* you."

Cut her off. Keep her out. She'd figured out his buttons, and he was tired of feeling guilty about leaving her.

What he needed was a nice quiet girl like the one across the street. Book Girl was probably steady and dependable. She'd have a smile on her face in the morning and make him coffee just to be nice. She might even have a sense of humor. She'd like his mom and his mom would like her. He might be bored to death, but at least he wouldn't worry about his bodily safety after he fell asleep at night.

Of course, that was never the kind of girl he went for. Because he was an idiot.

He glanced over his shoulder at Book Girl. Poor thing was staring out the window just like she had the week before when Ginger had started another fight. She was probably wondering what kind of lunatic neighbors from 7th Avenue she'd been stuck with when she'd bought Betsy's nice shop on Main Street.

"I'll leave your stuff by the front door," Ginger said. "I want you out."

"Fine." He was still staring at the bookstore. He'd seen people moving in and out all week. He'd been curious. Of course, watching them had spun Ginger into another jealous tirade. "Leave it by the front door and I'll get it."

"Good!" Ginger whirled around and stomped back into Bombshell.

A few minutes later, Russ walked out. The man was a friend; he was also Ginger's employee. He was an artist who also ran the office, and he was clearly conflicted. His hooded eyes had a hangdog expression and there was sweat on his forehead.

"Hey—"

"Don't." Ox held up a hand before Russ could say anything else. "I'm not gonna make a big deal about it. I'm relieved more than pissed."

"What are you gonna do? Go back to the ranch?"

"I don't know." He bent and picked up a pair of jeans. "For now. I'm sure my mom and Melissa could use the help. But I don't want to live in my sister's house forever. I'll find a place."

"You think your clients will come with you?"

Ox had already grabbed the small book where he kept his client list. "Most of 'em, but I gotta find a place to set up, you know? Anyone have space right now?"

Russ scratched the dark stubble on his chin. "I don't know, man. I think everyone's pretty full. Jolie's has four guys. I think Sacred Heart is full too, but I'll ask around."

"Thanks." Ox picked up a shirt and took an undershirt from the helpful—and amused—pedestrian crossing the sidewalk. "Let me know. For now I gotta go get some boxes from Book Girl over there."

"The girl in the bookshop?" Russ narrowed his eyes. "You're moving up."

"She offered me some boxes," Ox said. "That's all. Ginger's imagining things." Not that he hadn't been looking, but everyone looked, right?

"Book Girl looks sweet, man." Russ blew kisses at him. "I know what kinda sweet tooth you got."

"Shut up, Russ."

"Sweet tastes extra good after you've had that much sour."

Ginger opened a window upstairs and yelled, "Russ, am I paying you to talk to unemployed deadbeats?"

Russ rolled his eyes and walked back in the shop while Ox raised his hand to Ginger in a one-fingered salute.

Moving on, Miles Oxford. Moving on and moving up.

Hopefully.

CHAPTER FIVE

A FEW MINUTES after Ginger and Ox walked across the street, Ox walked back carrying a bundle of clothes. His expression was weary. And annoyed. This time when he opened the door, he poked his head in politely. "Hey."

"Hey yourself."

"I'm sorry about the scene earlier."

"Not your fault." Emmie waved him in from the stool behind the counter she'd set up when she moved the desk back to the office. "I put a couple of boxes by the door."

"You're a lifesaver." He dumped the armful of clothes in one then walked outside again and began picking up the clothes that Ginger had flung on the sidewalk.

"Things look a little calmer over there," Emmie called.

"For now." He walked back in. "You know the thing about artists being temperamental?"

"Uh-huh."

"Ginger likes to play into that."

Emmie smiled. "You called her Yvette."

"That's her real name, but don't use it. She told me in confidence and I shouldn't have called her that in front of other people."

Emmie leaned her chin on her hand. "You know, for an ex-boyfriend whose clothes are currently being thrown out a window, you seem awfully considerate."

Ox's head spun around. "The fuck?"

He stormed out the door and nearly walked into traffic before he made it across and started catching his stuff. After a few more shouts, he walked back to the store.

Emmie was trying really hard not to laugh. "So, I'm guessing this will not be another break up and make up, huh?"

"No." He let out a rueful laugh and tossed a sweatshirt in a box. "I am not cut out for that level of drama... Sorry, what's your name?"

"Emmie."

"I'm Ox. Miles Oxford, but everyone calls me Ox. You're a friend of Daisy's, right?"

"I am."

"She's a sweetheart. Spider's a lucky guy."

"You know Spider?"

"Everyone knows Spider. How many guys have a giant spider inked on their head?"

"Only one, as far as I know."

"Exactly." Ox narrowed his eyes. "I'm surprised *you* know Spider."

Emmie raised her eyebrows. "Why?"

"I..." He motioned vaguely to her. "You just don't seem like..."

...the type to know a quiet legend in the tattoo world.

Emmie didn't say it. It was none of Ox's business that Spider had been her tattoo artist for seven years and Emmie was the reason that Spider and Daisy had met. "Daisy and her family have rented Café Maya from my grandma for years."

"You're Betsy's granddaughter!" He shook his head. "I'm sorry. Of course you know Daisy and Spider."

"You knew my grandma?"

"Yeah." He gave her another half smile. "Betsy was friends with my mom. She's a big reader."

"Yeah?"

"She taught middle school out in Oakville." Ox wandered over to the bookshelves to peruse the books Emmie had been sorting. He picked up a battered copy of *Hatchet*. "Man, I loved this book hard. First book I really got hooked on."

Emmie was silently shocked and delighted. "You're a reader?"

Ox glanced down at his jeans and undershirt, then back up to Emmie. "Don't I look like one?"

"Everyone looks like a reader to someone who sells books." Emmie wondered why she was completely comfortable with this giant guy who had barged into her shop and brought so much chaos. His clothes were still flying out the window on the second floor across the street, but he was calmly perusing her books. "I try not to make assumptions."

He scratched the top of his head. "It's been a while since I've read anything other than trade magazines. When I was a kid, I lived in the country, so there wasn't much to do other than read." He tapped the paperback in his hand. "You know, I don't think I've ever been hooked on anything like I was hooked on this book. I got so into it I forgot to eat. I stayed up all night—"

"You were in another world," Emmie said. "Who wants to leave an adventure like that?"

Ox smiled slowly. "Exactly."

His smile did things to her stomach, and Emmie's nerves decided to reappear. "Sounds like you need to start reading again."

He glanced over his shoulder. Clothes were still flying out the window. "Since I don't have a girlfriend anymore and I'm unemployed, I'll probably have the time."

"I bet I could find something you'll love as much as *Hatchet*."

"Really?"

"Okay, probably not. I mean"—she gestured to the paperback

—"you never forget your first love. But there are some pretty great modern survival stories. Is that what you liked?"

"Yeah, I read 'em all. *Hatchet. Island of the Blue Dolphins. My Side of the Mountain.*" He tapped the book and stared at the bookshelves. "Man, I wanted a pet hawk. But who doesn't want a pet hawk, right?"

Emmie was shocked and charmed. Who was this guy? He looked like the last person on earth who would reminisce about childhood reading, but he seemed just as comfortable talking about books as he did joking with the bikers who parked in front of Bombshell.

"It looks like she might be winding down," Ox said, glancing out the window. "I didn't keep that much stuff at her place. Let me go grab the rest and then I'll get out of your hair."

You can stay in my hair.

"Sure." She waved her hand. "I'm just here. Sorting stuff. And cleaning. I needed some excitement."

"Yeah, there's no lack of excitement over at Bombshell. That's probably why I stuck it out for so long."

Emmie sighed as she watched her excitement walk out the door.

That's why she couldn't find a guy who kissed her the way Ox kissed Ginger. Emmie was the opposite of exciting. She was sensible and dependable. She was the comfy sweater on a rainy day, not the glamorous cocktail dress or the sexy shoes that looked so amazing you wore them even when they pinched your toes.

She watched Ox picking up the last of his clothes, chatting and laughing with people who passed him on the street, and wondered what it would be like to have just a little of that excitement in her life. Would it be invigorating or exhausting?

By the time he returned, Emmie's nerves had calmed down because she was resigned to never seeing Miles Oxford again.

He'd move on and find some other exciting person to kiss, and Main Street would be much less scenic, if a little quieter.

"So I was thinking," Ox said as he dropped the rest of his clothes in the boxes. "Would you mind if I left these overnight? I have a truck out at my sister's ranch, but I rode my bike here this morning."

"Oh sure, that's cool. What kind of bike do you have? I sold my car, so I was thinking about getting one of those cruisers they sell down at Valley Cycle."

He grinned. "Mine's a Harley type of bike."

"Oh." Her face heated up. "Of course." Of course he drove a motorcycle. Because guys who were tattooed muscle gods like Miles Oxford drove rumbly motorcycles with lots of chrome. Probably.

"I also need to box up my gear over at Bombshell. Can I bring it over here to store until I can get my truck? If it's a pain in the ass—"

"No, it's fine," Emmie said. "Like I said, I'm just cleaning and stuff. I'll be here."

He pulled out his phone. "Let me get your number. That way if I get delayed at the ranch, I can let you know so you're not waiting around."

"Who said I was going to wait around for you?"

Ox's eyebrows went up. "Fair enough. I'd still prefer to get your number. That way I can make sure you're here when I come back."

She walked over, took his phone, punched in her number, then waited while he dialed her phone to grab his. "There." She held up his digits on the screen. "We're connected."

"So we are." He took his phone and started typing. "And I am saving your number as... Emmie. Last name... Book Girl."

Her face went hot again. "For future reference, I prefer texting to calling unless it's an important conversation, and then you probably shouldn't be talking on the phone anyway because face-to-face conversations are better."

He looked down. "Are they?"

"A lot of nuance is lost over the phone."

"But not in texts?"

"That's what emojis are for." Emmie suddenly realized how close they were standing. She could feel the heat from his body.

Ox's voice was quiet. "You're kind of a little thing, aren't you?"

"I was going to say you're overgrown." Her face was on fire, but she couldn't stop her mouth. She didn't even come up to his shoulder. If he lifted his arm, he could probably rest his elbow on Emmie's head.

"I need to go pack up my gear," he said.

"Okay."

"Do you have any tattoos? Do you want any?"

Emmie backed away and went behind the counter. "None of your business."

His eyes narrowed. "If I texted you the question, would you answer?"

"No, it's not..." Her nerves had come back with a vengeance. "If I got a tattoo, I'd get it from Spider. So it's really none of your business."

Ox gave her another half smile. "Fair enough. Who wouldn't go to Spider?"

"He's family." Emmie flipped open the impossible espresso machine catalog and sighed. There was an old-fashioned copper machine she desperately wanted, but it was two grand, even on sale. It would match the shop perfectly, but she just couldn't afford to spend that kind of money on coffee, especially when she wasn't charging for it.

She heard the doorbell chime behind Ox as he walked back to the tattoo shop. She glanced up and watched his back as he walked away, half expecting Ginger to make her amends with Ox before he could pack up his gear. After all, Ginger might have been pissed at him, but even the most exciting girl didn't have a guy like Ox walk into her life that often.

Emmie looked back at the worn catalog and imagined the tall copper espresso machine polished and shining on the bookshop counter.

Why did she always want impossible things?

———

THE PAIN LANCED through her as the needle crossed her spine. She tried not to wince, but Spider sensed the movement.

"You better keep your ass still. If you mess up my design, I'm gonna be pissed."

"Isn't this my back?"

"Yeah, but it's my design. So keep still."

"Fine."

"I told you color was going to be the hardest part."

"I thought you were full of shit because the outline hurt so much."

Spider chuckled. It was his low, evil chuckle. "Have I ever lied to you?"

"No."

"That's right, Mimi. Don't forget it."

Spider Villalobos was the closest thing Emmie had to a big brother even though they were polar opposite in looks. She was a pale *gringa* and Spider had been born in the heart of Sinaloa. His copper-brown skin tanned dark in the valley sun while Emmie's burned. His hair—when he didn't shave his head—was thick and black while hers was a weird brown color that was reddish sometimes. With black tattoos covering most of his body—including his neck and head—Spider looked fierce to nearly everyone while Emmie was often overlooked by her own friends if she didn't wave at them in a crowd.

But they were family.

Spider had immigrated to LA when he was a baby named Manuel. When his dad passed away, he was thirteen. A tough age for anyone, it was even worse for a smart, bored kid in East LA. Within a few years, he'd fallen into gang life where he'd become the most skilled tattoo artist in a very specialized form of ink.

Then his mom had been killed in a drive-by shooting, and Spider ran.

Emmie didn't know the details like her grandmother had, but she knew twenty years later Spider still didn't go to Los Angeles. Ever. And he said he never would. He also wouldn't go to parts of Oakland and was wary in San Francisco.

He'd fled north, grown his hair out and covered his ink, living on the margins as an agricultural worker until he'd wandered into Emmie's grandmother's store asking about work in the winter.

Within weeks, Betsy had managed to set him up with a permanent job on a friend's ranch. He spent every holiday with Betsy, Emmie, and her mom, becoming part of the family. To ten-year-old Emmie, Spider was the *coolest*.

It was Emmie who'd seen his drawings first, but it was Betsy who loaned him the money to start his own tattoo business. Spider built a steady and discreet clientele over the years and even started shaving his head again, revealing the tattoo that had given him his nickname. Eventually clients started coming to Spider, some of them from a very long way away.

He didn't talk about his customers even though Emmie knew some of them were pretty famous. He didn't Instagram or Snapchat or Facebook. He didn't even have a mobile phone. He had a home phone and an answering machine.

It drove his wife absolutely crazy.

"Where's Daisy tonight?" Emmie stayed completely still as the needle moved back and forth over the same small area. He was shading on her lower back and it hurt like the devil. Tattoos were something Emmie loved, but not because of any kind of endorphin rush. She liked having them. She *hated* getting them.

"Taking dinner to Sandra tonight." He lifted the needle. "Do you need a break?"

"I'm okay. Sandra have the baby?"

"Yeah, last week. Little boy."

"Cool." Emmie knew Daisy and Spider had been trying for kids for a while. Daisy hadn't confided in Emmie, but she knew Spider worried. "That's cool for them."

"Yeah, they're pretty excited. Cute kid. Lots of hair. Danny keeps talking about the kid playing football, and he can't even lift his own head."

Emmie smiled. "Good to have dreams."

"I guess so. Dan played in high school I think."

"Did you?"

"Didn't have time for sports, Mimi."

And that was all he'd ever say about that.

"Do you know a guy named Miles Oxford?" she asked.

"Ox? Yeah, I know him. He's pretty good. Works for Ginger, right?"

"He did. They broke up. She was throwing his stuff out the window of her apartment yesterday."

The needle lifted, Spider sat up, and he busted up laughing. "She didn't."

Emmie smiled over her shoulder. "She did. He came into my shop to get some boxes to put his stuff in. Then she started throwing his stuff at my shop."

Spider was still laughing. "Welcome to Metlin."

"When did it turn into reality TV?"

"More like one of Eddie's telenovelas." He nudged her back into position. "More fill on this wing."

"Any of the purple yet?"

"It's not time for the purple. Be patient."

"Fine." Emmie turned her back and braced herself on the back of the chair. "So you know Ox."

"He's not a bad guy. Kinda stupid about women. He's a good

artist, but not as good as Ginger."

"Ginger's good?"

"Yeah, she's more than good. After me, she's the best in the area. She's just moody as hell and can't get a handle on her temper. But her portrait work is fucking amazing."

"Do you do portraits?"

"Nope. I've sent her some business over the years."

The needle was burning long lines in her back. Emmie bit her lip and closed her eyes. "What about Ox? You said he's good?"

"He's damn near as good as Ginger, especially in black and grey. His work is really... three-dimensional. Architectural. He's not as good at portraits though."

"Good thing I don't want to get a face on my ass then. I don't think Ginger likes me very much."

Spider snorted. "She'll get over it. She'll get over Ox too. Both of 'em oughta know not to shit where they eat."

"Not everyone is as wise as you."

"I know." He lifted the needle, set it down so he could rest, and reached for his beer. "And ain't that a fucking shame?"

CHAPTER SIX

EMMIE WAS SITTING at the counter and looking through her first inventory order when she saw the old black pickup pull into a spot on 7th Avenue. Ox stepped out of the truck, and Emmie tried not to straighten her sweater. She was wearing her new BOOK NERD T-shirt that morning. Sure, she'd chosen her outfit more carefully, but that was just because she knew she was having company in the store. She would have put in her contacts for Ethan or Jeremy too.

Probably.

Ox paused at the 7th Avenue door, looking it up and down before he pulled it open. He stepped inside and stood in the empty branch of the store. "I didn't realize that door was there."

Emmie nodded. "Yep. Two doors. The Main Street door is just the fancy one. It's a big shop. When my grandma was growing up, that part of the store was all toys and this half was books."

"Huh." He turned, taking in the space. "It's such a cool building. I think this is the coolest building on Main Street. I love that Betsy never tried to modernize it."

Emmie smiled. "Same. It needs some updating and new paint,

but I'm so glad she never covered the woodwork. I need to fix the tile in the entry though."

"I love what Daisy did with the tile in front of her place."

"With the different colors? Yeah, it's perfect for the café."

"Speaking of the café, I was going to grab a coffee," Ox said. "Can I get you one? My treat to say thanks for letting me keep my stuff here."

Emmie shrugged. "Sure. I'm ordering books this morning, so I've been stuck at the counter. A latte?"

"Regular?"

"Yep." That was her. Regular. Average. "You know what? Can I get an extra shot of espresso in that latte?"

"Your wish. My command. I'll start loading this stuff up as soon as I bring caffeine." He paused as he was leaving. "I see what you mean about the tile." He kicked a few loose pieces to the side.

"I think Ethan is going to help me with it."

"I'm sure it'll look great." He shook his head. "I'm gonna miss working downtown."

Emmie watched him walk out the door. She was staring at Ox's truck—an old Ford that reminded Emmie of her mom's truck—when two motorcycles roared south on 7th Avenue. Emmie turned back to the computer to check out the selections in the nonfiction section about motorcycles and custom cars. She was adding several automotive books to her shopping cart when Ox returned.

"*Auto Repair for Idiots* or *Basic Car Maintenance*?" Emmie asked as he walked to the counter.

"Excuse me?"

"I want a good automotive section in the shop," Emmie said. "Especially considering how many people in Metlin are into classic cars. I was gonna order a couple of basic manuals for newbies too. So *Autos for Idiots* or *Basic Car Maintenance*? Which one would you buy if you were learning how to fix your car?"

He set down her latte. "Seeing as I wouldn't buy a book that called me an idiot, I vote for *Basic Car Maintenance*."

"The 'for Idiots' series is very popular."

Ox leaned on the counter. "Well, idiots have no self-respect."

Emmie smiled and added both to her cart. "Thanks for the coffee."

"Daisy added something to the grounds when I told her it was for you."

"Oh!" Emmie perked up. "Roasted cloves probably."

"Cloves in coffee?"

"It's really good. If you suck up to her, she'll let you try it."

"I'll keep that in mind." He drummed his fingers on the counter and set his coffee down. "I better get started."

Ox walked over to the boxes and started sorting through some of the random stuff on top. After he'd left the day before, people from Bombshell kept bringing stuff over. A flannel shirt from the break room. A photo album. A borrowed tattoo gun. Emmie had pointed to Ox's stacked boxes with each new person and smiled. Ginger had not made another appearance.

Thank goodness.

Ox was muttering to himself and sorting through his stuff as Emmie worked. He plugged in the borrowed gun, and a soothing buzz filled the room. Emmie felt the smile curl her lips. She loved the sound of tattoo guns. The smell of ink.

The smell of ink…

Emmie looked at Ox's back and the line of dark ink down his spine where his shirt gaped in back.

Focus, Emmie.

She looked at his stuff. Then over at the empty half of the shop that opened onto 7th Avenue.

"Hey, Ox?"

"Yeah? Sorry about the noise. I just need to make sure this works before I—"

"Where were you planning to work?" Emmie interrupted him. "I mean, Ginger let you go, and Spider says you're good."

He smiled. "You asked Spider about me?"

"You have a clientele, right?" She ignored his question, thinking aloud. "I mean, if Spider moved halfway across the country, I'd still fly out to have him work on me. Do you have clients like that?"

He frowned. "I don't know if any of them would fly across the country, but yeah. I mean, most people like who they like."

The thought was nascent. Messy. But interesting. Maybe even a little... exciting?

"You already have a business," Emmie said quietly.

"Yeah. I'll do okay. I just need to find a space to rent. But all my clients have my number. I have theirs. Most of the ones I called last night want to reschedule as soon as I find a place."

A picture was forming in Emmie's mind. An unexpected picture, but was it the right kind of unexpected? Would the idea turn more conservative customers off? When you thought about it, everyone got tattoos these days. Her grandma had let Spider give her a tattoo of a book on her arm. In fact, Emmie would estimate half her customers in San Francisco had book or literary tattoos of some kind. Favorite book covers. Quotes. Scenes from stories.

Emmie smiled. "People love ink."

"What?" Ox dropped the tattoo gun back in the box.

"Huh?" She blinked.

"What did you say?"

"I didn't say anything."

Ox cocked his head. "Could have sworn you did. You're in your own world over there, aren't you?"

"I do that a lot."

"Daydreamer?"

"Always." Emmie hopped down off the barstool behind the

counter and walked around to the empty half of the shop. "You need a space to rent."

"Yeah." He pulled out another tangle of cords. "There are a few shops—"

"You need space." Emmie looked around. "I have space."

"Yeah, but..." He frowned. "I need tattoo-shop space."

"Why not bookshop space?"

"Because it's a bookshop. Not a tattoo shop," Ox said. "Are you feeling okay?"

"I'm feeling fine. I'm feeling *great*, in fact. And I think I have an idea that might work for both of us."

His eyebrows went up. "You want to put a tattoo shop in your bookstore?"

"I think I might."

He grinned. "You *are* a daydreamer. I mean, it's cute as shit but also kinda nuts." He put down the tangled cords. "But seriously cute."

Emmie ignored the cute comment and walked over to his stack of boxes, leaning on the side. "What kind of tattooing do you do?"

Ox crossed his arms. "The kind where I put ink into people's skin. What are you trying to get at?"

Emmie bit her lip. "Okay, here's the part where I confess I kinda looked through some of your stuff last night."

His eyes went wide. "What?"

"Just the photo albums! The bald guy brought them over."

"That's Russ."

"Okay, Russ brought over a stack of books and said, 'Ginger don't want his stuff on the counter anymore.' And he put a couple of photo albums and some business cards—you need new ones, by the way, the neon green is not a good look. Anyway, he put all this stuff on the top of the pile. And I was curious, so I looked through your albums. Your work is really good."

Ox looked more confused by the minute. "Thanks."

"And I noticed that you tend to do a lot of old-school stuff and a lot of black-and-grey work. Really artistic. Some Celtic knot work. But not anything too graphic."

He shrugged. "Not my thing. What are you trying to say?"

"You're an artist. Like, an original artist."

"I do a lot of custom work. What—"

"People love ink." Emmie held out her arms. "I'm saying my people—book people—love ink."

Ox looked at Emmie's bare arms. "Ink in books?"

"All kinds of ink."

Ox narrowed his eyes. "Are you serious about this?"

Emmie nodded. "Books and tattoos. Think about it."

"I am thinking about it. That is not... typical."

"But why not? Book people like tattoos. Who's to say tattoo people don't like books?"

Ox's face seemed to be set in permanent scowl mode. "I really don't think you're thinking things through."

"Why not?"

He raised a hand and his index finger went up. "One? Noise. Tattoo shops are noisy."

"But more so at night, when bookshops are closed. Unless we have an evening event like a signing or a book club, and we can work around stuff like that. Hell, we can probably have a book club tattoo party."

Ox closed his eyes and pressed his lips together. "Leaving that one alone for right now. Two, tattoo shops have to meet a shitload of health-code regulations. Are you prepared to do that? I need a sterile environment, and I don't see sinks or counters or—"

"We're putting in a lot of that stuff anyway because we're going to be serving coffee and sometimes food in here. Not for sale, but for events and stuff, so I wanted counters because it's more practical. And the floors are hardwood. We can add counters for you that fit the shop. In fact..."

Emmie walked over to the counter and held her arm out. "Everything from here over is going to be coffee and hangout area. Bulletin board. An area we can use for signings and that kind of thing." Emmie walked to the left. "Bookshop is here obviously." She walked to the center of the shop and held out her arms. "Sitting area that can be shared. Sofa. Low chairs. Coffee table. Hangout place." She walked over to the empty space. "Tattoo shop. Some low bookshelves here to define the area for you. Maybe put graphic novels over here. Mystery or horror or sci-fi. Whatever you think would appeal to your customers most. They could buy a book to read while they're waiting for an appointment or getting their tattoo."

Ox's frown was softening. "So you're saying we could overlap hours without sticking to the same schedule."

"I wouldn't want kids story hour to have a tattoo gun buzzing in the background, would I? So I'd put story hour in the morning when you were closed."

"And if I have a customer who curses like a sailor—"

"No problem. You book him for after bookshop hours and he can curse away."

Ox's face had moved from scowl to contemplation. "What's in this for you?"

"What do you mean?"

"Emmie, what you're talking about could be really expensive. Renovating this shop so it meets the regulations for tattoo parlors—"

"This has obvious benefits for my business," she broke in. "Any tattoo involves patience. You have to wait for a turn if you're a walk-in. You end up taking breaks for bigger pieces. And if they're waiting in the shop, your tattoo customers could buy a book to read while they wait or have a cup of coffee because… coffee goes with everything."

"Okay, I can kind of see it." Ox started nodding. "And your book traffic might bring in some walk-ins for me during the afternoon and early evening because those are usually my slow times."

"If you put up some book-related flash and some quotes from famous writers, you're going to hook a lot of new customers. I'm serious. Book readers can be huge tattoo fans."

"Really?"

Emmie nodded. "Really. Every single person who worked at Bay City Books had tattoos. Some of them had a lot. I know a lady that had an entire library inked on her back."

"Everyone, huh?" He looked her up and down. "What about you?"

Emmie ignored the question. "And can you imagine how much attention this could get for both of us? Have you ever heard of a bookstore with a tattoo shop inside?"

"I can honestly say no."

"Nobody in Metlin is going to make a big deal about me reopening Metlin Books. Nobody is going to care if you open another tattoo shop in town. But if we combine this? Everyone will be talking about it."

Ox glanced across the street. "Ginger is gonna be pissed."

That did give Emmie pause. She had no desire to piss off her neighbors. "Maybe at first, but she's losing your customers anyway, right? And the kind of new customers you're going to be attracting are—let's be honest—not the kind who are likely to go to her shop in the first place."

"You mean the hipster artsy tattoo crowd who want deer antlers instead of skulls and ironic butterflies on their asses instead of hearts that say Mom?"

"Yes, those people. Don't make a face; you can charge them more for their tattoos, and they probably won't bitch about it."

Ox pursed his lips. "There is that."

"But you *are* going to have to invest some stuff too," Emmie said. "I'm willing to put in the sinks and the counters so they'll match the rest of the store. But you'll need some dividers for privacy screens. Your own chairs and furniture. All that stuff. And it's going to need to match the look of the rest of the shop if we want this to work and not just be weird."

Ox said, "When I imagined my own shop, it always kinda looked like the old barber shop my grandpa took me to when I was a kid, you know? Weird art on the wall. Stuffed jackalope. Vintage beer signs."

"I'm cool with a stuffed jackalope," Emmie said. "Beer signs would be on an individual basis. Deer heads are a hard limit."

Ox raised an eyebrow. "We talking about hard limits now?"

She felt her face heat up. "Decorating limits. For our shop."

"*Our* shop." Ox rubbed his jaw. "I'd be opening my own shop."

"We're not going into business together. Not technically. We'd be two separate businesses sharing space. You'd have to pay rent."

Ox looked around the shop with newly appreciative eyes. "I'd be paying rent anyway no matter where I went. At least this building is cool. It's downtown. Good foot traffic. I'd need a new sign…"

Emmie nodded.

"And I'd need all the stuff to open my own shop. The licenses and all that."

He was starting to look skeptical again, but Emmie was more and more convinced that this was an idea that could catch serious attention. "Tayla is a genius at paperwork and she's helping me with the stuff for my place, so I'm sure she can help you with yours."

"Who's Tayla?"

"My best friend. I think I may have convinced her to move here from San Francisco. It was either my charm or the free apartment."

He turned around and sat on one of Emmie's kickstools. "This is a lot."

"Haven't you ever thought about opening your own shop?" Emmie asked.

"Kinda?" He shrugged. "Yeah, I have. But it was always one of those... in the future things, you know? I have... my family. Never mind." He shook his head. "Not important."

"I thought the same thing. *Someday.*" Emmie turned around in the empty store. "What do you think this is for me?"

He let out a slow breath. "I can't believe I'm considering this, but... I'm actually considering this. I've been saving up some money with this in mind. And I have a little from my grandpa."

Emmie refrained from jumping up and down in excitement. She couldn't shake the feeling that combining books and tattoos was a brilliant move. Gimmicky? A literary purist might say yes, but the entrepreneur in her said no. This was a strategic move to brand her shop as a hip and different kind of bookshop that targeted a younger crowd. Ox could brand himself as the artistic, not-quite-as-edgy tattoo shop that catered to the same crowd. If this worked right, both of them could profit.

"I need to check with my mom and my sister," Ox said. "Our family has a ranch, and doing this would take a lot more of my time than working for someone else."

Emmie nodded. "Totally fair and I completely understand."

"And Emmie, I do have one condition," Ox said.

"What's that?"

He stood, walked over, and put both his hands on her shoulders. "I just need you to know—because this has messed up way too many things for me in the past—that if we do this, if we start this shop together..."

She put her hands over his. "What?"

"You have to promise me we will *never* get involved."

CHAPTER SEVEN

HE WAS GOING to fuck this up. He was going to fuck this up so bad.

The slightly fallen expression on Book Girl's face was enough to tell him, so was the immediate mask to hide her reaction. Ox could have handled shocked and confused when he mentioned getting involved. He was hoping for surprised and amused. But slightly fallen told him that—at least on some level—Book Girl was attracted to him.

"Of course," Emmie said quickly. "Of course. I mean, that would be... Obviously, we'd be professionals first. This is business."

He was fucked. Because she was too damn cute to ignore for long. Sometime on the ride home yesterday, he'd reclassified Book Girl—Emmie—from cute and kind of boring to cute with a side of quirky and intriguing. She had a dry sense of humor and a quiet passion for her job. She'd subtly put him in his place enough to show him that she wasn't anyone's doormat. A little on the thin side, but she had a sweet body under the oversized clothes, and he wasn't pretending he hadn't noticed that. Plus she had thick brown hair almost down to her waist with all sorts of red colors in it when the sun hit it. Hair like that gave a man ideas.

So he was interested, and that presented a problem. Ox plus cute, intriguing girl equaled complications. Forget a bull in a china shop. He was an Ox in a bookshop and he was going to screw this up.

No. No, you can do this.

He had to. Because he agreed with Emmie. If they played this right, it could be killer, even if the idea of going out on his own was also slightly terrifying.

"Okay." He lifted his hands from her shoulders and rested them on his hips. Her shoulders were softer than his jeans, but he needed to get his hands off her. "Like I said, I need to think about this. Get some questions answered on my end. Talk to my mom and my sister, that sort of thing."

Emmie nodded.

"But I have your number. So I'll call you back by..."

"Tomorrow," she said decisively. "I totally respect wanting some time to think it over, but I'd like an answer from you by tomorrow. If you don't want to take the space, then I need to find someone else. So I don't want to be waiting weeks."

Ox nodded. He liked her attitude. "Fair enough. I'll talk it over with my family tonight and make sure they can spare me at the ranch. Then I'll call you."

"Okay." She smiled big, and he mentally cursed himself.

Ox, you are an idiot.

"Okay." He cleared his throat. "Well, I should..." He motioned toward the pile of boxes. "Should I leave these here?"

Emmie shrugged and turned back to the catalog she'd been flipping through. "I don't mind if you leave the boxes here. If you decide to rent that side of the shop, you'd just be moving them back. They're not in my way."

"Okay."

She was staring at the catalog and not at him. He glanced

down to see a tall, twisting copper-and-brass espresso machine with old-fashioned knobs and valves. It was cool as hell and would look amazing in the shop.

"Are you getting that? It's cool."

Color rose on her cheeks. "This one? No way. I wish. It's like two grand, and I'm not opening a café, just getting something customers can use to grab a cup, you know? It'll probably be used. This one is just..." She shrugged as if she was embarrassed for wanting something nice.

"That's the one I'd want for a place like this." He looked around at the huge windows edged by stained glass and the golden wood of the bookshelves. "It fits perfectly."

"I know." She turned the page. "But I don't have the budget for it. Maybe in a couple of years."

"You gotta indulge sometimes."

"Not when I'm the one paying the bills." Emmie closed the catalog. "I'm sure I'll find a used one that works for me."

Discussion closed, Mr. Oxford. The message couldn't be clearer. "Okay, well, if you're sure it's cool, I'll leave my stuff here and call you tomorrow."

"Totally cool." Emmie bobbed her head but didn't look at him. He'd lost her attention.

Which was fine. Because they were just going to be friends. Workmates. Associates of business.

Professionals. What had she said? *Obviously.*

He was definitely going to fuck this up.

———

"ARE you sure that this is what you want to do with your money from Grandpa?" Melissa sat on the fence with him, drinking a beer and watching the moon rise over the mountains. "You can only spend it once, Ox."

"I think I'm sure."

"I *think* is not I'm sure."

"I don't do *sure* as easily as you."

"No," she said. "You just don't know what you want."

Melissa wanted the ranch. Always had. Always would.

She'd used her money from their grandfather to plant orange groves on the lower hills. She'd been an agronomy major in college and had been preaching to her mother about utilizing some of the more fertile land in the lower part of their property for years. Orange groves were her first expansion of the ranch, and so far they'd been successful.

From the time she was a child, she'd sat on a horse and yelled at steers. She'd been able to grow anything in their mother's garden. She loved every inch of it. She'd mourned for their grandfather, but her determination had never wavered. Melissa was the ranch.

Before her husband had been killed in a car accident, Melissa and Calvin had worked it together. Calvin had been the youngest son of an old cattle family on the west side of the valley. He and Melissa had met in college and gotten married and pregnant with their daughter as soon as they graduated. Melissa's life had been planned out with ruthless and loving efficiency until an eighteen-wheeler and a foggy interstate had destroyed her small world.

But she still had the ranch.

Ox did not. "I know you've been counting on me to help with some of the winter—"

"Don't worry about us," Melissa said. "I can hire people. We've got cash right now."

"I can do my part."

Melissa turned to him and rubbed a hand over his buzz cut. "It's not your job. You have your own thing, and it's fine. It's good. I just want you to think it over carefully before you put a bunch of money into this and have that girl invest a lot of hers in you. Make sure it's really what you want."

Ox took a deep breath. "I've talked about my own shop."

"Yeah, but then you stopped talking a few years ago." Melissa cocked her head. "You stopped talking about your own shop… after Calvin died."

Ox didn't say anything. The wound where his brother-in-law's memory lived was deep, but it wasn't the aching void that Melissa carried. He didn't need to rake things up and make them all bleed again.

But of course Melissa wouldn't be his big sister if she didn't poke at him. "Why did you stop talking about your shop?"

He cleared his throat. "You know why."

"I didn't need your help."

"The fuck you didn't." He tossed his beer bottle in the bucket near the fence post. "Shut it, Lissa."

"Have you been putting this off because of me and Abby?"

"It's not like that."

She angled her shoulders toward him. "Then tell me how it is."

He forced a grin. "You're not my mom."

"No, I'm way meaner than Mom, so spill."

Ox hooked an arm around her neck and pulled her into a playful headlock. "Don't boss me around. I'm bigger than you."

Melissa dug her knuckle into the sensitive flesh just above his knee on the inside of his leg, causing Ox to yelp and almost lose his balance.

"Ow! You little… *Mo-om!*"

Melissa snorted with laughter and Ox couldn't hold back. He started laughing too. He laughed so hard his sides ached.

His sister was wiping tears from her eyes when Ox said, "I wanted to be close. I wanted you close. Wanted Abby close. She was still a baby. I needed… I just needed to be here. That's why I moved back from Metlin."

"If you need to be here, you're always welcome. You know that. Always. But if starting your own place, running your own shop, is what you really want, then you need to go for it. You need to put everything you have into it. Use your money from Grandpa.

Dedicate the time. Make it something special that you're proud of."

Ox nodded.

"And tell me about the girl."

"There's nothing to tell about the girl." He glanced at her. "I told you. She's nice, but we're business only if I do this. Strictly business."

Melissa finished her beer, tossed her empty into the bucket, and narrowed her eyes. "She's cute, isn't she?"

"Melissa..." He couldn't say anything. If he said no, he'd be lying. If he said yes, his sister would never let up.

"She's Betsy's granddaughter. Owns a bookstore. I bet Mom would love her."

Ox shook his head. "I'm not telling you—"

"Don't make me hurt you again, Ox. You know I can."

"You are so mean."

CHAPTER EIGHT

THE SIGN OX was painting in the alley would hang over the 7th Avenue door. It simply read INK.

INK. What else could they call it? Books and tattoos. Tattoos and books. INK.

They were doing this, and Emmie asked herself every morning if she was making a horrible, awful mistake.

"It's not too late to call it off," Daisy said. "Then you can find a nice children's retailer to work with while I convince Ox that the two of you are meant for each other."

Daisy had hopped on the INK train and immediately hopped off when Emmie had told her about Ox's condition.

"Don't be ridiculous, and keep your voice down," Emmie said. The shop was finally clean, the shelves were empty with all salvable stock boxed and organized, and Emmie was standing on a ladder, starting the new coat of vanilla-cream paint that would set off the dark oak bookshelves and the counters that Ethan and his dad had ordered.

"You and Ox would be great together," Daisy hissed, glancing toward the back hallway that led to the alley. "I was thinking about setting you up. I was just waiting for him to break up with Ginger."

"You are full of shit. He may be hot, but I am the opposite of his type." Emmie started the paint and immediately let out a happy sigh. Everything was better with fresh paint. She'd cleaned out her old bedroom upstairs and painted it a fresh green that reminded her of the mountains. The bathroom was sky blue. The living room she was waiting to paint until Tayla moved south next month.

"He is a twenty-eight-year-old man," Daisy said. "Trust me, he doesn't know what type is good for him."

"Good for *him*? What about me?"

"Trust me. That man would be *very* good for you. Or parts of you at least."

Emmie rolled her eyes. "We are starting a business together. Not getting involved was a smart condition, and I agreed immediately because I am a grown-up and business is more important than my hormones."

"And then you died a little inside," Daisy said sadly. "Because you will linger alone, a poor village girl, slave to her virtue, never having felt the fire of passion in your too-short life."

Emmie laughed so hard she snorted and almost smudged the woodwork. "Have you been watching telenovelas in the kitchen again?"

"I swear, Eddie works faster when they're on in the background," Daisy said. "I think I'm absorbing them subconsciously. Spider thinks you're nuts."

"For not hooking up with Ox? That seems like none of his business."

"No, about putting a tattoo shop in your bookstore."

Emmie spun around. "He told me he liked the idea!"

"He does. He just thinks you're nuts."

Emmie turned back to the wall. "Well, all you doubters can stuff it. Tayla did some research and tattoo shops combined with other businesses are cropping up all over the country. We're just pushing Metlin to the cutting edge."

"Because Metlin was just begging to be pushed to the edge."

"I am determined to make this town cool," Emmie said. "I may go broke in the process, but I'm going to try. And Ox is going to help me."

"Help you what?" Ox walked down the hallway, unsnapping the air filter from his face. "Sign is painted. Looks good. Want me to start on the next one?"

Emmie bit her lip and nodded.

Ox held up a hand. "Are you sure?"

"We're not getting rid of the old sign," she said. "I need to let it go."

Emmie had decided that with a new look and a new theme, they needed new signs. One for Main Street and one for 7th. But removing the Metlin Books sign that had hung over her family shop for generations was difficult. In the end, it had been Ox who had suggested cleaning up the old sign and hanging it inside over the built-in bookshelves. He'd already brought some of his grandfather's old cattle brands and a few signs from his family's ranch for his section of the shop. The Metlin Books sign tied in perfectly while giving space for the new branding outside.

"Let's do it," Emmie said. "Do you need the ladder?"

He nodded and Emmie climbed down, setting her paint roller in the tray. Together, they carried the ladder outside and steadied it as Ox climbed up with the electric screwdriver and started removing the brackets.

"Help you with what?" Ox said.

"What?"

"What was Daisy talking about when I walked inside? Was there something else you needed help with?"

Emmie bit her tongue. Her eyes had been stuck on the edge of skin peeking from Ox's shirt, and her very first thought would probably have made Daisy very, very happy. While also violating workplace sexual harassment standards. *Yes, Mr. Oxford, I need some help taking off your shirt so I can see what delicious thing you have inked on your back.*

"I need help making Metlin cool."

He turned and smiled at her, his eyes squinting in the afternoon sun. "Silly Emmie. Didn't you know? Metlin is already cool."

"When did that happen?"

"When you and I decided to start this shop."

She smiled and Ox winked at her before he turned back to the sign.

Emmie's eyes landed on his ass. She forced them away because she was smart and focused. Business, not hormones.

Daisy was holding up a sign inside the shop. *Lingering alone. A slave to your virtue.*

Emmie held up her hand and showed Daisy a different kind of sign.

———

THE FIRST CONFRONTATION with Ginger wasn't nearly as dramatic as Ox had predicted, though it left Emmie rattled in completely unexpected ways.

Emmie was kneeling in the children's book section, painting the display platforms Ethan had built to go under the Main Street windows. She'd decided the back of the platforms could be turned into chalkboards since the children's section faced the Main Street windows. The new platforms also protected the original trim from crayons and chalk.

Emmie was painting the last side when she saw Ginger walking across the street from Bombshell.

"Oh shit." Emmie glanced over to the parking on 7th, but Ox's truck was nowhere in sight. He was helping at the ranch that morning.

Ginger pushed open the door and walked in, her hair perfectly coiffed and her makeup precise. Ginger was every inch the glamour girl. She totally sold her shop's name. She looked like the bombshell painted on the window. In fact, she'd probably been the model.

"Hey." Emmie cleared her throat. "Can I help you?"

Ginger spun around, her assessing gaze raking over Emmie, who was wearing work jeans and an old flannel. Her hair was up in a bun on top of her head and likely dotted with paint.

Ginger's gaze moved quickly from assessing to patronizing. "Look at you. You're a mess."

Emmie forced a tight smile to her lips. "Well, that's generally what happens when you paint."

Ginger strolled around the shop, which was beginning to take shape. The furniture had come, a mix of the old couch from Daisy's aunt and some vintage wingback chairs Emmie had collected in San Francisco. Paired with a midcentury coffee table and a Persian rug Emmie had stolen from upstairs, the shop was beginning to look eclectic, bohemian, and cozy, exactly the kind of place customers would want to linger and hang out while they drank coffee and chatted about book recommendations.

It was not coiffed, precise, or glamorous, however.

"Well, this is... interesting," Ginger said, staring at Ox's side. "Letting the country boy out, I see."

Emmie stood and set her paintbrush down. "Can I help you? We're not open yet. Ox isn't here. But if you want to leave him a message, there's a notepad on the counter over there."

Ginger spun and smiled at her. "No message for him. He's a handsome one, isn't he?"

Emmie forced herself to keep smiling. "I suppose so. But we're business partners; it's not personal."

"Oh." Ginger cocked her head. "I guess you wouldn't be, would you?"

Bitch. "If you don't have a message for Ox—"

"He at his mom's this morning?"

Emmie didn't want to tell this woman anything, so she just stood there with a hand on her hip, trying for an expression that said bored and impatient without being rude.

"Miles Oxford." Ginger ran a finger along his counter, her mouth curling around Ox's name. "So handsome. So sexy. So... *devoted.*" Her voice fell on the last word. "He'll always pick them over you, by the way. You know that, right? I hope you're not too invested in this little business because at some point they *will* make him choose, and he *will* choose them."

The punch landed exactly as Ginger had intended. Emmie felt sick to her stomach. She had invested everything in the shop, and she thought she had a partner as dedicated as she was. Ox had talked about his family—his mom, sister, and niece—with affection, but there'd been no indication that they depended on him. He always seemed like his own man.

But what did Emmie know? Did she know Miles Oxford as well as his ex-girlfriend who'd been with him for over a year? She knew Ginger was trying to unnerve her, but how much of what she said was true? Emmie had no idea.

If Ox abandoned INK, she'd have spent a large percentage of her renovation money on a part of the shop she had no way of using. She'd be up shit creek. She needed him to pay rent and bring in business. She needed him to make her vision work.

"Well," Ginger said. "This has been informative. Nice to meet you..."

"Emmie," she said through gritted teeth.

"Emmie." Ginger smiled, all bubbles and sweetness. "Isn't that cute? Emmie. Like a little doll." She waved over her shoulder as she sauntered out the door and across the street.

No, her first meeting with Ginger was not at all what Emmie had expected.

CHAPTER NINE

EMMIE CLUTCHED the back of the chair, wincing at the bite of the needle against her shoulder blade.

"You need a break?" Spider asked.

She gritted her teeth and squeezed her eyes shut. "I'm fine."

Daisy called from the kitchen. "Take a break and we'll have dinner, babe."

Spider patted Emmie's shoulder. "The boss speaks. We'll eat and then finish that shoulder."

"And the left?"

"Probably next week. Then you're done."

Spider left the room and Emmie eased a loose tank top over her head. One of the downsides to having Spider do her tattoo was that he had to fit her in around his regular clients and his commissions. Spider's shop was low-key, tucked into a quiet residential area near his and Daisy's house. He didn't even have a sign, but it was always busy. When he wasn't working on tattoos, he worked on paintings. He'd sold a dozen of his pieces in a gallery in Las Vegas last year, and he and Daisy had refinished the hardwood floors. When he worked on Emmie's tattoo, he worked at home.

Emmie unwound the tight bun at the top of her head and braided her hair over her shoulder, leaving her back clear. She heard Tayla and Daisy laughing in the kitchen and followed the sound.

"Something smells good," she said. "Can I get a beer?"

"There's a growler of Metlin's in the fridge," Daisy said.

Emmie grabbed a glass from the cabinet and poured herself a glass of brown ale from the local brewing company. Daisy had given control of the kitchen to Tayla, who was baking something in the oven. It smelled like cheese. Emmie approved.

"How's the back going?" Tayla asked.

"Fine. After he's finished filling in this shoulder, we just have the left one to go. Then a little shading and it's finally done." Emmie looked her up and down. "Are you always coordinated?"

Tayla spun around, her cherry-patterned apron whirling around her. "Daisy found one that matched my dress! Isn't it cute? Not all of us can look great in hobo-chic or whatever you're calling that outfit."

Emmie glanced down at her yoga pants and loose tank. "Oh yeah. I'm Instagram-ready."

"You're pretty, have amazing skin, and gobs of auburn hair. You can wear anything and be cute. Appreciate your power."

Daisy made a spin-around motion with her hand. "Let me see."

Emmie turned and let Daisy see the growing pattern of vines, leaves, and butterflies on her back. The outline was in deep green and the whole design, when it was finished, would look more like a pre-Raphaelite painting than a traditional tattoo. It had been Spider's idea to turn the silly butterfly tattoo she'd gotten in college into something more. Emmie would never forget the look of disappointment on his face when she'd come home for Thanksgiving.

Some college kids worried about disappointing their parents with bad grades. Emmie had disappointed Spider with substandard tattoo work.

"It's going to be so incredible," Daisy murmured. "I love this look. I wonder if he'd be willing to do more."

"Yes." Spider walked into the kitchen and slapped Daisy on her backside. "For you, mama? Anything, you stubborn girl."

Daisy smiled and lifted her face for a kiss Spider quickly granted. "I'm picky," she said. "Not stubborn."

He slid his arms around her and lifted her up. "You picked the best one, so I know you got good taste."

Emmie rolled her eyes, but secretly? She loved watching them. Spider and Daisy adored each other. "Get a room."

"I got a house." He set Daisy down, grabbed a kitchen towel, and flicked it at Emmie. "And you're in it. So mind your manners."

A timer buzzed on the stove. Tayla clapped her hands. "Okay, everyone in the dining room. I'll grab the casserole. Emmie, grab the salad?"

They settled in the small dining room attached to the living area. Daisy and Spider's house was an old Spanish bungalow from the 1930s they'd been fixing up since they bought it. Ethan pitched in for free beer, but the young couple had done most of the work themselves.

Tayla set the steaming chicken casserole on the table, and Spider refilled everyone's drinks. Daisy said a quick grace, then everyone dug in. Tayla had made something with green chilies, chicken, and cheese. As far as Emmie was concerned, that was never a bad combination.

Spider asked, "How's the shop coming? When you guys gonna open? I had someone asking after Ox the other day."

"Probably three weeks?" Emmie said. "I might do a light open a week or so before, but I know he's still waiting on his chair."

"We need to plan an event," Tayla said. She'd started moving her things down the weekend before. "Grand-opening reception or something, you know? Do cocktails. Wine and cheese."

Spider raised an eyebrow. "I'll bring the beer."

"That's a good idea," Daisy said. "You should call Hugh over at

Metlin Brewing. If you do some cross-promotion with local businesses, you'd get more customers in because they'll promote your event too."

"That's an idea," Emmie said. "I just know that it can't come soon enough."

"Is the shop done though?" Tayla asked. "I thought Ethan was still installing the counters."

"He is, but that'll be done this week." Emmie's car money was officially gone with the finished counters. She hadn't been able to buy the beautiful copper espresso maker she'd longed for, but as Tayla reminded her, she wasn't opening a café. The counters were a wiser investment.

That was Emmie. Always making the wise investment.

"Two more weeks," Tayla said, "and I'll be your willing servant."

"Ox been pulling his weight around the shop?" Spider asked quietly.

"He's been great," Emmie said, trying to rid her mind of the doubts Ginger's visit had planted. "Really. He's working just as hard as Ethan and me. He's been sanding all the cabinets this week while he waits for his stuff. Ethan says they'll be ready for finishing next week."

"Good." Spider finished his serving of casserole and reached for seconds. "Tayla, this is great. Thanks for cooking."

"I plan on hitting you up for tattoos after seeing your work on Emmie." Tayla peeked over Emmie's shoulder again. "It's amazing."

Daisy said, "Now if she'd just wear anything that showed it off."

Emmie muttered, "Not this again."

Tayla set down her fork, clearly recognizing an ally. "Right? She's the queen of unflattering career dress."

"I have tried to take her shopping so many times."

"Me too!"

Emmie tried to catch Spider's eye. "Make them stop."

He shook his head. "I'm out of this one."

She scowled. "Worst pretend brother ever."

"I'm just sitting here drinking my beer." He finished his glass and Emmie could swear he was fighting back a smile.

"I am not your guinea pig," Emmie said to Tayla. "I wear professional clothes because I'm a professional."

"But you don't work in San Francisco anymore," Daisy said. "You own a bookshop in Metlin. There is no reason for high-necked dress shirts to be part of your wardrobe."

Tayla said, "Like it or not, you are part of your marketing when you own the business."

"I don't even know what that means," Emmie said.

Tayla pulled on her braid. "That means Instagram-ready, *chica*. Not just your shop, but you too."

"That is superficial and horrible and an indictment of our sexist culture," Emmie said. "Forget it. I'm selling books. Not myself."

"It's not sexist," Daisy said. "You know how the girls flock to Ox's chair? It's not just because his work is good."

Emmie rolled her eyes. "Yeah, he's good-looking. So?"

"Has he taken his shirt off yet?" Tayla asked. "I feel like there have to be some abs happening there based on the muscle tone everywhere else."

Spider rose. "Pretty sure that's my cue to leave. I'm not talking about some dude's abs. Why am I always the only guy at dinner?"

"Because you're a lucky, lucky man?" Daisy handed him her empty plate. "Thank you, babe."

"I'm inviting Ethan next week," he said. "We need more testosterone in here."

"What about Jeremy?" Tayla asked. "You know, cute comic shop Jeremy?"

"Definitely my cue to leave." He took their plates to the kitchen, leaving Emmie alone with her tormentors.

"I don't care that Ox is hot," Emmie said. "Remember? I'm very carefully *not* noticing."

"But you're just as hot as he is," Tayla said. "That's the point. The nerdy-cute bookseller with the superhot tattoo artist." She set down her fork. "Oh my God, you guys could be on a romance-novel cover. You have to make this happen. You know writers."

Daisy said, "They would look hot on a book cover."

"I'm never, ever going to do that," Emmie said, tugging nervously on her braid. "Just stop. I'm not supposed to be noticing how hot Ox is, remember?"

"I wonder how he got that name," Tayla said. "Come on, I can't be the only one."

"Oxford. Miles *Oxford*." Emmie stood. "Okay, I'm out. Getting a needle poked in my back a thousand times a minute is less painful than this conversation."

"We're giving you a makeover before the grand opening!" Daisy said as Emmie cleared her plate. "Don't try to fight us. You know you'll lose."

————

EMMIE KEPT on *not* noticing how attractive Ox was for most of the next week. She was in her own little world in the shop, sorting books, ordering supplies, and cleaning. Always, always cleaning. Most of the woodwork had been done, but it seemed like fine sawdust still hovered in the air, just waiting for an even surface to settle on. Emmie was determined that the books wouldn't come out until the air cleared.

She was standing on a short ladder, dusting in time with the music blaring from her laptop, when she felt a draft on the small of her back. She spun around and nearly fell over in shock; Ox's arms came around her hips.

"Sorry! I noticed your tattoo and—"

"You thought it was okay to sneak up on me and lift my shirt?" Emmie glared at him.

"Shit." His mouth fell open and he backed away. "No. Sorry. I called your name a couple of times, but you didn't hear me, so I walked over and... I just noticed— I shouldn't have looked. Is that Spider's work?"

"That's not okay," she said, her cheeks flushed. "That's really not okay."

"You're right." He wiped a hand over his face. "I was curious, but I should have asked."

"It's personal," she said. "And it's not finished."

Ox pressed his lips together. "You're right, and I'm sorry. I was surprised by it and impressed with the work, but that's not an excuse. Will you forgive me?"

Emmie saw sincere regret in his expression. "Fine. Yes. I forgive you. Don't do it again."

"I promise I won't. I should know better. People touch mine all the time and it's not cool."

"Exactly." She stared his chest. "So are you going to take your shirt off? It's not like I'm not curious about your ink too."

Ox ripped his shirt over his head. "Sure, what did you want to see?"

Emmie slapped a hand over her eyes, but not before she'd gotten a whole heaping eyeful of hard muscles and intricate ink. "I was joking!"

"You asked."

She parted her fingers, positive her face was bright red. "I was joking."

His skin begged to be touched. A three-dimensional geometric pattern covered the left side of his chest, flexing with the muscle as he moved. Each piece of his ink was a different optical illusion that fed into the next. Cubes and lines intersected with stylized chess pieces and an old-fashioned clock. Emmie wanted to stare, but she was equally afraid of being rude and getting dizzy.

He caught her gaze. "Careful what you joke about. I'm not shy."

"Clearly."

Ox slung his T-shirt over his shoulder.

"You're just going to leave your shirt off?" She forced her hand down, trying to keep her eyes on his face.

"It suddenly feels hot in here." His tongue peeked out and licked his lower lip. "I have to say, you don't seem like the type."

"What type?"

He looked her up and down. Emmie was still standing on the short ladder, so he didn't have to look far down. "Hair in a bun. Collared shirts. Big sweaters. You're all buttoned-down. It does make me wonder."

She didn't ask about what. She had a feeling it would destroy her sanity. "Well, I... like buttons."

I like buttons? What the hell, Emmie?

"Buttons can be fun," Ox said. "For all sorts of things."

Emmie frowned. "What are we talking about?"

"Buttons." He reached over and flicked the bottom button of her cardigan. "Okay, Buttons, I better get back to work."

He stretched his arms up and yanked his T-shirt back over his chest. Emmie tried not to whimper as the beautiful, beautiful skin was covered up. Then his words registered.

"You're not calling me Buttons," she said. "That is not a good nickname."

He walked back to his corner of the shop. "You don't get to pick your nickname."

"Buttons is like a nickname for a cat or something."

He bent over and picked up his sanding block, muttering something under his breath that sounded like, "Here, kitty kitty."

"What?"

"Nothing." Ox started sanding the cupboard door. "So, that's Spider's work, right?"

"Yes."

"It looks good. Again, really sorry about not asking. That was rude. But when you're ready to show it to me, I'd love to see the whole piece."

When you're ready to show it to me...

Ha! That would be... roughly never.

CHAPTER TEN

HE WAS an idiot and he was surprised she hadn't slapped him for nosing in where he didn't belong. He was as bad as one of Abby's goats.

The tattoo had been a shocker, but the more he thought about it, the more it made sense. Emmie had grown up with Spider, she likely didn't have any qualms about tattooing. He'd spotted her examining his ink more than once. It was one of the reasons he'd been so quick to pull off his shirt. She liked it.

But her work?

He'd only gotten an impression of it. Leaves and the edge of a wing. A bird? The vivid red had been the first thing to catch his eye. He didn't work in color much even though he'd been trained across all different styles—his specialty was black and grey.

But he wanted to press his lips to that red.

She kept it secret, and he wanted to see it. She was pale. The colors would be vivid. And the design started right at the top of her supremely excellent ass. She kept it hidden, but he knew it was there.

Ox had a sudden mental picture of Emmie back up on the

ladder, her lower back at eye level. He wanted to lift her shirt and lick up her spine in that warm soft curve at the small of her back where he'd seen vines and leaves curling. He wanted to press his hands into the soft swell of her—

"Fuck." Ox rammed his toe into the base of his counter. He had to stop thinking about her.

"What was that?" she yelled.

"Just kicked my counter. Accident. No big deal... Buttons."

"Stop calling me that."

Buttons. The name made him smile. *"I like buttons."*

Yeah, so do I, Emmie. Bet I could find a few of yours if I tried.

She was fucking adorable and unintentionally hilarious. How was he going to get this chick out of his head? He flipped open the catalog and started jotting down a list to start an order when he got back to the ranch. He needed to bring his laptop in to the shop, but he'd been letting Abby use it for school and was using it to watch TV in his room. Maybe he'd get a separate one for the shop. He pulled out his phone and looked at prices.

Shiiiiit. Maybe not. Abby would have to use her mom's computer.

Emmie left the shop and walked upstairs to her apartment. Every now and then when he'd been working late over the past few weeks, he'd heard her up there, puttering around. She played music. He heard the TV every now and then, but not often. Mostly it was music. Folksy stuff with guitars and banjos and shit. She probably listened to music while she read. Sometimes it was just a piano. He wanted to sit in a corner and sketch her while she read. Sometimes he'd catch her reading a book, and he liked the tiny expressions that crossed her face when she was deep in concentration.

Ox vaguely remembered a time when he'd thought Emmie would be boring. He didn't remember *why* he'd thought that, but he'd been wrong. With some people, quiet meant boring. With

Emmie, it just meant he couldn't quite figure her out. And that was interesting as hell.

She came down a few minutes later wearing another baggy sweater. "Hey, I'm going out for lunch. You want anything?"

For you to take off that god-awful sweater? "You going to Café Maya?"

"Yeah."

"Coffee would be great."

She flashed him a smile before she slipped out the door. "You got it."

A few minutes after she left, Adrian Saroyan, the asshole real estate guy, walked past on Main.

"Keep walking," Ox muttered. "She's not here."

Sadly, Adrian walked in, his designer suit spotless and his shoes shined. Ox glanced down at his boots.

They were not shiny.

"Hey!" Adrian said in a newly familiar greeting. "Emmie around?" The first time he'd come by it had been "Good afternoon." The second time, it had been "Nice to see you again." And now it was simply "Hey." Ox wished the guy would get the hint.

He flipped past the piercing supplies in the catalog. "She's not here."

The bright white smile didn't waver and the man's hair didn't move. "I sure wish I knew what her hours were. I'd really like to speak to Emmie."

Ox could have told him she'd just left for lunch and she'd be back in an hour, but... he didn't want to. "She's the boss," he said simply. "Keeps her own hours."

"You've been giving her my messages?"

"Yep."

Adrian nodded slowly. "And you're sure she has my card?"

"You can leave another one on the counter if you want. I'll let her know it's there."

The man's friendly demeanor cracked just a little. "No, that's fine. I'm afraid…"

Ox looked up.

Adrian continued, "I'm afraid I made a bad first impression the last time we spoke."

"Didn't you go to school with her or something?"

"I did."

"So when was the bad first impression?" Ox asked. "Back in first grade or something?"

He knew exactly what Adrian was talking about, but he didn't feel like cutting the man any slack. According to Emmie, the first time she'd run into the guy after she'd moved back to town, he'd pressured her into selling her building or letting him rent it out as a property manager, basically implying her business was doomed before it started. That kind of shit pissed Ox off. You think someone was fooling themselves and taking a bad risk? Keep it to yourself unless they ask you for your opinion. Every damn person thought their opinion was like gold these days.

Ox blamed Facebook.

Adrian said, "I haven't had a chance to talk to her again after our first meeting. Since I only ever seem to find you here, just tell her I stopped by and that I'd really like to speak to her again. Not about anything to do with selling or renting the place. I'd just like to see… her."

Ox narrowed his eyes on the man.

Shit.

He didn't want Emmie's shop. He wanted Emmie.

And Ox should not have had a problem with that. In fact, if Emmie hooked up with Mr. Shiny Shoes, it would be best. Then she'd be off-limits and Ox could stop thinking about her. He didn't fool around with women who were in relationships. Adrian Saroyan, real estate agent, was probably the kind of guy she'd go for anyway. Girls like Emmie fooled around with guys like Ox, but they didn't get serious about them. They got serious with guys who wore ties, gelled their hair, and had office hours.

Adrian's frown made Ox realize his lip was curled. He cleared his throat and flipped the catalog closed. "Yeah, I'll let her know you came by. Sorry, man, that's all I can do."

And I will not be giving her your heartfelt sentiments about seeing her. Fuck you.

Ox smiled and put his hands in his pockets, glancing meaningfully at the door.

"Right," Adrian said. "Thanks for all your… help."

"You're very welcome."

But don't come back until you wash the shit out of your hair.

———

AN HOUR LATER, like clockwork, Emmie returned from lunch. Ox was working on screwing his counters into the wall, wincing as he drilled through the old plasterwork, when she set his coffee on the floor.

"One large coffee. Black with two sugars."

He rolled up to sitting and set the drill down. "Buttons, you are my coffee angel."

She rolled her eyes. "If you tell Tayla that name—"

"I won't." He grinned. "It's my own special name just for you."

"Thanks." She walked back to her shelves. "I feel so honored."

She took off her oversized sweater and tossed it on the wing-back chair in the lounge area. Beneath it, she'd changed into a slightly-less-baggy-than-normal green T-shirt that read ONE MORE CHAPTER across the bust like a nerdy sorority shirt.

"Your friend Adrian came by again."

"Not my friend." She made a face. "Can that guy not get a hint?"

The face made Ox smile inside. *Suck it, Shiny Shoes.*

She climbed up the ladder and started dusting again. When she lifted her arms, the shirt rode up and he could see the edge of her tattoo.

He tore his eyes away from that sliver of skin.

Business. Strictly. Business.

CHAPTER ELEVEN

THE WEEK BEFORE THE OPENING, everything about INK was in full motion and Emmie was trying not to lose her mind. Ox and Ethan were putting the final touches on the tattoo shop, hanging newly refinished doors on the cabinets, waxing the floors, and perfecting the plumbing in the sinks Ethan had installed. Emmie and Tayla were cataloging inventory, sorting shelves, and creating displays for the opening-day reception.

Ethan and Emmie had driven out to Metlin Brewing Company to work out a deal for the microbrewer to serve their seasonal ale, cider, and root beer at the opening reception while Daisy was baking dozens of book cookies decorated like the covers of classic books. Ads were already in place in the *Metlin Gazette*, and Ox's phone was ringing off the hook with clients booking appointments for when he was ready to open.

The old barber chair Ox had bought was the centerpiece of his shop, but a new rolling stool and a massage table hid behind a discreet screen for privacy. The walls were hung with his art, and yes, he had found a stuffed jackalope. The tattoo shop had a distinctly masculine feel, but it was still open and friendly with windows Ox had painted facing 7th Avenue. A sign advertising his hours and website was ready to be placed on the sidewalk outside.

The coffee station was ready for business. They had a drip machine to make larger pots for things like book clubs and a single-serve machine for those times in between. An eclectic selection of mugs lined the counter along with assorted sweeteners. Cream and milk was in the small fridge beneath the counter.

It was all a bit overwhelming, but she'd be fine in a week.

Probably.

The shared lounge area was the centerpiece of the shop, sitting right in the middle of the tattoo shop and the bookshelves. The long couch had been re-covered and was joined by two chairs, a coffee table, and several stools. A mix of art books and tattoo magazines littered the table. Bookmarks, stickers, and journals sat in racks by the register.

Emmie stood at the door, trying not to be overwhelmed. It was seven days till the grand opening, and she had nothing to be worried about. Tayla had already been updating the shop's social media accounts and posting pictures. Over three hundred people followed them already, and they weren't even open. Emmie had sent postcards announcing the opening to her grandmother's old mailing list. It was only a few hundred people, but she'd already had a few excited calls asking about book clubs.

Emmie turned when the bell over the door rang and saw Daisy walking in with another pillow for the couch.

"Hey," Daisy said. "Finished the last one."

"Thanks."

"Why do you have a scared-shitless expression on your face?" Daisy asked.

"Probably because I'm scared shitless." Emmie tugged on the sleeve of her cardigan. "What if no one comes?"

"Didn't Tayla say that over one hundred people had already responded to the online invite?"

"Is that enough? I have no idea." She was trying not to panic. "I remember running the numbers and doing the projections, but somehow none of that is coming to mind right now. I just look at my grandma's shop which"—she turned and put her hands in a frame position—"does not look like my grandma's shop anymore. At all. And I'm now almost positive this was the stupidest thing I've ever done and I should have taken Adrian's advice to sell or rent this place to Banana Gap or something."

Daisy bit her lower lip, trying not to laugh. "Banana Gap?"

"Or something."

Daisy came beside Emmie and put an arm around her. "Okay, deep breaths."

Emmie forced a breath in and out. Then she let her eyes rest on Ox, who was hanging upper cabinet doors. His shirt—the evil shirt that covered his beautiful inked muscles—rode up over his waistband as he stretched his arms over his head. She shouldn't have been so hard on him. If she was standing behind him, she'd be sorely tempted to run her tongue along the small of his back, not just her fingers.

Daisy followed Emmie's eyes. "Are you in your happy place now?"

Emmie kept her voice low. "I know I shouldn't, but..."

"This is judgment-free space between us right now." Daisy patted her shoulder.

"I'm judging myself." She closed her eyes and pressed the heels of her hands to her forehead. "Okay, what am I forgetting?"

"That shopping trip we were taking today to revamp your wardrobe before the grand opening."

Emmie squinted. "Nope. That is not what I'm forgetting because I never agreed to that."

Tayla walked over with her purse. "Yep, pretty sure that's it. Hi, Daisy."

"Hey, Tayla."

Emmie looked between her two best friends. "Is this a setup?"

"No," Tayla said. "This is a kidnapping."

TWO HOURS LATER, Emmie was still in hell, but it was starting to feel cozy warm instead of sweltering. Of course, that might have had something to do with the three margaritas she'd had at lunch.

She tried to wiggle out of the trendy, torn jeans they'd forced her into. "These are too tight. And they're torn. I'm pretty sure they make my butt look huge."

"They do not. And they're *artfully* torn," Tayla said. "Since we're going for the nerdy bohemian look for you, artfully torn jeans are a must."

"What is nerdy bohemian?" She tugged on the jeans, which she had to admit were comfortable but also fitted to her butt, which she hated. Of all the areas of her body to be oversized, it had to be her ass. Not her boobs. Her butt.

Luckily, margaritas had been invented by the patron saint of long lunches.

"Nerdy bohemian?" Daisy sipped on an iced coffee. "Let's see, you watch sappy period drama but also you might fly off to Budapest at the last minute to visit a friend who's preparing for fashion week in Milan."

Emmie's eyes bugged out. "I don't know anyone who's going to fashion week in any city. What—"

"You watch *Doctor Who*," Tayla interrupted, "but only while drinking absinthe."

"You drink craft beer and listen to K-pop."

"You guys are ridiculous." Emmie caught a filmy kimono thing that Daisy threw at her head. "What am I supposed to do with this? Is this a robe? Where do I wear something like this?"

"You wear it to work! Listen, *you* in cool torn-up jeans, that vintage *Great Gatsby* T-shirt you're wearing—we should see about stocking that kind of thing in the shop, by the way—and a coordinating wrap like this." Tayla squared Emmie to the mirror and put the kimono over her shoulders. "Rock and roll jeans. Nerd-girl T-shirt. Bohemian shrug." She tugged Emmie's braid over her shoulder. "Loose braid of amazing hair. Mismatched earrings. Maybe add a scarf or a chunky necklace."

Emmie stared at the more stylish version of herself in the mirror. "This is mostly stuff I have."

"You have a lot of T-shirts—you need good jeans and cool accessories," Tayla said. "But it's not a makeover because you don't need to be remade. You have cool stuff, you just need to learn how to put it together. Will you trust me? This is a thing I do, okay?"

Emmie wavered. She did look nice in the mirror. Still herself, but more put together. And the jeans were torn, but they did look cool. And they were definitely more comfortable than her regular work clothes.

Daisy added, "You've been wearing old jeans and T-shirts for the renovation, but you can't wear those *or* your Bay City wardrobe when you open. This is Metlin, not Union Square. I get itchy just hearing the word *slacks*."

"That's because slacks is an awful word," Tayla said. "But Daisy is right. You need to let your hair down."

"Literally?"

"And we really need to show off your ink," Daisy said.

Emmie glared at her in the mirror. "It's my whole back. No."

"One shirt!" Daisy said. "There's this amazing burgundy velvet shirt at Marcella's you need to see. It's got an open draped back—"

"I'm not going braless!"

Tayla rolled her eyes. "You have adorable teacup boobs. You can wear one of those sticky bras and be fine."

"Spider is going to finish your back—your beautiful, amazing piece-of-art back tattoo—this Friday night," Daisy said. "Which gives you a week to heal. And this shirt would show it off perfectly. It's high-necked in front, so it's still modest. It's just totally open at the back and the colors would be amazing with the butterfly wings."

Tayla rested her chin on Emmie's shoulder. "Please let me

dress you up. You wear a size six. There are a million clothes that fit you. Let me live vicariously."

"Don't pull that. You have way more clothes than me, and you always look amazing."

"But it takes much more effort. Trust me on this." Tayla gave her puppy dog eyes. "Please, Emmie. Please please please—"

"Fine." She looked at the price tag on the kimono thing and her eyes went wide. "How many of these am I supposed to buy?"

"This one is your birthday present. Two more and then some cool scarves and you'll be fine. Think of it as an investment. In you. In the shop. In your nonexistent sex life—"

"Hey!"

"You know you want Ox to look at you and drool," Tayla whispered. "Even if you never do anything about it, you want to make his eyes bug out."

Emmie took a deep breath, glanced at Daisy's hopeful eyes in the mirror, and gave in. "Okay, I'll try on the shirt."

Daisy stood up and clapped. "And you can try on the leather pants that go with it."

"I did not agree to leather pants!"

———

EMMIE STUMBLED BACK to the shop with four bags of clothes including the backless shirt. Despite begging and pleading, she hadn't given in to the leather pants, but she did have three new pair of jeans that "did justice to her legs" according to her friends.

It was dark and she was more than a little off-balance from a combination of shopping bags and the steady stream of margaritas Tayla and Daisy had been dosing her with all afternoon. Her head swam nicely as she waved at them in the car. As she opened the Main Street door, she saw a light in Ox's corner of INK. He was still working. He had a pile of frames on the counter, and it looked like he was mounting flash to hang on the wall.

"Hey!" she said. "You're still here."

Ox glanced up. "Hey yourself. Where have you been?"

"Tayla and Daisy are evil and made me buy girl-clothes."

"I thought chicks liked buying clothes," he muttered.

"I do like buying clothes. I order sarcastic T-shirts online and…" She blinked. "I forgot what I was going to say."

Ox looked up and smiled. "Buttons, you're drunk."

"No, I'm… relaxed. And you should do that more. But stop calling me Buttons."

"Do what?" He put a screwdriver down and walked over. "What should I do more?" He reached for her bags.

"Smile." Emmie handed them over because they were heavy enough to be cutting into her hands. "Smile more. That's what I noticed about you first."

"Oh yeah?"

"When I first saw you, I thought you were mean. Then you smiled at this old lady and helped her load stuff in her car. And then I thought you were nice."

Ox's smile turned softer. "I am nice."

"I know that *now*. But when I first saw you, you were always yelling at Ginger."

He put a hand on the small of her back and herded her toward the stairs that led to the second-floor apartment. "Some people bring out the worst in each other." His voice dropped. "Some people bring out the best."

They started up the stairs, Ox walking behind Emmie and holding her shopping bags. Her head was swimming just enough to destroy her filter. She'd be embarrassed tomorrow. Tonight, she was too curious. "Which kind am I?"

He tugged on her waistband. "What do you think?"

Emmie turned and they were almost nose to nose. "I like you."

Some expression moved over his face, but it was too dark to read it. "Probably a good thing since we'll be working together."

"I picked out books for you. I ordered them yesterday."

He smiled again, and his eyes crinkled in the corners. "What kind of books?"

"Adventure books. Like *Hatchet*, but adult fiction. Some nonfiction. And a sci-fi novel. You didn't mention sci-fi, but this one is kind of more steampunk and I think you might like it." She blinked and tried to reach for one of her bags. He shouldn't be carrying all of them. "I mean, I hope you'll like it. I tried—"

"I'll like it." He held the bag away from her. "What are you doing?"

"Trying to get my shirt. It's very embarrassed. It doesn't have a back."

"The shirt is embarrassed?"

"No, I am. When I wear it."

He frowned. "So why did you buy it?"

"Because Daisy wants me to show off my tattoo."

He glanced at the bag. "Do you *want* to show off your tattoo?"

"Kind of." She leaned forward and nearly lost her balance.

Ox dropped the bags in his right hand. "Careful." He slid his arm around her waist, his fingers skimming along the skin at the small of her back.

Emmie shivered and goose bumps rose on her arms. "Sorry."

"We should get you upstairs."

Neither of them moved. Emmie stared at the ink along his collarbone and saw his throat move as he swallowed.

"Maybe you should show me." His finger was stroking along the softly raised lines of ink along her spine. "Just to practice before you debut it to the world. I'm a professional."

"Huh?" Her head was swimming, and she was pretty sure it wasn't just from the margaritas anymore.

"If you're going to show your ink to the world"—his finger kept moving back and forth, back and forth—"maybe you should let me see first."

She blinked. "You want me to take my shirt off?"

He closed his eyes and his shoulders shook in silent laughter. "Upstairs, Buttons."

"That's kind of unprofessional. You shouldn't ask me to take my shirt off. That might be sexual harassment."

"You're my landlord." He nudged her around and up the stairs, leaving the bags on the floor and keeping one hand on her. "So I kind of work at your pleasure. I think sexual harassment works the other way in this situation."

She shook her head. "I don't think so."

"Also, you're drunk, so I'm definitely not asking you to take your shirt off."

"Okay, that's good." She managed to get the door open and the lights on.

Ox set down the bags and went back for the others. He put them all in the small entry where Emmie dropped her keys on the antique dressing table she'd moved from the bedroom.

"Turn around," she said.

He frowned. "What?"

"Turn." She spun her finger in a circle. "Turn your back."

"Ooookay." He turned his back and Emmie turned hers, counting on liquid courage to get her through the first reveal. She pulled up her shirt and removed her bra before she held both bundled over her front, revealing her back to the chilled air of the apartment.

"Emmie?"

She stared at the streetlights reflecting on the windows of the apartment across the street, realizing that somewhere in the opposite building, Ginger had her own apartment where she and Ox had shared a bed.

She almost lost her nerve. She was no voluptuous beauty. She was skinny. She was pale. There was cellulite on her thighs and she was only twenty-seven, for heaven's sake. She definitely needed to start exercising.

Do it, Emmie.

"Okay, you can look."

She heard him turn and then the quick inhalation of breath. A slow exhalation.

"Wow." He moved closer. "Can I turn on this lamp?"

She nodded.

The lamp on the kitchen counter clicked on, and warm gold light filled the apartment. She could hear Ox coming closer.

"Fucking gorgeous. That deep burgundy on the wings. That's"—he cleared his throat—"really beautiful." His voice dropped. "Really, really beautiful." She heard him kneel down, felt the heat of his hands near the small of her back. "Do you mind if I…?"

She shook her head, still speechless. She knew if she wore the backless shirt, people would look. Somehow having Ox examine her with an artist's eye was easier. She could hear the appreciation in his voice, but it wasn't about her. It was about the ink.

It was about the ink.

What Ox was seeing was an intricate tapestry of vines, flowers, and butterflies, all in the pre-Raphaelite style. Deep green and blue shading covered her back, turning her pale skin into a garden. Butterflies flitted from shoulder to shoulder as vines and leaves crawled up the nape of her neck.

He tapped on her spine. "Is this a cover?"

"The roots?"

"Yeah."

She nodded. "The stupidity of youth. I wanted a butterfly, and I didn't want to ask Spider to do it."

"Mistake."

"Trust me, he's never let me forget it."

Ox's low laugh soothed her nerves, but it didn't get rid of the goose bumps on her skin. Hopefully he'd think they were from the cool air.

"Your skin is fair; the colors show up well." He brushed his fingertips over her left lower back. "And his shading here is so good. That brown almost looks like velvet. How does he do that?"

"I wish I could see it from your perspective. I only get mirrors."

A single finger trailed up the right side of her back to her shoulder. "You could have him extend this vine at some point, curl this branch over your shoulder and down your arm."

Emmie's mouth dropped open and her eyes closed. *Dear Lord...* His hands were warm and a little rough. Her skin felt every tiny movement. She wanted him to continue the line he was drawing, over her shoulder, across her collarbone, down to her—

"At least"—he took his fingers off her skin and Emmie tried not to cry—"that's what I'd do if it were my design, but it's yours. And"—she felt a warm thumb make one last brush over her shoulder—"it's amazing. Fucking gorgeous, Emmie."

"Thank you."

He stood up and put his hand on her shoulder before he leaned down to her ear. "Thank *you*," he whispered. "I should probably go now."

Emmie couldn't speak.

"I'd rethink that backless shirt though."

"What?" She looked over her shoulder. "Why?"

"Trust me." He skimmed a hand over her shoulders before he walked to the door. "Everyone will want to touch."

CHAPTER TWELVE

EMMIE HAD JUST UNPACKED the order of books that contained the adventure novels she'd ordered for Ox when she heard unfamiliar voices in the shop. She grabbed Ox's books, walked downstairs, and peeked through the door, curious who had come to visit. According to Ox, she'd successfully avoided Adrian Saroyan three times now. She didn't want to break her streak.

"So you're going to Sierra Community now?" Ox asked. "What are you studying?"

"Just general ed right now," a girl said. "But I'm going to be a psychologist."

Emily peeked farther. No Adrian. Three college girls sitting in the lounge. Ox being inadvertently charming.

Emmie was pretty sure he didn't try to be charming, but she'd seen the same phenomenon too often to consider it a coincidence. The more Ox ignored the girls who flirted with him, the more they liked him. To Emmie, it was really confusing.

Ox held up a hand. "Better not tell you too much then. You'll start analyzing me."

All three girls giggled.

It wasn't that funny.

Emmie examined them. They were all in their late teens or early twenties and dressed for winter, throwing on stylish wraps and boots even though the temperature had barely dipped below sixty the night before. They'd be sweating by afternoon, but for the moment they looked cool and clever and impossibly stylish. Emmie glanced down at her clothes. INK wasn't officially open, so she wasn't wearing her new wardrobe. Her oversized T-shirt sported a cat with laser-beam eyes, and her jeans were the baggy variety.

Get over yourself, Em.

This wasn't high school even if the girls in the lounge reminded her of it. She was a business owner and these were potential customers, though from the look of things, they were way more interested in Ox than in books. Still, three coffee cups from Café Maya littered the table between them, people were in the shop, chatting and laughing. It wasn't a bad way to start her working day.

Emmie straightened her shoulders and walked out of the hallway. "Hey!" she said cheerfully. "Welcome to INK. We're not officially open, but can I help you?"

"Girls, this is Emmie. She runs the bookshop." Ox stood. "Remember Russ across the street? Kim is his sister, and these are some of her friends."

All three girls waved at once. "Hey."

"Hi." Emmie waved back. "Did you need help with anything?"

"We just came by to say hi to Ox. My brother said him and Ginger broke up."

He and Ginger. Emmie smiled and reined in any grammar-correcting urges. "Yeah, I'm pretty excited to be working with him here at INK."

The girl who'd spoken was the blonde studying psychology. She pulled out her phone and started taking pictures of the shop. "This place is so cute."

INK

The next girl pulled out her phone too. "It's supercute. I need to buy a book and some winter stuff to go with that really furry blanket my mom got me. That would make such a cute picture, right?"

The third girl said, "Oh my God, Amber, that would look amazing. Like coffee and books and cute socks?"

Emmie quietly counted the number of times they included "cute" in the conversation.

Too many.

"Cocoa," Kim said. "Use cocoa instead. Cocoa is cuter than coffee."

"You're so smart." Amber turned to Emmie. "What's your Instagram? We'll tag you."

Emmie's brain was scrambled and she'd lost count of how many *cutes* they'd uttered. "Sorry, what?"

"Hey!" Tayla walked downstairs just in time. "I love your boots!" she said to Kim. "Did you just get those this season?"

"They're vintage," Kim said. "My mom had them."

"You're so lucky." Tayla immediately walked to the counter and grabbed three business cards. "So, all our information is on there. Instagram. Snapchat. We totally follow back. We don't have a YouTube channel up yet, but Emmie and I are going to be doing online book reviews eventually."

They were?

Tayla was still talking to the three girls "Do any of you have tattoos from Ox already?"

"I do!" Kim held up her hand. "I have this little star on my wrist. I got it last year."

Ox had come over to the counter and was leaning against it with Emmie, fighting off a smile. "They invaded at dawn," he said quietly. "I couldn't turn them away. Kim brought me coffee, and you weren't awake yet."

"I'm so confused, but I'm letting Tayla do this part. She speaks cute."

93

"Trust me, you speak cute fluently."

Tayla had walked to the YA section and grabbed a new fantasy romance with stars on the cover. It was a stunning hardback and one that Emmie had been planning to feature at the opening because the online reviews were glowing.

"Do you like fantasy?" Tayla asked.

"I watch *Game of Thrones*," Kim said. "Oh, I love that cover!"

"Right? Okay, so let's give you this and hold it with the hand where the tattoo is—"

"Got it." Kim took over immediately, grabbing the book and angling her phone to snag a shot of her right hand holding the book, the small black star peeking from the corner of her wrist.

"That looks amazing," Tayla said over her shoulder. "Now you can say you get all your ink at INK."

"Caption!" Kim said. "So. Cute."

"Tag us and I'll repost."

Tayla kept chatting with the girls while Emmie started the coffeepot.

Ox grabbed the books Emmie had forgotten on the counter. "Hey, are these for me?"

"Yeah." She glanced at him nervously. "I hope you like them."

He was already reading the back covers, his brow wrinkled in concentration. Had he looked at her bare skin with that same look? Because she was melting a little inside thinking about that.

It had been two days since she'd drunkenly bared her back to Ox. She'd been expecting him to mention it, but he'd been totally silent. Hadn't brought it up once. If not for a quick question about her head the next morning, she might have thought she'd imagined the whole thing.

"How's your back?" he muttered. "Spider finished last night, right?"

"Are you a mind reader?"

He looked up. "What?"

"Nothing." She shook her head. "It's fine. He finished all the details on the shading, so it's slightly sore all over, but not as intense as when he did the fill." And that sticky bra Tayla had forced on her was already coming in handy.

Ox asked, "Do you toss and turn at night?"

"Nope, I sleep like the dead."

"I'll keep that in mind." he muttered.

"What?"

"Nothing." He nodded at the girls. "This is good, right? Russ asked if they could come by, and I said it was cool."

"Yeah, totally cool. They clearly shop a lot. We just need to make sure they think books are photo-worthy accessories."

Ox chuckled. "Accessories. Right."

He was holding his books like they were shiny new toys. It warmed Emmie to her toes. He really was going to read them. He really was excited.

And he just got hotter. Great.

"So when is your opening?" Amber asked Tayla. "Kim, we should totally go."

"I don't know..."

Ox looked up from his books. "If you girls come and bring some friends, I'll give you little stars like Kim has."

The three girls lit up. "Oh em gee, Kim, how cute would that be?"

"We could take pictures."

Tayla said, "Take pictures holding books!"

"The cutest," Kim said. "We'll be here." She held up her phone. "Look! You already have two hundred and eighty likes."

Emmie blinked. "What?"

"On the picture of me with the book."

"Holy shit, that's awesome. Thank you!"

Kim beamed.

Tayla wandered over to Emmie and whispered, "Get all your

ink at INK. Remember that one." Tayla plucked at the edge of Emmie's laser-cat T-shirt. "What are you wearing? Picture ready, remember?"

Emmie rolled her eyes. "Fine, I'll go change."

Ox was still reading the backs of his new books. "She looks fine to me."

"She's wearing laser cats."

"And?" Ox bumped her shoulder. "Thanks for the new reads, Buttons. That sci-fi one looks good."

Tayla waited for Ox to get back to his side of the shop. "Buttons?"

"As in, pushing all of them this morning."

"*Chica*, you've got it bad."

"You have no idea."

———

EMMIE WAS GETTING her afternoon pick-me-up at Café Maya when she heard the voice she'd been avoiding for weeks.

"Hey, Emmie."

Oh no. She'd changed her clothes, but she still wasn't prepared to meet Adrian Saroyan.

She looked over her shoulder and feigned surprise. "Adrian! How are you?"

He still looked amazing, if a bit overdressed. Emmie wondered if he always met clients that way. Maybe he had to visit the bank. She'd quickly gotten used to being in Metlin again with its more relaxed dress code. Seeing a man in a suit—even a nicely tailored one—was jarring.

"I've been trying to get ahold of you," he said. "Did your friend tell you I'd stopped by?"

"Who, Ox?"

"I don't know." Adrian chuckled, his white teeth gleaming

against a dark tan. "The big guy with lots of..." He motioned over his arms.

Emmie frowned. "Lots of muscles?"

Adrian's smile turned stiff. "Tattoos."

"Oh! Yeah, that's Ox."

"Ox?" He nodded. "Okay. I was there last week and told him I needed to speak to you. I left a card."

"I got it. I've just been super busy with all the prep for the opening next week." *And also avoiding you.*

"Everything in the shop looks great."

"We're getting good advance buzz," Emmie said. "We're very optimistic."

"Moving a tattoo shop into the other side of the store was... innovative." Adrian shuffled his feet. "I really hope it works out for you."

Emmie nodded and smiled. It was hard to forget Adrian's initial reaction to Emmie's reopening the shop.

"I'm serious," he said. "I feel like we got off on the wrong foot, and I'd like to make it up to you. Buy you a coffee?"

"I don't know. I'm really bus—"

"Just to catch up," he said. "Also, my mom was asking about you. She's so excited Metlin is going to have a bookstore again. Plus her birthday is in a couple of weeks. I was hoping you could recommend a book."

"Okay." *Curses!* She couldn't say no when someone asked for a book recommendation. It was a compulsion.

He stepped to her side. "What can I get you?"

A few minutes later, they were settled into a corner table at Café Maya while Daisy shot them laser looks from behind the counter. Emmie ignored her and focused on Adrian, who was drinking tea while she sipped her latte.

"So... San Francisco, right?" he asked.

She nodded. "I was up there for school and working part-time at a big bookstore."

"A chain?"

"No, an independent place. An institution, really. Lots of big-name authors would come in for signings. Major events. It was pretty cool." She smiled. "Well, pretty cool for a book person."

Adrian smiled. "Sounds pretty cool for anyone. That was always your thing in school. Books, right? Smartest girl in class."

Oh yeah, because that had been the title her sixteen-year-old self had wanted. "They hired me on full time after I graduated. I was an assistant manager and did all their displays." She shrugged. "It was good. They paid well."

"And now you're your own boss," he said. "Was that something you wanted?"

Emmie thought about it. "Not consciously. But I guess when you grow up with your grandma and your mom working for themselves, it feels like a natural transition."

"Your mom still doing the...?" He played air guitar.

Emmie laughed. "Yeah. A lot of studio stuff lately. Some of her own pieces. Some covers. She keeps busy. She's touring with a band next year. She won't tell me who yet."

"Sounds cool."

"She is cool." Emmie sipped her coffee. "I was always the straight arrow in the family."

Adrian looked at her and a smile touched his lips. "Straight arrow looks good on you, Marianne Elliot."

Emmie covered her face. "I forgot you knew my real name."

"Perks of working in the high school office."

Emmie groaned. "Why?"

"Why do you hate it?" he asked. "Marianne is a beautiful name."

"Marianne Elliot sounds like a sad Jane Austen character who gets passed over for a more witty cousin."

"That's not true." He laughed. "At all."

"That's because you don't read Austen."

"So tell me what to read. You're the professional."

Emmie smiled. "Funny."

"I'm serious." He leaned forward. "You were right. I don't read enough. How am I supposed to impress beautiful women at dinner if I don't read books?"

Emmie was speechless.

"So what Jane Austen novel should I read? Pick one, I'll read it, and then... we can go to dinner and talk about it."

Emmie stammered, "Are... are you using Jane Austen to ask me on a date?"

"Yes." He raised an eyebrow. "Did it work?"

"Sure." She spoke before she thought twice. Her eyes went wide. What was she doing? She'd just accepted a date with Adrian Saroyan. If she were sixteen, she'd be ecstatic. At twenty-seven, she didn't know what she was thinking.

He asked, "Did you surprise yourself by saying yes?"

"You surprised me first, so I'm blaming it on you."

Adrian smiled and brought his mug to his lips. "So the Jane Austen thing worked."

"*Sense and Sensibility.*"

"Is that the book?" He took out his phone. "I'm making a note now."

"You better not buy that online," she said. "I have a copy at the shop."

"But you're not open yet."

"I'll make an exception, and you can pay me back later."

"Cool." He leaned on the table. "So when are we going to dinner?"

"How fast do you read?"

"Pretty fast when I'm motivated."

Emmie's head was starting to spin. Was this real life? Why was Adrian Saroyan asking her out? She grabbed her cup of coffee and stood. "I need to get back to work."

"Great." He stood and slung his coat over his shoulder. "I'll follow you over and get my book."

He followed Emmie out of the shop and she studiously avoided both Daisy's laser eyes and the phone buzzing relentlessly in her pocket.

Oh, she was going to have some explaining to do by the time all this was over.

CHAPTER THIRTEEN

FUCKING ADRIAN SAROYAN and his shiny fucking shoes and his ruthless smile hidden by veneers.

Ox glanced up from his sketch book and just as quickly looked away. *What the hell, Emmie? That guy?*

A voice that sounded a hell of a lot like his late brother-in-law said, *Then get off your ass and make a move, idiot. Your excuses are bullshit.*

She was his partner. His landlord. Hooking up with Emmie would be catastrophic when it ended.

If it ended?

Maybe it wouldn't end. Maybe she was the one.

Getting way ahead of yourself there, Oxford.

How did you pursue someone when the consequences of it going bad were so very, *very* bad? At this point they'd both invested thousands of dollars and the shop wasn't even open. They had to make this work. Getting involved would complicate everything. It could be great, but the chances were much greater that at some point, he'd fuck up and she'd hate him.

"Some people bring out the worst in each other. Some people bring out the best."

"Which kind am I?"

"What do you think?"

It didn't matter. It didn't fucking matter how much he wanted her. He couldn't have her. He couldn't have her and the shop, and he needed to want the shop. He needed to get his shit together and make a real go of running his own business. Screwing around with his landlady was not part of the plan.

But Adrian Saroyan?

Ox's brain was a jumble. He broke his pencil twice trying to sketch out new book flash for the walls near the café.

Adrian had followed Emmie back to the shop, trailing after her like a puppy. Sadly, she hadn't been scowling. Adrian waved at Ox as he walked in and wandered around her bookshelves, making dumb jokes that somehow made her laugh. Then he'd picked up a book and said something about how fast he could finish like he was bragging.

Finishing fast is not something you brag about, asshole.

Ox knew he was probably talking about the book, but his mood was foul and he didn't want to think about the asshole even touching Emmie. He was already standing too close.

Anywhere in the shop is too close.

Ox stood and grabbed his jacket. "I'm going out."

Emmie looked away from Adrian. "Okay."

"Can I grab you a coffee on my way back?"

She shook her head. "I just had coffee with Adrian, but thanks."

"Right." Ox glared at Adrian. "See ya."

"Nice to see you again." There was a triumphant glint in the asshole's eye.

Ox grunted and quickly left through the 7th Avenue door, walking down the street to his truck. He climbed in and started it, banging on the dashboard when it hiccuped. He'd put a new starter in the week before. It shouldn't still be doing that. It had been rebuilt, but Sergio assured him that he'd done it himself and Sergio was the best mechanic in Metlin. Ox drove south on 7th, turned left on Sequoia and then north on 6th Avenue, taking the back alley into Supreme Automotive, the shop Sergio ran with his uncle Beto.

Sergio walked out, wiping his hands on a red rag and frowning at Ox when he rolled the window down. "What'd you do to my truck this time?"

"Not your truck, asshole."

The older Sergio got, the more he looked like his dad, barrel-chested and burly. Sergio wouldn't win any beauty contests, but he had a never-ending parade of cute girls dropping their cars off at the shop, so he wasn't a stranger to problems with women.

"Someone's been spending too much time with pretty girls on Main. Frustrated much?" He thumped the hood and unbuttoned his coveralls, tying the arms around his waist when Ox turned off the engine. "It's too warm for this time of year. I'm dying in the bay. What's wrong with it?"

"I just want to check the starter. Make sure I didn't forget something."

"We rebuilt this thing with Stu when we were kids," Sergio said. "You know what you're doing."

Stu Oxford, his grandfather, and Sergio's uncle Beto had taught both Sergio and Ox the basics of auto repair on the old Ford pickup. Sergio had kept learning. Ox had lost interest.

"What's wrong?" Sergio asked.

"I don't know." Ox climbed out and lifted the hood. He leaned over the passenger side and rested his elbows on the edge, reaching down to check his work as Sergio looked over his shoulder.

"Dude, there's nothing wrong with that starter. I did it myself."

Ox knew that. He knew it was nothing but a hiccup. He just wanted to talk to Sergio. "I think I'm screwing up my shop."

"The tattoo shop? Dude, you haven't even opened yet. That's not a good sign." Sergio frowned. "How could you be screwing it up? You out of money already?"

"No." He kicked his boot against the tire. "It's this girl."

"Is Ginger messing with you?"

Ox frowned. "No."

"Oh." Sergio smiled. "Book Girl?"

"Yeah."

Sergio leaned against the grill and ran the rag over his manifold. "You know, there's a reason I don't have a girlfriend."

"Because you're a workaholic who doesn't know how to take a vacation and all your girlfriends break up with you because they get sick of it and also your mom and your sisters scare them away?"

Sergio opened his mouth. Closed it. He mumbled, "Yeah, probably that's part of it."

"I know the smart thing to do is stay away from her. I know that. Don't shit where you eat, right?"

Sergio squinted. "I never got that saying. I mean, hooking up with someone is nothing like shitting. It's like the opposite."

"I think it's more the breaking up with someone that's the shitty part."

He shrugged. "Who says you have to break up with her? You said she's a sweetheart. Why would you break up with that? I mean, we're not kids anymore. When my dad was my age, he had three kids already. You find a nice girl, it's a sign."

"Dude, this is me." Ox leaned back and reached up, waiting for Sergio's hands to clear before he let the hood fall. "When have I ever not screwed up with a woman?"

Sergio threw the rag over his shoulder. "I don't know, man. Everyone screws up until they find the right person, don't they?"

Ox considered that. It had a certain amount of logic. Of course he'd screwed things up with Ginger. He'd known from the beginning that hooking up with her was a bad idea. He'd known that in his gut. With Emmie, he didn't get the same sense of dread. But it was still a huge risk.

He curled his lip. "I think she might have a thing for Adrian Saroyan."

"The real estate douchebag who's trying to sell everything on Main and 7th?"

"Yeah. They knew each other in school."

"Huh." Sergio shrugged. "Well, if that's her type, I don't see her going for you."

"I know." He leaned on the hood. "She's not my type anyway."

"Yeah, probably not. You said she was nice and smart and brings you coffee. Definitely not your type. If you said she was a drama queen who liked to throw shit at you and pick fights in bars, then I'd say you definitely had a shot."

"Fuck you, Sergio."

CHAPTER FOURTEEN

"DAMN."

Emmie turned around. "What?"

Ox stood in the doorway of the 7th Avenue entrance, staring at her.

"Ox?"

"Damn... I forgot my book at home." He dragged his eyes away from her and over to his side of the shop. "You look nice today."

"Thanks." Emmie frowned, glancing down at the skinny black jeans and T-shirt she was wearing. "Tayla picked it out."

"That shirt comfortable on your back?"

"Yeah, the scabbing isn't too bad."

"Let me know if you need anything for it." He took off the old leather jacket he wore when he rode his bike and hung his helmet on the hook by the closet door. "It's getting cold out there."

Ox was living at his mom's ranch in Oakville, about a thirty-minute drive from Metlin, but she had to imagine the wind was vicious when he was driving in the country. He'd spoken about his mom Joan, his sister Melissa, and his niece, who was nine, but Emmie had yet to meet any of them.

"No truck today?"

"My sister needed it. She was taking some goats to Abby's class today."

"Goats?"

He turned and grinned. "You like goats?"

"Sure." Her face heated up. "Who doesn't like goats?"

"Me." Ox laughed. "They're devils."

"They are not." She turned around and got back shelving books. "They're just misunderstood."

"Okay, you get your favorite shirt eaten and tell me how misunderstood they are," he growled. "Just don't show up at the ranch in those jeans. There's hardly anything left of them as it is."

"Tayla calls them 'artfully torn.'"

"Okay, sure." He cleared his throat. "By the way, my mom might be coming by today. She's been begging to see the shop, and she claims it's unfair to make her wait until the opening."

"Oh cool! Can't wait to meet her." Emmie reached for the top shelf in the science fiction section. "Ox, were you looking at these?"

"Yeah, sorry." He walked over and reached over her head. "Last night. I probably got them out of order."

"Did you already finish *The Martian*?"

"I did. I couldn't put it down. Melissa's reading it now."

"Cool. He has a new one out. I already ordered a couple of copies."

"Nice," he said, flipping through a collection of Asimov short stories. "Maybe I can start some kind of account. That way I can pick up stuff for my mom too. I no longer have control of the television remote."

"Reading more?"

He scraped at the stubble on his chin. "Since I prefer that to Disney channel? Yes."

"Just let me know what you want."

"Do those go up there?" He pointed to the books in her hand. "Hand them here."

"I can get a stool."

"Or I can do it because I'm right here." He smiled and grabbed the books. Ox towered over her, quickly putting the books in the correct order. "Anything else?"

Do that again, but shirtless.

Emmie smiled. "Nope."

Ox ran a finger along the spines of the new books. "You got me hooked on reading again, and now I don't have enough time."

Emmie watched his finger. She was a bad person. She was a very bad person. She cleared her throat and forced her eyes away from his hands. "Your mom was a teacher, right?"

"Yep."

"But no college for you?"

"Oh, she wanted me to go." He shook his head as he walked back to his side of the shop. "My grades were okay, but I hated school. Well, I liked art, welding, and shop class. Other than that, I hated it. Melissa went. She has a degree in biology."

"Fair enough." She opened a box of new historical romances. "So how did you start tattooing?"

"My high school girlfriend suggested it after seeing my sketchbook," he said. "I checked it out and decided it would be fun to train. Figured I could help out on the ranch and make some extra money during the slow season."

"But it ended up being a full-time job, huh?"

He shrugged and opened his laptop. "Melissa and my mom don't need much help, so they let me coast."

"And now you're a business owner."

"Yeah, I am." His expression turned grim. "It's gonna be good."

"It's gonna be great." She wished she could feel more enthusiastic, but as they counted down the last days till the opening, her nerves were as jumpy as his.

"Are we crazy?"

Emmie turned to see Ox staring at her. "What?"

"You and me." He leaned on the counter, his eyes locked on

her. "Are we crazy? We don't have business degrees. I've never run a business before. Neither have you. Are we nuts to think we can do this?"

"No." She said it with more confidence than she felt. "We'll run into problems we don't expect, but we're smart. We work hard. We'll figure it out. And there's two of us. We can back each other up, right? That's more than what a lot of new businesses have."

He smiled slowly. "I got your back."

"And I got yours." She nodded. "See, we'll be fine."

His eyes drifted across the street. "I'm surprised Ginger hasn't been blowing up my phone."

Emmie hadn't told him about Ginger's visit. It wasn't necessary, and she didn't want to talk about it.

"Maybe she just realizes that there's room in Metlin for another shop. You're certainly not her only competition."

"Yeah, maybe." His expression said he didn't believe her. "Anything I can help with?"

"Most of the books are shelved. My windows are done." She looked around at the nearly finished shop. "Help me set up the tables for the opening?"

He smiled. "Anything for you, Buttons."

"You really need to stop."

"Never."

———

IT WAS the night before the opening. Everything was set up. Tayla, Daisy, Emmie, Ox, Ethan, and Spider were gathered in the lounge, sharing the bottle of bourbon Ox had opened from his grandpa's stash.

Spider nodded at the first taste. "This is nice, man." He held up his glass. "To Emmie and Ox. To INK. Mountains of success, you two. Seriously. You guys have worked your asses off."

Everyone raised their glass. "To INK."

Emmie raised her glass again and looked at Ox. "To new friends and old ones."

Ox nodded. "To friends."

They all drank and wandered around, Tayla fussing with the decorations for the next day's grand opening while Ethan showed Daisy the refinished woodwork. Ox, Emmie, and Spider gathered around his chair.

"This is nice, man." Spider ran a hand along the old leather. "Did you get this from Brewster's?"

Ox nodded. "Mr. Brewster and my pop were buddies and I know his son. He had it stored in their barn, but they didn't know what to do with it. No new barber shops opening in town, you know?"

"Give it time," Spider said. "Guys like us don't use the fancy barber, but look at Ethan."

Emmie snickered. "Ethan spends more on his hair than I do."

Ox tugged her braid. "Your hair is perfect. You don't need to do anything fancy to it."

She tried to ignore the rush of pleasure and Spider's curious expression.

What you up to, Mimi? his eyebrow said.

None of your business, her eyes answered.

"So!" Emmie patted Ox's chair. "Who's your first appointment?"

"You." Ox put his bourbon down on the counter. "Sit."

"What?"

Spider nodded. "Good call."

"I just finished getting ink less than a week ago." She held up her hand. "I'm done for a while."

"Come on," Ox said. "Something small."

Spider said, "You don't want the first tattoo in a new place to be a stranger. Good luck for it to be a friend."

She crossed her arms and glared at Spider. "You told me you were the only one allowed to tattoo me from now on."

"I'll make an exception for your partner. I trust Ox." Spider locked eyes with the bigger man. "Conditionally."

Ox smiled a little. "Understood." He slapped the back of the chair. "Sit, Buttons. You got me hooked on sci-fi. I'm giving you ink. My treat."

"Ox—"

"The first tattoo in my own place," he said quietly. "I don't want to share this with everyone. Just friends."

"Okay," she said, trying to ignore the flutter in her belly. "But I have no idea what to get."

Ox reached for her wrist. "Something small. Something you can see." He ran his thumb over her wrist. "Here?"

Emmie had been thinking about a wrist tattoo. "That sounds good."

Spider stood back while Emmie sat in Ox's chair. He pulled out a pen and held her wrist in his hand. "I work in black and grey."

"That's fine."

"Okay, let me…" He bent over her wrist and drew on Emmie's skin, the angle hiding his pen from her eyes.

After a few minutes, he lifted his pen and showed Emmie what he'd drawn. It was a single book lying open. Above the book, in an outline mirroring the curve of the pages, was a set of wings. It was as if a bird had lifted from the page and taken flight into the distance.

"Wow." It was bigger than she'd expected, but it was perfect. Totally perfect.

"You like it?"

"I like it."

Spider looked over her shoulder. "That'll look nice on your wrist. Good size."

Ox ignored Spider and locked eyes with her. "Is this it?"

Emmie nodded. "I want it."

"Cool." He smiled and grabbed a piece of paper, quickly

copying the book and the bird, adding shading and dimension until the small drawing looked like it would leap off the page.

The stencil was printed and placed. She nodded and watched Ox's face as he started his gun.

Emmie hissed when the needle touched her skin, but she remained perfectly still, her left arm resting on the warm leather of the chair as Ox worked in silence. The wrist wasn't as painful as the spine. She could deal.

Their friends had gathered in the lounge, Tayla switching the music from rock to an oldies station. Spider pulled Daisy into a slow dance as the sound of Ritchie Valens singing "Donna" filled the shop and Ethan opened a growler of beer.

Ox lifted his needle and wiped away the blood and ink staining her skin. "This is it," he said, catching her eye. "This is the beginning."

"Excited or scared?"

"Since I'm not an idiot, a little of both." He glanced up. "Thanks, Emmie."

She smiled. "For what? I'm the one getting a free tattoo."

He bent over her wrist again, working the needle over the delicate skin. "Thanks for dreaming big enough for both of us."

Her heart pounded hard. "And thanks for having my back."

Ox lifted his head and locked his eyes with hers. "Always."

CHAPTER FIFTEEN

EMMIE FACED herself in the mirror.

First day.

Grand reopening.

"You can do this." She heard Tayla walking down the short hall of the apartment. Emmie opened the door and hooked her best friend around the waist.

"Oh hi!" Tayla laughed. "Nervous a little?"

"Stop." Emmie enveloped her in a hug. "I will never be able to thank you enough for doing this. You completely uprooted your life, quit your job, and have been working your ass off for a shop that's not even yours."

"I like to think the office is mine though. You're total crap at filing and inventory."

"I'm trying to be grateful. Cut the sarcasm."

Tayla hugged her back. "I'm having a blast, Em. Seriously."

"I know you miss good sushi."

She shrugged. "The Japanese cuisine in town could definitely use some improving, but the Thai restaurant won me over." She patted Emmie's back. "Seriously, this has been good for me too."

Emmie took a deep breath and released Tayla from her stranglehold. "Okay."

Tayla put her hands on Emmie's shoulders. "I love seeing you so happy. And despite your anxiety about coming back here, you are happy. You're still the professional you were up in the city, but you've relaxed. And you needed to relax. You're... God, it sounds so cheesy, but you're really blooming here."

Emmie stared at Tayla. "That does sound cheesy."

"I know. I warned you."

"We haven't had coffee yet. I'll excuse you on those grounds alone."

"Fine." Tayla walked to the kitchen. "Coffee here or downstairs?"

"Downstairs. Ox will be here soon, and he'll want some too."

Tayla bumped Emmie's hip as she walked by. "You're so thoughtful about your *partner*."

"Stop."

"Heya, *partner*, want some coffee? How about I grab lunch? Oh thank you, Ox! You're such a good *partner*."

"Shut it." Emmie stepped into the knee-high boots Tayla had convinced her to buy. "We work together. That's all it is. We're just friends too. Isn't that a good thing?"

Tayla leaned against the counter. "You will never convince me that Miles Oxford would not be hitting that *daily*—maybe hourly on weekends—if he had not made that stupid pledge about never sleeping with you. Don't lie. You have to have noticed."

Her cheeks burned. "Nope. You're imagining things."

"Come on! There's all these little sizzle-sparks between you guys." Tayla's fingers danced in the air. "The longing looks. The flirty glances. The late nights talking about books that you pick out for him? I mean... did you see the way he was staring at you last night?"

"He was giving me a tattoo," Emmie hissed. "Of course he was staring at me. He was staring at my wrist."

"Nope." Tayla twirled into the cardigan that matched her polka-dot dress. "He was giving you the sexy-eyes all night. Know why he's always Mr. Considerate about getting you a coffee or grabbing lunch?"

Emmie wound a thin scarf around her neck. "Because his shop is ready and he doesn't have as much to do and he's simply a nice person?"

"Because he watches you constantly," Tayla said. "Because he luuuuu—"

Emmie slapped a hand over Tayla's mouth. "Stop. Seriously, stop."

Tayla pried her hand away. "You have feelings for him."

"I am... very attracted to him. You know that. But that's a stupid reason to complicate things when we're just getting started with a business. He laid down the rules at the beginning for a good reason. We need to be able to work together, and dating would just complicate that, and honestly I am so not his type."

"You are blind," Tayla said. "But sure. Okay. You're going to let the simmering tension simmer for a little while longer. All the best romances have to bubble under the surface for a while. At least admit you also see how much he's also attracted to you. Do not sell yourself short."

"I'm not selling myself short, I just don't think I'm his type. But I'm other people's type and I'm fine with that. Adrian Saroyan asked me out, didn't he?"

Tayla rolled her eyes. "He's boring. Why did you say yes?"

"Because..." *I had a huge crush on him in high school and I was flattered.* Okay, that sounded kind of sad. "Adrian is a very nice guy. He's smart, and he was very sweet. And he's reading Jane Austen for me."

"Ox has probably already read Jane Austen."

"Required reading in high school doesn't count."

"So Ox is reading something else that he likes more than

regency romance! But at least he's not doing it to get in your pants."

"Adrian's not reading Jane Austen to get in my pants."

Tayla blinked. "That is *exactly* why he's doing it. I'm not saying it's not a good move. I'm just saying it's not…"

Emmie crossed her arms. "Oh, do tell, woman who is suddenly interested in comics and tabletop games and has to wander down to Jeremy's shop on the regular."

Tayla grinned. "Like I said, it's not a bad move."

Emmie grabbed the long-sleeved kimono that Tayla had bought for her. It matched the scarf and the deep purple in her My Weekend Is Booked T-shirt. She quickly braided her hair over her shoulder and slicked on some lip gloss.

"Okay," she said. "Downstairs. Coffee. Customers."

Tayla had her business face back on. "What time is Ox coming in?"

"Today he said he'll be in early, but normally his shop won't open until noon."

"Cool." Tayla stood behind her and rested her chin on Emmie's shoulder. "This is going to be amazing."

"I am scared shitless."

"It's going to be great. You know books. You know how to sell the right book to the right person. You're like a book yenta. The ultimate matchmaker. And now you're using your superpower for good."

"You're ridiculous and I love you."

"I love you too." Tayla smiled. "And you're ready."

———

THE GRAND REOPENING of the bookshop started with… a fizzle. As Tayla pointed out, it was ten in the morning on a Friday. Their first real customer came in at ten thirty and stayed to chat. Cornelia was one of her grandmother's old customers who'd responded to the mailing-list invitation. She picked up a new Elizabeth George mystery while also grabbing a few used historical romances "for a friend."

She was sweet and darling even as her eyes went wide when she saw Ox sitting in his chair drinking a coffee and reading *Popular Mechanics*.

"Ma'am," Ox said with a nod. "Thanks for stopping by."

"Oh my," Cornelia said quietly. "That's different."

Emmie smiled big. "It's a new part of the shop. But Ox will have tattoo appointments in the afternoons, so the bookstore will still be quiet in the mornings."

Cornelia patted Emmie's arm. "Betsy did like a handsome sailor in her day."

Tayla waited until Cornelia was well out the door before she burst into laughter. "Go, Betsy!"

Ox was chuckling in the corner. "I second that. Go, Betsy."

Emmie couldn't stop the laugh that bubbled up. "Yeah, she's not lying. Grandma did like a man in uniform."

"Your family is so much more fun than mine," Tayla said. "Ox, how about you? Does your mom like a man in uniform?"

He shook his head. "Not going there. My dad split when I was a baby. As far as know, my mom is a nun and I don't want to know different. It's bad enough I know about my sister's dating life."

"What happened to Abby's dad?"

"Tayla." Emmie shook her head.

"It's fine," Ox said. "Car accident about five years ago. It was shit. Calvin was awesome, and Abby hardly remembers him."

"I am so sorry."

Ox shrugged and went back to reading his magazine.

His mom, Joan Oxford, had been an open book when she'd stopped by the shop the other day. Emmie had heard most of the family history before Ox returned with sandwiches. It had added a lot of depth to the still waters that were Miles Oxford. The depth of responsibility and love for his family made sense when Emmie realized he was the sole man in the house since his brother-in-law had died.

"Anyway," Emmie said. "Kind of cool that Cornelia was the first one to come by. She and my grandma were friends for a long time. She seemed happy, right?"

Tayla nodded from behind the counter. "Four books. Nothing wrong with that. And she signed up for the email list."

"Cool." Emmie wandered over to Ox. "You don't have to stay if you don't want. Clearly it's not going to be a stampede."

He looked up and gave her an easy smile. "No worries."

The rest of the day passed a little more quickly. After lunch more customers trickled in along with Ox's first clients. Soon the buzz of the tattoo needle was joined by the hiss and bubble of the coffee maker and the chatter of book people. One o'clock swiftly turned to six o'clock, and they were hustling people out the door for an hour so they could prepare the shop for the official grand-opening night.

"I got the beer," Ethan called as he walked in the 7th Avenue door. "Hey, Ox."

Tayla stopped in her tracks. "Are you wearing that?"

Ethan looked down at his jeans and plaid shirt. "Yeah."

Tayla made a small strangled noise in her throat.

"What's wrong with this?" he asked.

"Dude," Ox said. "The girls are dressing up and shit."

"What are you wearing?"

"I have a black button-down in my truck. Black jeans. Black button-down. That's all you need."

Ethan sighed. "Let me bring the beer in and I'll go grab a clean shirt." He looked at Tayla. "Just remember, this is Metlin, not San Francisco. People are going to show up in jeans and plaid."

Tayla smiled. "And if they're customers, that's totally fine."

Ethan grumbled, but he walked out to grab the beer just as Daisy thumped on the Main Street door with her foot. She was carrying a huge tray of cookies. Emmie jumped to open the door as Ox cleared a space on the table nearest his counter. Emmie had already set out trays of crackers and cheese along with some cut fruit and other finger food. The lounge was quickly being turned into a reception space, and Emmie could only hope people would show up.

She fussed with napkins and paper plates until Tayla shoved her toward the stairs.

"Go get dressed." Tayla was already in a fitted grey dress with a wide pink belt. Her hair was pinned up and her lips matched her belt. She was wearing pink polka-dot heels and looked amazing.

Emmie stared at her, feeling helplessly unfashionable. "Should I wear a dress? I have a couple of dresses."

"Absolutely not," Tayla said. "Not until I take care of your little black dress situation. I laid out your outfit on your bed. Hair up. Show off the beautiful art on your back. And please put at least a little makeup on?"

Emmie nodded. When it came to following fashion orders, she could do that. Then again, thinking about the completely backless shirt Tayla had laid out made Emmie feel like running and hiding.

She glanced at Ox, who was helping Ethan with the kegs from Metlin Brewing Company.

"Trust me. Everyone will want to touch."

That thought made her shudder. Maybe the backless shirt was a bad idea. She didn't want anyone touching her but Ox.

Not Adrian?

He was coming to the party and claimed he was almost done with *Sense and Sensibility*, which meant she was going to have to go out with him soon.

Wait, *have* to go out with him?

Emmie fled to her apartment before she could make herself any crazier. She'd wear the backless shirt and ask Ox to stay behind her for the entire evening. No one was going to touch her if he glared at them. Of course, glaring at customers was probably the opposite of what they needed to do. She was supposed to be selling books and trying to sign people up for the book clubs and promotional events Tayla and she had brainstormed. Ox was supposed to be booking appointments and showing off his previous clients who'd promised to come.

So many people. So. Many. People.

Emmie shut the door to her bedroom and wondered if she could hide from her own grand opening.

CHAPTER SIXTEEN

OX SAW HER DISAPPEAR UPSTAIRS, tried not to think about her coming back downstairs in a shirt that would show off her entire back. He was jealous of people seeing her ink, which was ridiculous. That thought led to him thinking about inking her wrist the other night, which led him to imagine his needle in other places. Other places where he was the only one allowed to see.

Not your girl.

Emmie was not his girl.

Adrian the douchebag Saroyan was supposed to be coming to the reception. He wondered if he could pay Kim and her buddies to keep the man occupied. They'd probably think it was hilarious.

What the fuck was he doing?

Ox rose from his chair when he saw Spider walking down 7th Avenue. It was far from the first time he'd met the man, but a little thrill still went through him every time Ox thought about hanging out with him. Spider Villalobos was a legend in the tattoo community. He'd been featured in magazines though it was under his proper name, Manuel Villalobos. Only friends and clients called him Spider anymore. Ox wondered if Emmie knew that.

He was also one of the most badass men Ox had ever met. It

wasn't his size. Spider barely came to Ox's chest. It wasn't his attitude, because the man was practically a Zen master of calm. But something about the cool expression in Spider's baby face and the creeping tattoos on his neck and head warned others that you did not cross the man. If you were a friend, that expression warmed. To everyone else, Spider was an enigma. An enigma that could probably kill you.

"Hey." Ox pushed the door open. "As always, I'm honored, man. Thanks for coming."

Spider stuck his hand out. "Ox, good to see you." He stepped inside and looked around. "The place is looking good. How'd the first day go?"

"Slow for me, pretty busy for her. I didn't want to book anyone that might overlap with the opening, but I have appointments going the rest of the week."

"Cool." Spider nodded. "I might have a client to send your way. Not sure, but I'll let you know. His girl likes the Irish stuff, and it's not my deal."

"I'd be happy to talk to her."

They chatted for a few moments until Ox noticed Spider adjusting his neat black tie and smoothing a hand over his vest.

"Shit," Ox said. "I gotta change."

Spider looked over Ox's faded jeans and T-shirt. "Yeah, you do."

"Hey, not all of us dress to impress."

Spider grinned and nodded toward Daisy on the other side of the shop. "When you're married to a woman like that, you dress however the hell she wants you to."

Ox noticed that Daisy was wearing a sharp, retro-looking red dress with black polka dots and some fancy thing in her hair. She spotted Spider and Ox and waved with a huge smile.

"You know you're a lucky bastard, right?"

Spider looked around the shop. "Look who's talking."

Ox ducked outside and grabbed the clothes his mom had

pressed for him that morning. It was just black jeans and a black button-down shirt like he'd told Ethan, but it looked good and it wouldn't stand out in this crowd. If he were still over at Bombshell, Ginger would sneer at him for trying to impress. At INK, it was just part of the image.

He slipped back into the shop as more and more people started to arrive, ducking into the office at the end of the hall only to find Tayla sitting at the desk and typing rapidly on her phone.

"Uh, hey Tayla." Emmie's best friend both intimidated and amused Ox. She reminded him a little of Ginger, only without any of the bitterness or claws.

"Don't mind me," she said with a wave. "I've imagined you naked plenty of times, and my imagination is usually pretty accurate."

Ox felt an unexpected blush. "Why are you imagining me naked again?"

Tayla looked him up and down with a critical eye. "This is when I say duh. I imagine all good-looking men without their clothes. It's one of the benefits of reading a lot." She closed her eyes and circled her hand beside her temple. "I have cultivated my mental camera."

"And that mental camera leaves off the clothes?"

"Mostly." She opened her eyes and stood up. "Don't pretend you don't do it with women. And don't pretend you're not wondering if Emmie's mental camera is as fine-tuned as mine."

Well, now he wouldn't be able to think about anything else. Did Emmie imagine him naked every time she looked at him?

"The girl has a good imagination, Ox. And that's all I'll say about that," Tayla continued. "I need to get out there again, so I will allow you your privacy. Please be social media ready by the time you leave this room."

"You're too kind, madam." Ox bowed as she passed by.

Tayla paused. "You're good. You will be devastating when you get your head out of your ass and make a move on the girl. Don't think I haven't noticed."

Ox straightened. "Noticed what?"

"Are you going to make me say duh again?"

Best friends saw too much.

"We both agreed it was a bad idea to get involved," Ox said.

"Who was the one who suggested it?"

Him. Clearly Tayla already knew that.

"So who has to be the one to put an end to this foolishness?" she continued.

Ox didn't say a word.

"I wouldn't waste time if I were you." Tayla leaned closer. "You're far from the only one who's noticed."

She patted Ox on the shoulder and walked out of the office. Ox shut the door, locked it, and took a minute to recover from the experience that was Tayla McKinnon.

Then he thought about Emmie's "mental camera" again.

Damn it.

CHAPTER SEVENTEEN

THE FIRST FACE Emmie saw when she walked down the stairs was Jeremy standing next to Tayla and wearing a huge smile. Both of them were dressed to the nines, Jeremy in a waistcoat and snazzy bow tie, Tayla in her sleek sheath with a wide belt and heels. Emmie walked toward them and stopped a few feet away as Jeremy let out a low whistle.

"You look great!"

Tayla nodded firmly. "You really do. That color is perfect with your hair."

The red burgundy of the shirt brought out all the red in Emmie's hair. She had to admit she loved that part of it. The back, however... "I feel naked," she hissed.

"You're not naked. You're beautiful."

Jeremy nodded. "Promise. You look great."

"And you two match," Emmie said, looking between the two of them. "Tayla, are you going to ask him out or not?"

Tayla ignored the faint red on Jeremy's cheeks. "You have no appreciation for the dance, Emmie. Anticipation is everything." She slid a finger down Jeremy's arm, tossed him a wink, and hooked Emmie by the arm. "Okay, let's go show you off."

Emmie could feel the cool air on her back as she walked through the growing crowd. They passed by the counter, and Tayla grabbed a handful of business cards and shoved them in Emmie's back pocket.

"This is showing me off?" she asked.

"Give it a minute." Tayla squared her to the room and stood behind her. "For now, I want you to look at this and appreciate what you've done."

Emmie took a deep breath and looked around.

By the bookshelves, customers were enjoying short glasses of brown ale and wine as they looked through the titles on the shelves. Everyone had a book or books in their hands, many using the totes Ethan was handing out at the door as people came in. The couch and chairs in the lounge were full, a mix of people congregating as they drank and looked through the stack of coffee-table books and Ox's albums on the table.

Speaking of Ox...

Emmie looked to the right, expecting to see Ox surrounded by a gaggle of female customers asking about his tattoos. The gaggle was there, but he was ignoring them and his eyes were locked on her. His black button-down was open at the neck and his sleeves were rolled up, displaying the grey-and-black ink on his forearms.

He stared at her with an inscrutable expression, and Emmie felt her cheeks growing hot, but she couldn't look away. He broke away from the chattering group of customers and walked slowly toward her.

"Resolutions crumbling...," Tayla whispered at her side. "In three... two..."

"Hey," Ox said when he reached them. "Emmie, you look—" He shook his head. "Forget what I said about the shirt being a bad idea. You look wonderful."

"Thanks."

Tayla patted her shoulder. "I'm going to go flirt shamelessly with other men to make Jeremy jealous. See you later."

Emmie tried looking around the shop, but she still felt Ox's eyes on her. "How many people so far?"

"Ethan handed out forty bags last time I checked, but not everyone took a bag, so he thinks it's closer to fifty."

"And we ordered one hundred?"

He nodded. "Did you do something different with your hair?"

She shook her head. "Sometimes it's just redder than other times. It kind of depends on what I wear. It's really brown, but when I wear wine colors it kind of…"

Ox tucked a loose strand behind her ear. "I like the braid."

You can use it as a handle if you want.

Bad Emmie!

She forced a smile. "You look nice too."

"Thanks."

Emmie finally braved looking at him full in the face, and the punch of his expression made her forget what she was going to say.

Okay, maybe Tayla was on to something, because Ox looked hungry, and she didn't think it was from a lack of mini egg rolls at the buffet.

She swallowed the lump in her throat. "Forty bags, huh?"

He nodded.

"Have you booked some appointments already?"

"Yeah." His eyes left hers and traveled down to somewhere in the vicinity of her lips. "Are you hungry?"

"No, I'm okay."

He stepped closer, glancing over her shoulder, letting his eyes linger on her skin. "You should eat."

"I think I'm too nervous to eat." Was it possible to actually feel someone's eyes? Because she felt Ox's eyes. "Besides, we probably need to mingle. Talk to people and stuff, right?"

"Uh-huh." His tongue peeked out and tasted his lower lip.

"Ox?"

He cleared his throat and blinked. "Yeah, why don't we get you a beer or something?" Ox put a hand on the small of Emmie's back, sliding his fingers under the edge of her shirt so his palm was pressed to her skin.

"Okay." *Oh my.*

His hand was huge and warm and suddenly Emmie didn't feel quite as exposed. Ox led her to the bar that Hugh and Carly from Metlin Brewing Company had set up at Ox's tattoo counter. Just as he grabbed their beers, Emmie heard the bell she kept on the register ringing over the hum of the crowded shop.

Emmie turned and saw the last thing she expected. Spider was standing on one of her kickstools, holding a beer.

Everyone quieted at the sight of him. Whoever had control of the music paused it.

"Hey," he said. "I'm Spider. I don't give speeches."

A light smattering of laughter.

"But I'm looking around this place and it's cool," he said. "Lots of people hanging out. Lots of people you might not put together. This is Metlin, right? We kind of stick to our own sometimes. But"—he looked at Emmie—"change is good. Emmie started this place with Ox, and it feels like a place where everyone is welcome." He raised his glass. "So, to Emmie and Ox. To INK."

"To INK!" the crowd answered back before everyone drank and clapped. The music started again, and the strange vibe that had buzzed between Emmie and Ox seemed to dissipate as they walked through the crowd.

First they visited the people gathered around the tattoo chair looking through catalogs and admiring the art on each other's skin. Then they wandered over to the books, and a few of the girls whom Emmie recognized from earlier in the day took turns showing Ox the most scandalous book covers in the romance section that featured tattooed heroes.

From the badly smothered smile on his face, he was eating it up, but not once did he leave her side. Most of the night he stood behind her and to the side, letting her lead the way as they visited customers and introduced themselves to many of the other businesspeople from Main Street and 7th.

There was Hugh and Carly from Metlin Brewing, of course, but they were also joined by Junior, who ran the Ice House across from Bombshell Tattoos. Cynthia and Esther Nixon dropped in from the antique shop south of Main. The Nixon sisters had to have been in business for fifty years at least, but they were still the life of the party. Esther was flirting with Marco Ventura and his father, who ran the paint shop across the street on 7th. Trang and Julie Nguyen from the T-shirt shop next to Jeremy's place had come, as had Don from the welding shop. He'd mumbled a quick hello before he grabbed a beer and escaped to a corner near the biography section, his grey head bent over the books, ignoring anyone who tried to make conversation.

It was a glorious and confusing mix of old and new, and Emmie loved it. It was way more fun than the stuffy readings and receptions she'd hosted at Bay City where everyone tried to impress everyone else by what books they read as they traded opinions about wine.

Ox leaned over and whispered, "Are you happy?"

Emmie nodded. "You?"

"Yeah." He was staring at her again. "You look happy."

She couldn't keep the heat from marking her face. "Ox, what are you—"

"You gotta be fucking kidding me," he muttered.

"What?"

Emmie looked up, but Ox wasn't looking at her anymore. He was staring at the door with a scowl on his face. Turning to follow his eyes, Emmie realized why he looked so angry.

Ginger had walked into the shop with Russ and two other artists from Bombshell. Though the crowd didn't go silent, the room definitely got quieter.

"Oh no." Emmie sighed. "She's not going to—"

"Let me take care of this." Ox slid an arm around Emmie's

waist and slid his thumb back and forth over her spine. "I don't want... I'll get rid of her."

"Don't be rude," she said quickly.

Ox turned and gave her an incredulous look.

"She is our neighbor," Emmie continued. "I have to live across the street from her. The last thing I need is to start some kind of feud. Just... be polite."

Ox leaned down. "Are you serious right now?"

"As polite as you can," she whispered.

"I'm not the one who started the fights," he said under his breath. "I'm sick of her shit, and she decided to bring it over here."

"But—"

"Is this my shop too?" he asked, his eyes flashing. "Is it?"

"Of course it is."

"Then I don't want her here." He sliced out his hand. "At all. I don't have to be polite to her. You have no idea how she will mess with you, Emmie. Trust me on this: you do not want to have sympathy for this woman. She feeds on it."

Ginger had strolled to the bar and ordered a beer while Emmie and Ox were talking. She leaned on the bar and watched Ox and Emmie with a smug expression on her face.

"She's watching us," Emmie muttered.

"What?"

"She's. Watching. Us."

"Don't care. Let her watch." Ox drew her up and kissed her temple. "I'll take care of this."

Emmie might have imagined the collective sigh that emanated from the romance section of the bookstore, but she didn't think so. She also didn't think she imagined the daggers that shot from Ginger's eyes or the swirling feeling in her own head.

Did that just happen?

Ox walked over to Ginger and stood in front of her, keeping his voice low. Ginger, of course, didn't suffer from the same problem.

"I thought this was a grand opening." She managed to make "grand opening" sound sarcastic. "Just wanted to check out the competition."

The group behind her looked uncomfortable, and Emmie couldn't help feeling sympathetic. These were people Ox had worked with. They probably wanted to be excited for him. A couple were looking around the shop with obvious curiosity.

Ox spoke again, but Emmie couldn't hear his words above the chatter of the crowd and the music that Tayla kept playing. Her friend shot her a look across the shop, but Emmie could only shake her head. She had no idea what Ox was saying, but Ginger had settled a mutinous look on her face and was clearly ignoring him. She scanned the crowd, her lip curled slightly at the corner.

She looked amazing, of course. Ginger always looked amazing. *Glamorous heels, not comfortable slippers.*

Emmie looked away and wandered to the book section, determined to ignore whatever was developing at the tattoo counter. She chatted with happy customers about books and fielded questions about book clubs and events. She'd already had a couple of people suggest movie nights and she loved the idea, wondering if Ox would be willing to host a joint party.

She heard a voice raised across the room and couldn't help but look.

"You think you're too good for us," Ginger said over the music. "You always did. But you're not, Miles. Not even close. At least I don't lie about who I am. But hey, I'm glad you found a pretty little thing you could trick into supporting you. I wonder how long that will last. And when you'll show her your true colors."

Guests had stopped chatting and turned to look. Emmie felt a surge of embarrassment as Ox and Ginger once again took center stage in their own personal drama. She felt like she was going to cry.

"Cut it out and stop talking out your ass," Ox said.

Tayla and Jeremy were standing by the speakers, whispering

furiously, all flirtation gone from their expressions. Daisy's eyes were wide behind the refreshment table as she rearranged cookies. And Spider...

Was walking over to the drama in the tattoo shop.

"Ginger," he said quietly. Spider leaned over and said something in Ginger's ear.

Her expression calmed as he spoke, and the tension in the room began to ease. Everyone watched as she nodded toward the door, then the cadre from Bombshell walked out the door. One shot a small wave at Ox while another—the bald guy Emmie remembered—nodded at him.

"Whoa." A breathy voice behind Emmie spoke as the music changed. "That was superintense, right?"

"So intense."

Emmie turned and saw the Instagram gang from the day before. "Hey. Sorry about the drama."

"No way," Kim said. "Are you kidding? Everyone is going to be talking about this. It just made your grand opening a story." She bumped Emmie's shoulder. "Don't worry. I'm totally Team Emmie. Ginger's a bitch and a half."

Emmie tried not to wrinkle her nose. "Eh, it's no big deal. I mean, everyone gets weird about exes, right?"

"Right. But it's pretty obvious that Ox has moved on, right?"

"Moved on?"

"I mean, I love my brother, but it'd be so much cooler if he worked at a place like this." Kim looked around the shop. "Bombshell smells like beer. Like, all the time."

"Right." Emmie glanced over at the tattoo counter, but she didn't see Ox anywhere.

Or Spider.

"Oh no."

"What's up?" Kim asked.

"Sorry, I just have to..." Emmie never finished her sentence.

She walked down the hall and into the office near the alley door. She heard voices as soon as she approached.

"...what the fuck you're doing," Spider said. "Grow up, man. You couldn't just leave her alone? You did exactly what she wanted."

"I don't want her here. I don't want her around Emmie."

She leaned against the wall next to the door and listened. She didn't care if she was eavesdropping. After all, it was her shop and they were talking about her.

"Emmie's been around plenty worse. That girl may look shy, but she's tougher than you think."

"I'm... I'm trying to leave that shit in the past, Spider. Start new. You of all people should understand that."

"You think I left my shit in the past?" Spider snorted. "Your past never leaves you all the way. That's not the way it works. Not unless you cut it out, and you don't want to go there. Resolve shit with Ginger. She's your neighbor and she's not a bad person. But you were a dick to her."

"*I* was a dick?"

"Did you cheat on her?"

"Fuck no! She's just suspicious as shit. She knew for months I wanted out. She was picking fights all the damn time."

"If you didn't cheat on her, she'll get over it. But for fuck's sake, man, just leave her alone. You could have let her hang out for a while and ignored her. She would have gotten bored—this isn't her crowd anyway—and then she'd go. Instead, you had to make a big deal about it."

Emmie heard shuffling feet.

"I don't like her around Emmie."

"Get over it. Emmie's a big girl and she can take care of herself. What are you really worried about? Ginger talking shit about you?"

Emmie leaned toward the door. Ox didn't say anything.

Spider continued, "Emmie's not going to listen to shit about you from Ginger. That's not who she is. But you better decide what you want, man. And you better not be playing my girl."

"I'm not. I just don't want—"

"Man, you don't know what you want." Spider's voice got louder, as if he was walking toward the door. "But you better figure it out."

Emmie tiptoed down the hall before anyone came out of the office. She turned left and walked up the stairs before she went back to the party. Her mind was whirling, and she needed a few minutes on her own. Unfortunately, she heard Ox's voice from the hall just as she reached the landing.

"Emmie?" Ox was looking up the stairs. "Where are you going?"

CHAPTER EIGHTEEN

HE STARTED WALKING up the stairs. "Where are you going?"

Emmie cleared her throat. "I just need a second to breathe, you know? So many people out there."

"So you're running away? Is this because of Ginger?"

"Of course not." Did he think she was a ninny? "I just... I need time. Alone time."

He'd reached the step before the landing. They were eye to eye. "You need alone time."

"On a fairly regular basis, yeah."

Ox frowned. "Why did you go into retail again?"

She shrugged. "I can talk about books. I can always talk about books. But stuff like this? It wears me out. Big crowds are not—"

"What's your favorite book? I've never asked you that."

Emmie blinked. "My favorite book?"

"Yeah, what's your favorite book?"

He was trying to distract her. It was a nice thought, but an impossible question. "What's your favorite tattoo? Can you pick one?"

Ox smiled. "No."

"Kind of the same thing." Ox kept looking in her eyes, and Emmie was starting to feel scrutinized. "I'm fine."

"You sure that's all it is?" he asked. "You just need a breather?"

"I told you I'm fine."

"I'm sorry about Ginger. I should have just ignored her." He was examining her face like he was searching for something. "I fucked up. Did she ruin it?"

Emmie shook her head. "Of course not. Everyone's out there having a great time. Daisy's food rocks. We haven't run out of beer. Everything is fine."

The corner of his mouth twitched. "I think I hate the word fine when it's coming from you."

"That's too bad, because it's a really useful word that most English speakers use regularly."

"It's a useless word that doesn't describe anything. People use it when they want to shut you up."

Emmie frowned. "We'll have to agree to disagree on that."

"Have I told you I like it when you act all fussy?"

"I don't act fussy. What does that even mean?"

"And you use punctuation when you text." His searching eyes landed on her lips. "Nobody does that."

"I do that." She squirmed under his gaze. "Ox—"

"You look amazing tonight."

"Thank you." Her chest was tight. Why was it so hard to breathe? "I think you were wrong about the shirt though."

"Oh yeah?" His voice was soft, nearly a whisper.

"Yeah." She swallowed. "Nobody's tried to touch my back. Everyone has been really cool."

"That's good, 'cause I don't want to have to break any fingers."

Emmie blinked. "Which would be a complete overreaction."

"Really?" He slid his hand along her waist and around her back, teasing his fingers along her spine. "We'll have to agree to disagree on that."

She could feel the heat from his chest, feel his hand resting hot on her skin. "Ox, what are you doing?" She put a hand on his chest. "You said—"

"I really want to kiss you right now," he said. "And I know I shouldn't."

Her mouth fell open, but she couldn't speak. *Did he just say...?*

"That mouth is not helping." He leaned closer to her, their lips a breath apart.

Emmie's fingers curled into the muscle on his chest. "Ox—"

He closed the inches between them and softly bit her lower lip, closing his mouth around it and flicking the sensitive edge with his tongue. Everything in Emmie's body heated. She raised her other hand to draw him closer just as he pulled away.

"That wasn't a kiss," he said, his breath still hot on her lips. "So I didn't break the rules."

"You didn't?" Her lip felt marked and swollen. She wanted to taste him, wanted to feel the rub of stubble against her jaw. "I feel like that's a technicality."

A low, frustrated sound rumbled in his throat. "Emmie."

"Ox?"

He let her go and stepped back. "Take your minute. One of us needs to go back to the party."

Emmie blinked and tried to clear the fog in her head. "Right." She started down the stairs only to have Ox put a hand on her hip, blocking her and nudging her back toward her apartment.

"Me." He was fighting a smile. "I'll go down. You take a minute to enjoy the quiet." He nodded at her door. "I'll send Tayla up if you disappear for too long."

Emmie nodded. "Okay." She turned to the door but turned back before he walked away. "That just happened in real life, right? I didn't imagine that?"

The corner of his mouth turned up. "Have you imagined it?"

"Not that. Precisely." Her face was burning. "I have a good imagination; I read a lot." She cleared her throat. "And I am going in my apartment before this gets any worse."

He backed down the stairs, bracing himself on the railing. "You mean any better?"

She raised a finger. "You should not be saying things like that, Miles Oxford."

He pursed his lips. "Are you sure?"

"Your rule. This was *your* rule."

He gave her a slow smile. "Yeah. But I forgot to tell you I was always shit about following the rules."

Emmie opened the door to her apartment and escaped before she did something really, really stupid.

————

BY THE END of the weekend, Emmie had formed two different book clubs, an adult romance group and a YA fantasy group. She'd added over 150 names to her mailing list. She'd scheduled the first movie night and taken the card of a local historical writer who wanted to organize a signing.

She'd also managed to avoid any more narrow hallways occupied by Miles Oxford.

It hadn't been too difficult. Ox had been as busy as Emmie. He had half a dozen regular clients he'd had to reschedule who were eager to get back in his chair, along with new appointments for custom pieces and some of the new "book art" he was advertising.

Monday was her day off, and Emmie was treating Tayla to a massage at Duchess Day Spa, a small storefront on the other end of Main Street. It was a tiny place, heavily decorated in pink, with a royal theme that reminded Emmie of some of the new modern royal romance covers she'd seen lately.

Tayla groaned loudly from behind the curtain where Jocelyn, the owner of the shop, was giving her a massage.

"I needed this so much," Tayla whimpered. "It hurts so good."

"When was the last time you had a massage?" Jocelyn asked.

"Far too long."

Jocelyn called, "Emmie, you next?"

Emmie looked up from her book. "Are you going to beat me up?"

Jocelyn poked her head out from behind the curtain. She was a smiling woman in her forties with smooth brown skin and hair she usually wore in braids. This month the braids were threaded with purple and pink extensions. "Of course I'm not going to beat you up. This one asked for deep tissue."

Emmie smiled. "Then yes. But more the 'relax my troubles away' massage, please."

Jocelyn nodded and ducked back behind the curtain.

"You know, Emmie doesn't need a massage to relax," Tayla said. "She needs to bang her business partner."

"Oh really?" Jocelyn said, "You better spill, missy."

Emmie was grateful Jocelyn's manicurist had already gone to lunch. "Jocelyn, does banging one's business partner *ever* seem like a good idea?"

"Depends on what the business partner looks like."

Tayla laughed. "Right? And this one is smoking and looks at her like he wants to bite."

He did bite. Emmie didn't say it. She hadn't told Tayla anything about opening night, and she wasn't planning to.

"I like the sound of this boy," Jocelyn said. "Who is it?"

"Miles Oxford," Emmie said.

Jocelyn tore the curtain back. "You're in business with Ox? I thought he worked at Ginger's place. Weren't they together?"

"They were, but they broke up over a month ago. He reopened his shop in my bookstore. In that corner where Betsy was always thinking about putting a café."

Jocelyn closed the curtain again. "This is what happens when I take a vacation to my mama's house. I miss everything."

"Aren't day spas where everyone in a small town trades gossip?" Tayla asked.

Emmie opened her book again. "No, that's the beauty parlor."

"Truth," Jocelyn said. "You hear everything at Vivi's. But that's what I get for letting my sister do my hair. Emmie, I don't know about that Ox boy. He's hot as sin, but he's got poor taste in women from what I can see. You need a *man*. You're too mature to settle for less."

Tayla asked, "Are you married?"

"Twenty years next anniversary."

"Wow, that's awesome!"

"Not all of us are lucky enough to find a Reggie," Emmie said. "And since I'm not going to be banging Ox, this is a stupid discussion."

"This isn't a stupid discussion," Tayla said, "because you have not seen the zings."

"Zings?" Jocelyn asked.

"So much zinging. Like little stars shooting all over that place. I'm surprised they haven't lit all those books on fire."

Jocelyn laughed out loud. "Well, I will say this: Ox comes from a nice family. His mother and sister are very good women. And he's started his own business now. Maybe he'll get his head screwed on right. Don't get me wrong. He's a nice boy, but I don't think he knows what he wants. Mind you, lots of 'em don't until they find the right woman, so there's that."

Emmie stood. "Does anyone want coffee? I'm going to get coffee."

She walked out the door before either of them could respond, dying to leave the chatter about her and Ox.

The problem was, Emmie had a sneaking suspicion that both Jocelyn and Spider were right. Ox *didn't* know what he wanted. She'd pushed him into opening the shop with her. He'd set down rules and then teased her into breaking them. Did he want a lover or a business partner? She wondered if he'd had the same rule with Ginger at the beginning. Maybe this was all a game to him.

Emmie nearly ran into another pedestrian she was concentrating on the ground so intently. "Sorry!" She almost swerved into a lamppost before he caught her arm.

"Emmie?" Adrian Saroyan smiled. "Hey!"

"Hi!" She righted herself and hooked her purse higher on her shoulder. "I'm so sorry. I was thinking about something, and I just didn't..."

"No worries. I'm glad I ran into you." He laughed. "Or I caught you." He leaned forward and cocked an eyebrow. "Not unlike Mr. Willoughby and Marianne."

"Oh!" Emmie smiled. "Have you finished *Sense and Sensibility* already?"

"Not yet, but I'm liking it so far."

Well, that would explain the positive Willoughby reference. "Cool. I'm just headed down to the café."

"Bookshop closed today?"

Emmie nodded.

"Yeah, most of the shops downtown are closed on Monday."

"Ox might be working, but we're at Duchess. Jocelyn's currently beating Tayla up. It's my turn next."

"Nice." He laughed. "You deserve a day off after how hard you've worked. The opening was great. I'm sorry we didn't get to talk more, but I really liked everything I saw. Great atmosphere. I picked up a few books and that one for my mom. It looked like everyone was having a great time."

Adrian was smiling, and Emmie was wondering if his teeth had been capped. Had they always been that white? He was wearing another suit and another pair of immaculate shoes. Emmie was wearing jeans again, but Tayla had forced a stylish sweater over her Edgar Allen Poe I PUT THE LIT IN LITERATURE T-shirt.

He was just so... nice. Was it an act? Was she too cynical? Was she reading too much into character motivations that might not be anything more than straightforward interest?

Adrian cocked his head. "Are you all right?"

"Coffee," she blurted. "I need coffee. I only had one cup this morning."

"I don't drink it," he said. "I try to get up and run in every morning. That's what wakes me up."

Oh dear Lord, that sounded disgustingly healthy.

"Well, that's... great. For you."

Adrian smiled bigger. "I know I'm abnormal. You're not the first person who's given me that look. Come on, I'll walk you to Café Maya." He cocked his arm. "I wouldn't want you running into anyone else."

"I promise I'm not that clumsy."

"So it's just around me?" He shrugged. "I'll take that."

Emmie couldn't stop the smile; she linked her arm with his. "You know that's not what I meant."

"Sorry, I couldn't hear you over my heroism," he said. "I've been reading Austen, and you're the first woman I've met who came close to swooning. I think it might be a sign."

CHAPTER NINETEEN

CARY NAKAMURA WALKED into the shop and paused just inside the door, looking around and nodding. "This is good."

"Yeah?" Ox walked over to shake his neighbor's hand. "You like it?"

"I do." He glanced over behind the book counter. "There any coffee made?"

"No. You want a latte, go down to Daisy's. I'm not your mom."

"My mom could beat you up." Cary was about fifteen years older than Ox, but he'd been a client as long as Ox had been tattooing. He was a neighbor from Oakville and had orange groves just north of their acreage. When Melissa had started planting, she'd turned to Cary for help. Ox had more than once wondered if the older guy had a thing for his sister, but he didn't ask. It was none of his business. Cary had been friends with Calvin. It was complicated.

"How's your crop looking this year?" Ox asked.

"If I wanted to talk about my oranges, I'd call your sister. That's all she wants to talk about. Ever."

"Fair point." Ox sat down on his rolling stool. "I know jack shit about oranges."

"Stick with what you know." Cary flipped a chair around and pulled out a piece of paper. "So this is the only picture I have of my dad's shoulder. You can see the chrysanthemum is pretty faded, but—"

"I can definitely see the look you're going for."

"He got it for my mom. It was her favorite flower. Now that he's passed, I want to get one too."

"That's beautiful, man. We can definitely work something up." He glanced at Cary. "The traditional Japanese designs are not my specialty. I just want to warn you. I've done a few, but I'm not a master."

"Man, I've seen your sketches, and the dragon turned out perfect. I'm not worried." He handed Ox the paper. "Sketch it out. See what you can do. For now let's keep going on my back."

"Cool."

Cary had been working on a full back tattoo for over a year. The dragon was almost done, and it was one of Ox's favorite custom pieces. It wasn't strictly a Japanese dragon, but it was inspired by classical art with a few modern tweaks that Cary had asked for. The clean lines and deep shading made it a striking piece, and it would blend well with the more traditional Japanese pieces Cary already had.

The needle started buzzing, and Cary relaxed into the chair, and Ox started to shade his left shoulder.

"The place is nice. Your pop would like the jackalope."

"You remember Brewster's?"

"Are you kidding? I always passed by that place as a kid, wishing my dad would take me there, but my mom refused to spend the money. Barber shops were for men. She buzz cut my head every month until I was sixteen."

"They had a stuffed jackalope in there. I found one online."

"How about the chair? Online too?"

"Nope, that's from Brewster's. Salvage."

"Very cool."

"Thanks."

"This is a good place, man. Business going well so far?"

"So far."

They chatted for the next thirty minutes, and Ox tried to imagine what it would be like to tattoo a client like Cary when the bookshop was open. Emmie would be sitting behind the counter, probably reading a book unless a customer wandered in. Or making coffee, letting the coffee grinder and bubbling machine join the buzz of the tattoo needle.

Quiet music played from the speaker on his counter. It was nice. None of the pounding metal that was common across the street at Bombshell. No one was cursing and yelling or whining about how big a cut Ginger was taking. It was just peace and quiet, minimal conversation, and a buzzing tattoo needle set to Johnny Cash.

Ox lifted the needle from Cary's back. "This shop is exactly what I want."

Cary said, "That's good. That's great, man."

It felt like a revelation, even if it was a quiet one.

A couple of high school kids passed by the Main Street door and pulled on it, not trusting the CLOSED sign. Emmie had made the decision, like most of Main Street, to stay closed on Monday. It was a good move and allowed Ox some peace and quiet in the shop. At least one day a week he would be free from the distraction of her presence.

"That wasn't a kiss, so I didn't break the rules."

"You didn't?"

He had broken every rule. He couldn't get the taste of her off his tongue. Her lip had been soft. Delicious. He'd wanted to devour her.

I was always shit about following the rules.

Ox had stepped back, immediately regretting his actions. And not regretting them. He regretted muddying the waters between him and Emmie, and he also regretted not backing her into her

145

apartment, stripping her naked, and finishing what he'd started with a bite. He'd had a taste of her now, and he couldn't get the idea out of his mind when she was anywhere near.

Hell, she was gone and he still couldn't get the idea off his mind.

Ox muttered, "Cary, my friend. I love this place, but I am so fucked."

"Let me guess. A woman?"

"How'd you know?"

"Because I'm older and smarter than you."

"Really?"

"Yeah. But also your sister said something. And your mom. And Abby."

Ox didn't know whether to be annoyed with the women in his life or flattered that they cared.

CHAPTER TWENTY

FINISHED with her *relaxing* massage after having coffee with Adrian, Emmie wandered back to the bookshop with Tayla midafternoon. They slipped in the Main Street door, making sure the sign remained turned to CLOSED. Her grandma had always been adamant that taking at least one day off every week was vital to long-term success. It led to happy employees and happy owners, and customers got used to it.

She realized as soon as she went inside that they weren't alone. The low buzz of the tattoo needle hummed in Ox's corner over the sound of Johnny Cash playing on the speakers. Emmie looked over and waved a hand. "Hey."

A lean Asian man leaned forward on Ox's black tattoo chair, his silver-grey hair pulled into a short ponytail while Ox inked his back. "Ladies," he said in a low voice.

"Hi there," Tayla said, scoping the man out. "Silver foxes are always welcome at INK."

The man smiled, and his dark brown eyes creased in the corners. "Ox, you got a couple of live ones, huh?"

Ox glanced up. "Cary," he muttered, "these two ladies are

Emmie and Tayla. Emmie runs the bookstore and is my partner, so don't even think about it. Approach Tayla at your own risk."

"Interesting." Cary's muscled arms were covered by black-and-grey sleeves. They crossed in front of his chest, which was bare since Ox was working on his back. "You ladies having a nice day?"

"We are now," Tayla said.

"Shameless," Emmie said, pulling Tayla back. "Ox, we'll get out of your hair."

"He doesn't have much hair," Cary said, "but I'm pretty sure he wouldn't mind you in it."

Tayla laughed, and Ox glanced up with a smile.

"Get outta here," he said. "I know it's your day off."

Emmie said, "Nice to meet you, Cary."

"You too." Cary winked at Tayla. "And it's definitely nice to meet you."

Tayla put a hand to her chest. "Swear to God, the men in this town are gonna kill me."

Emmie walked upstairs and the music grew softer. The men's voices were muted by the time she reached her door. Tayla was nearly hanging on her back.

"Did you hear him?" Tayla said. *"Don't even think about it."*

"Hush." Emmie unlocked the door. "Leave it alone."

"Please. You so do not want to leave any of that alone."

Emmie shook her head. "And you flirt with *everyone*. I mean, come on. That guy had to be forty. At least."

"And?" Tayla glanced at the door. "He was hot. Nothing wrong with experience."

"What about Jeremy?" Emmie asked, pulling off her purse and hanging it on the hooks they'd installed by the door. "I guess I thought you guys..."

Tayla rolled her eyes. "Oh, come on. He's a sweetheart, but I just moved here. I'm getting to know people. I don't even know if I'm going to stay past a year, Em."

Emmie went to the kitchen and grabbed two glasses. Jocelyn

had told them to drink a lot of water after their massage, and she didn't want to get sore. "I'm just saying I think he really likes you, and he's a good friend of mine, and... it would be cool. That's all."

"I really like him too," Tayla said. "But that boy has forever heart-eyes when he looks my way. And I just don't know if that's in the cards for me right now, you know?"

"Don't you want to meet someone? Get married? Have kids? That kind of thing?"

"Eventually." Tayla flung herself on the couch. "We're not even thirty yet."

Emmie handed her the water. "But soon. *Soon.*"

"Don't say it. I'm going to be twenty-seven forever. Hush." Tayla gulped the water. "There's nothing in this water."

"No. It's water. It's good for you just like it is."

Tayla stuck out her tongue. "You can take the wholesome country girl out of the country—"

"And then you can bring her back and she still believes in things like hydration." Emmie sat next to Tayla and leaned against her shoulder. "We're going to be *thirty.*"

"Never."

"In three years."

Tayla patted her head. "And look at everything you're doing with your life. You have your own shop. You have a new and fabulous wardrobe."

"I have new jeans and sweaters."

"And dangly earrings. Don't forget the earrings. You have multiple men chasing you—"

"I wouldn't call impromptu coffee dates and random, vague comments *chasing*, but okay." Emmie snuggled closer. "What are you trying to say?"

"You're doing it, Marianne Elliot. How many of our friends in the city were spinning their wheels, waiting for that big thing to happen?"

Most. All?

"It's a bookshop," she said. "I'm not inventing the next great app or anything."

"It's a thing that you're making and you're running. And it's better than an app."

Emmie finished her water. "If only it made me as much money."

"Well, there's that." Tayla drank her water and made a face. "Nothing? Don't you have any of those little drops or something? Did this actually come out of a tap?"

"You're hopeless."

"I'm adorable."

"Adorably hopeless."

———

IT WAS NEARLY FOUR, and the afternoon sun was streaming through the long windows, bathing the sofa with a warm light. Not even the fast-paced paranormal romance Emmie was reading could keep her from nodding off like a cat. Tayla had hidden in her room, a mud mask plastered over her face and bubblegum pop blaring from her speakers.

Someone knocked on the door, making Emmie start from her half-asleep state. "Hello?"

"It's me."

Ox. Of course it was Ox. Who else had keys to the shop and could get upstairs without using the buzzer by the side door?

"Give me a second." Emmie scrambled to her feet, tugged her hair into a messy bun, and briefly debated putting her bra back on. Instead, she just threw a sweater over her T-shirt. Bras were evil.

She opened the door. "Hey."

"Hey." His smile was warm. "Did I wake you up?"

"A little." She glanced over her shoulder. "There's this sunbeam that comes in the window around three— You don't want to know about the sunbeam. Why are you here?"

He crossed his arms. "I'm kind of interested in the sunbeam, but I'm actually here to invite you and Tayla to dinner at the ranch."

"Oh!" That was nice. "Uh, when? Thanks, that's really sweet."

"Tonight if you can make it. And it's kind of self-serving. My mom and Melissa have been bugging me for weeks now. They say I'm being rude."

"I didn't think that." But she would definitely have to put a bra back on.

Hmmmm.

"Emmie, who's— *Eek!*" Tayla had stomped into the living room with black mud all over her face and décolletage only to abruptly spin and run back to her room.

"Tayla?"

"Men must never see how the magic happens!"

Ox's eyebrows went up. "I was not expecting that."

Emmie nodded toward Tayla's door. "Let me go ask."

She cracked the door open to see Tayla sitting on the edge of the bed, looking at her mask in a small compact.

"Did I smudge it? I don't think I did." She patted her chest. "Maybe around my boobs."

"Why do you have charcoal on your boobs?"

"The skin in this area"—she waved at her chest—"is just as delicate as the skin on your face. You can't ignore it."

"Uh-huh. Ox invited us out to his mom's for dinner. Do you want to come?"

"Yes and no. I want to, but I can't. I have a video call with my parents tonight. They're visiting my granny and I'm required to be there, so I have to stay in." She shooed Emmie. "But you should go. Meet the sister. Have fun. His niece looks adorable in pictures."

Emmie hadn't seen any pictures of Ox's niece. "He has pictures of his niece?"

"Of course he does. He's not a monster." Tayla lowered the compact. "You haven't asked to see pictures of his niece?"

She threw up her hands. "Apparently I *am* a monster. I'll ask to see pictures."

"No, just go. Besides, what were you going to make for dinner?"

"Meatless chili."

Tayla made a face. "No thank you. Go. Scoot." She rose and shoved Emmie to the door. "Make kissy faces at each other behind the kid's back. That's always fun. But put on a bra. You shouldn't meet anyone's parents without a bra."

Emmie was unceremoniously shoved out the door and into the living area. Ox was leaning against the counter, and Emmie was pretty sure he was staring at her chest.

Thanks, Tayla.

Emmie crossed her arms and Ox looked up. "Uh, so she can't go. But I can."

"My mom's a good cook. She might even be making chili."

Emmie nodded. "So you heard..."

"Pretty much all that. The walls aren't very thick."

"Right." *Kill me now.* "Okay. I'm going to go put a bra on now, and then I will stop saying the word bra for the rest of my life."

Ox smiled. "I'm curious what making kissy faces will be like though. Is that as fun as it sounds?"

Emmie spun around and marched to her room. "Maybe you should ask Tayla about that one."

———

EMMIE INSISTED on driving herself until Ox reminded her she no longer had a car.

"Right," she said. "So you're going to drive me thirty miles out to your family ranch, drive me back, and then drive home again?"

"Don't be silly," he said, throwing his jacket on as he turned off the lights in his shop. "I'll pack some clothes and sleep in town. I have a friend I can crash with."

"Oh." Was it a woman? Did he have another Ginger already? "That's cool."

It wasn't any of her business. She kept telling herself that even as Ox ushered her out to his old truck with his hand at the small of her back, reminding Emmie of the night of the opening.

"That wasn't a kiss, so I didn't break the rules."

It was *so* against the rules. Everything about that night—even his protective posturing—had been against the rules. Because whether Ox had kissed her or not, she was jealous of him with imaginary women. She was relentlessly curious about him. She loved spending time with him and listening for his quiet humor.

Her heart, whether she wanted it to be or not, was already involved.

Ox opened the door. "What are you thinking about?"

Emmie hopped in the truck, glad she'd decided to go with jeans and boots. "Nothing."

"Didn't look like nothing."

"Maybe this isn't a good idea," she said.

"What isn't?" Ox reached over and pulled the seat belt across her body before she could leave the truck. Emmie sucked in a breath at the warm scent of him: skin and ink and a hint of something cedar at his neck.

"Me," she said. "Going to meet your family."

The belt clicked in place, but Ox didn't move. "You're my friend, aren't you?"

"Yes."

"And you've already met my mom."

"Just for a few minutes and she—"

"My mom likes for me to bring my friends over. It's one of her things." He still hadn't moved.

"What are you doing?" she asked.

He cocked his head, his lips hovering inches from hers. "Did you tell Tayla about last Friday?"

"No." Emmie felt like she could barely breathe. "Did you tell anyone?"

He shook his head, his eyes falling to her lips. "What would I tell?"

"Exactly. You didn't kiss me."

"Nope." His eyes rose and met hers. "Not yet."

"Rules, remember?"

His smile was slow and smug. "I told you I wasn't very good about following the rules."

She closed her eyes and allowed herself to imagine it. Imagine the luxury of his full mouth and how solid his arms would feel around her. A man didn't move like Ox without knowing what he was doing. She'd observed him for weeks. Knew what kind of attention he paid to detail. He was a man who didn't rush. Who knew how to take his time. With the physical chemistry between them, she was aware enough to know it would be good. It would be *really* good.

Until it wasn't. And then what?

Ox started to lean in, and Emmie quickly put a hand on his chest. "I need this to work, Ox."

He froze. "What?"

"INK. The shop. This idea. I've sunk all my money into it. I sold my car. I used my savings. I need it to work."

He took a deep breath and pulled away. "Yeah, me too."

She stuck her hand out. "Friends. Please say friends."

Ox took her hand, grasped it, and covered her knuckles with the palm of his other hand. "Friends."

She let out a long breath. "Okay."

"For now." He smiled, leaned back, and slammed the door shut.

Damn you, Miles Oxford.

He was going to be the death of her, but a little voice in the back of her head told her to just lean back and enjoy the ride.

CHAPTER TWENTY-ONE

THE REST of the ride out to Ox's family ranch was spent arguing playfully over the radio. Ox changed the station from song to song, driving Emmie nuts.

"Just leave it on—"

"You said you don't like country."

"That was Johnny Cash." She switched the radio back to the classic country station. "Only monsters don't like Johnny Cash."

"Or ask for pictures of my niece apparently."

Emmie grimaced. "According to Tayla. I'm sorry if I offended you. I didn't mean to. I just think of family pictures as being personal and—"

"And you have a sense of boundaries." Ox smiled. "Unlike Tayla, who does not."

She barked out a laugh. "No. To be fair, if she did, we probably wouldn't be friends."

"How did you meet?"

"She used to work for a bookkeeper who did the accounts for a small bookshop where I worked when I was a freshman. She badgered me enough that I eventually gave in and started talking to her."

"Huh. I wonder if she'd help me with my books." Ox glanced at her. "Have you always worked in bookshops? Weren't you working in one before you moved?"

"At Bay City Books. But that wasn't where I was working when I met Tayla. The old bookshop went out of business," Emmie said. "Lots do. But yeah. I guess that's just what feels familiar."

He nodded but didn't say anything else.

Sensing he was waiting for her to speak, Emmie asked, "Why don't you get a new radio for the truck so you can use your phone and stuff?"

Ox shrugged. "It was my grandpa's. I learned how to fix cars on it, so I try to keep it as original as possible."

"That makes sense. And the ranch was his?"

"It was his mom's first. Came from her family. And then to him and then to my mom. She's an only child, so after he passed, it was hers. They don't keep as many cattle anymore. Mom and Melissa rent out the land for grazing and planted orange groves on the rest. Mom knows ranching, but my sister was always more into the farm side."

"Cool."

"I hope you like oranges, because once they're in season, they're going to send me into work with boxes of them. In the summer they usually have a stand at the summer farmers' market downtown."

Emmie smiled. "I like oranges."

They were passing through dark hills covered with orange groves and orchards with red leaves. Fall was coming, and while the fruit trees looked tired, the dense citrus groves were invigorated. A smattering of rain had fallen in the foothills, leaving a haze of green along the dusty roads. They wound through tiny burgs and into dark hills, turning from pavement to gravel.

Ox jumped out and swung open a long gate. Emmie scooted over the bench and put the truck in gear, driving over the cattle grate and stopping on the other side as he swung the gate and latched it.

He was smiling as he opened his door. "You've done this before."

"Sorry, I should have asked." She was back safe on her side of the truck. "It's just habit. My mom—"

"No worries." He put the truck in gear and bounced over the gravel. "You can drive a stick."

"That's what I learned on."

"Not bad for a city girl."

"I was a small-town girl first." Emmie was starting to feel nervous. She was just meeting Ox's family as his friend, right? What had he told them about her? Had he told them anything? What if they thought she and Ox were together? What if they thought she was a snob because she'd lived in San Francisco?

"Don't worry." He reached over and squeezed her hand. He suddenly frowned. "Meatless chili."

"What?" Emmie asked.

"You're not a vegetarian, are you?"

"No."

His face relaxed. "You'll be fine then."

———

THE RANCH-STYLE HOUSE was tucked into a small valley in the foothills with the Sierra Nevada mountains towering in the distance. It had a long porch that wrapped around the outside and brightly lit windows that gleamed in the twilight. Ox ushered her up the porch steps and opened the door without a knock.

"Mom? Melissa?"

Emmie understood the vegetarian concern the second they walked through the door. The whole place smelled like barbecue, and her stomach rumbled.

Ox looked over his shoulder and grinned. "Well, that's a relief. I think you eat salad every day."

"Just because I like salad doesn't mean I don't like tri-tip." Holy smoky deliciousness, it smelled amazing. It was impossible to get real, true Santa Maria–style barbecue in San Francisco, and Emmie hadn't had any since she'd gotten back to Metlin. She could smell the savory garlic salt and peppered beef and the spicy aroma of pinquito beans coming from the kitchen.

"Miles?" A female voice came from the kitchen a second before Emmie heard the thump of small feet hurling toward them. As if on command, Ox knelt down as a small girl flung herself onto his back, peeking her grubby face over his shoulder.

"Hi!" the little girl said. "You're Uncle Ox's friend."

Ox grunted and shifted the little girl on his back. "Emmie, this is Abigail, the small wild creature that lives in this house and breaks into my room when I'm not here."

"You said I could!"

"I told you that one time. Now you're just being nosy."

Emmie couldn't help but smile. "Hey, Abigail. It's nice to meet you."

"Are you the one who picks out the books Uncle Ox gets me?" She glanced at Ox. "Uh…"

"Yes, she does." Ox walked toward the adult voices. "Mom, I'm home. Lissa, your kid is stuck to my back again."

"Have you tried throwing water on her?" a voice replied. "That works for me sometimes. She's awfully hard to unstick."

Abigail giggled.

Ox said, "I haven't. I need to try that. Get a pitcher and some ice so I can—"

"No!" Abigail jumped off her uncle's back and sped down the hall again. "I don't want to get wet."

A woman stuck her head out of the kitchen and yelled, "Face and hands, Abby! I want them clean. Dinner in five minutes." She turned to Emmie and Ox. "Hey! Welcome to the ranch. We raise cattle, goats, and eight-year-olds. The eight-year-old isn't domesticated though."

Emmie smiled. "No eight-year-old should be domesticated."

"That's a matter of opinion." Ox took off his jacket and hung it on a hook in the hallway. He helped Emmie out of her cardigan before she realized what he was doing and had her grey sweater hung next to his before she could speak. "Lissa, you need anything before I wash up?"

"Can you double-check the goat pens? Abby fed, and I just want to make sure—"

"No problem." He put a hand on Emmie's back and shoved her toward the woman. "Emmie, Melissa. Melissa, Emmie." Then he touched Emmie's shoulder and said, "I'll be right back."

The woman held out a hand. "Nice to meet you."

The front door slammed and Emmie was left in the hallway with Melissa. The radio was playing gospel music, and Abby was singing at the top of her lungs down the hall.

"I'd say it's usually not this crazy, but I'd be lying," Melissa said. "I'm glad you came! Ox has told us so much about you."

"He has?"

Another voice called from the kitchen. "Is that Emmie?"

Emmie recognized Ox's mother's voice. They'd met the one time when she dropped by the shop, but Ox said his mom didn't drive into Metlin if she could avoid it. Emmie's impression had been that of a small, sturdy woman in work boots and a flannel shirt. When she walked into the kitchen, the memory was confirmed. Ox looked nothing like his mom, though his sister was the spitting image.

"Hi, Mrs. Oxford." Emmie set her purse on a corner of the counter. "It's nice to see you again."

"I told you to call me Joan." She looked over her shoulder from the pot she was stirring. "I think I talked your ear off about your grandma when I saw you. I apologize for that. It hasn't been that long. How you doing?"

The question brought an unexpected wave of emotion. "You know, I've been so busy... Thanks for asking." Emmie blinked away a few unexpected tears.

Joan rattled on. "Working in her shop must bring back so many memories. I can't imagine what that must be like. I think of Betsy every time I drive by."

Emmie couldn't remember the last time anyone had asked about her grandmother. When Emmie talked to her mom, it was only about her mother's grief. There was so much to do, so many details to take care of. Then, after she'd decided to start the shop...

"Emmie?"

She sniffed. "Yeah, I'm doing okay."

The empty place sat like a lump in her belly.

"Oh, hon." Joan turned and handed the spoon to Melissa. "I'm so sorry. I shouldn't have brought it up."

"It's okay," Emmie said. "Really. It's nice to hear that she's missed."

Joan wrapped strong arms around Emmie and gave her a long hug. "You call me anytime you want to reminisce. She was a gem of a person, and everyone just loved her."

The hug was unexpected, but Joan Oxford was so maternal Emmie accepted the gesture without question. "Thank you. I guess I'm worried about disappointing her. I hope she'd like the shop. It looks so different now."

"Different times!" Joan said. "I'm sure Betsy would love it. She was always trying new things."

"She was?"

Ox's mother smelled like barbecue and warm bread. Her hug felt like being wrapped in a very warm sweater. Joan was everything Emmie's free-spirited mother wasn't. Not that she didn't love her mom. Joan just felt... comfortable.

Ox walked in just ask Joan released her. "Mom, what are you doing?"

Emmie pulled away and wiped her eyes. "I'm fine."

"I hate it *so much* when you say that," Ox muttered under his breath. "Mom, what's going on?"

Joan walked over and patted Ox's cheek. "We were just talking a little about her grandma, baby. Go wash up. We'll take care of your girl."

Ox was frowning, but he left the kitchen while Emmie silently repeated, *Not his girl. Not his girl. I am not his girl and this is not my family.*

Melissa and Joan started chattering about what needed to be done for dinner, brushing off Emmie's offers of help. Abby ran in a moment later, hair pulled into a fresh ponytail and face washed. She went to a drawer under the counter and pulled out placemats for the table. Within minutes, food was appearing and the table was set. Ox returned and sliced the tri-tip while Melissa badgered Abby about her homework.

"Hey." Ox set the platter of tri-tip on the table and sat next to Emmie. "We driving you crazy yet?"

Not your family, but if you lean any closer, I might take a bite out of you.

Emmie smiled. "I'm—"

"Don't say fine." He speared two thick slices of steak and put them on her plate. "If you say fine, I won't believe you."

"I'm hungry."

The corner of his mouth inched up. "Then you've come to the right place, Buttons."

"Did you call her Buttons?" Abby burst into laughter. "Uncle Ox, that's not a good nickname."

Emmie turned to him. "See?"

"Says who?" Ox scowled at Abby. "What do you know? You're eight and you named a goat Mr. Hummus."

"Mr. Tumnus!" Abby yelled. "Stop calling him Mr. Hummus."

Melissa passed the rolls to Emmie. "No yelling at the table, Abby."

Emmie took the rolls. "Mr. Tumnus from *The Lion, the Witch, and the Wardrobe?"* She turned to Ox. "That's an excellent goat name."

"I told you, Uncle Ox." Abby picked at her salad. "I like you, Emmie."

"Thank you. I like you too." Emmie liked any little kid imaginative enough to name a goat Mr. Tumnus. "Does Mr. Tumnus like books?"

"Mr. Hummus likes books," Ox said. "Flannel shirts. Tin cans."

"Aprons," Joan added. "My tomato plants."

"Wooden fence posts." Melissa chimed in. "Dog food. Cardboard boxes."

Abby met Emmie's eyes with a very earnest expression. "Mr. Tumnus is a very curious goat."

"It sounds like it."

CHAPTER TWENTY-TWO

THAT WAS IT. He was done for. Ox knew it the minute he walked into the kitchen and nearly attacked his mom when he saw Emmie crying. His mother was the closest thing he knew to a saint. Even during his obnoxious adolescent years, he'd worshipped her. The fact that his immediate reaction to seeing Emmie cry was a spike of anger at his *mother* knocked him sideways.

He was silent through dinner as Emmie chatted about books with Abby and asked genuinely curious questions about the ranch and the orange groves. She and Melissa chattered away while Ox's head spun.

What was he going to do?

It was obvious things couldn't continue the way they were. Their chemistry was too intense. Their attraction tangible. He'd nearly kissed her again when he buckled her into his truck, but her words had stopped him in his tracks.

"I need this to work, Ox."

She was right. They both needed INK to work. But desire and excitement twisted his gut. He was being honest with her. He was shit about following rules, and he was gone for her. He'd never thought about a woman the way he thought about Emmie. He'd never wanted one the same way, especially one he'd barely touched.

Ox dug his fingers into his leg under the table, resisting the urge to grab her hand.

He was thinking about holding her hand at the fucking dinner table.

"Ox?"

"Hmm?"

"You're quieter than normal."

Emmie pursed her pretty mouth. She had the same expression when she was reading and she was really into a book. That mouth was one of the reasons he couldn't resist biting her lower lip the week before.

"Careful," he muttered.

"What?"

He leaned over and whispered, "You're going to get bitten again if you're not careful."

Emmie's cheeks reddened, and she turned back to the dinner table. "So do you guys get any snow here in winter?"

It was obvious Melissa knew something was going on. Her expression was amused. "We do, but it doesn't tend to stick. We're not high enough."

"Oh." Emmie pushed the beans around her plate. "I like snow."

"Me too," Abby said. "Last year we got to sled."

Melissa nodded. "Last year was heavier than normal. Pain in the ass with the cows, but fun for Abby."

"Mr. Tumnus got really excited."

His mom was playing dumb. "Is everything all right, Ox?"

"Yep." He cut into a piece of tri-tip. "Just remembered something about work I needed to ask Emmie."

"Oh?"

"Yeah." He glanced at her. "There's a clause in the employee manual we need to clear up."

The one about sexual harassment and how she needs to be doing more of it.

Melissa asked, "You have an employee manual?"

Emmie's cheeks turned redder. "Kind of. We have some guidelines and *rules* that have been pretty clear from the beginning. We've just never written them down. Maybe we need to."

"Or we could keep things casual," Ox said. "Like we have been."

She smiled. "Yes. Exactly like we have been."

"Maybe not exactly," Ox said.

"Exactly is working great for me." Emmie reached for the pepper. Picked it up. Set it down. "Excuse me, Joan. Where's the bathroom?"

"Right down the hall, sweetie." Joan was biting back a smile. "Second door on your right."

"Thanks." Emmie rose and left the room.

Ox watched her until she disappeared down the hall. He reached for another roll.

"You're either really stupid," Melissa said quietly, "or brilliant."

"Ask me tomorrow."

Joan asked, "So will you be staying in town tonight?"

Ox thought about the sweet swing of Emmie's hips as she hustled down the hall. "Yep."

"Are you having a sleepover?" Abby asked. "Whose house are you going to?"

Melissa snorted before she could turn it into a cough. "Yeah, Uncle Ox. Whose house are you going to?"

Ox smiled at Abby. "A friend's."

———

THE TENSION in the truck was thick on the drive back to town.

Ox could navigate the twisting roads in his sleep, he'd driven them so many times. He had a duffel bag thrown near Emmie's feet and every intention of talking his way into her apartment even if he was sleeping on the couch.

Emmie hadn't said a word. She wasn't a chatterbox, but he could tell she was dying to say something. Or maybe she was waiting for him to laugh off what he'd said at the table or make a joke to relieve the tension.

Nope. Not this time, Buttons.

"I like your family," she finally said.

"Thanks. I do too."

She glanced at the duffel bag. So you have a friend you can stay with in Metlin? It's really late."

It wasn't that late, but Ox played along. "I know. I'm pretty tired."

Emmie was dying to ask who. He knew it.

"It's nice you're still friends with some people from Bombshell," she said.

Nice try, sweetheart. "I'm not staying with anyone from Bombshell. Still kind of awkward between me and the guys over there. Though Ginger gave me a slight nod the other day instead of flipping me off, so I'm hopeful."

"Oh."

She had no idea what he had in mind. Ox almost felt sorry for her. Almost.

"I have a girl I can stay with." Melissa was right. He was either really stupid or brilliant.

Ox glanced over at Emmie. Her mouth was open and she was staring at him.

"You bastard," she said quietly.

He set his face in a hard line. "Why does that make me a bastard?"

"Because you... you said, when we were at the table"—her face was turning red, but it wasn't a blush this time—"you talk about biting me—biting me!—one minute, and then you casually mention some girl you're sleeping with."

"I'm not sleeping with her." He pulled the truck over on the side of the road. "Too soon for that. She needs some time to get used to the idea." In fact, the idea of making her wait put him in a perversely good mood.

Emmie hadn't even noticed that the truck stopped. "You're unbelievable! You arrogant—"

"I'm not taking anything for granted. She hasn't invited me to her bed. I don't go there unless everyone's on the same page. How does that make me arrogant?"

"You think you can just wind me up, walking around the shop, flirting with me—"

"I'm not a flirt." He unbuckled his seat belt and turned toward her. "I don't flirt."

"You bite my lip. You talk about breaking rules. This was your rule! You're the one who said it was a bad idea to… to—" Emmie suddenly realized the truck was stopped in the middle of an orange grove and Ox was moving toward her. "Where are we? What are you doing?"

God bless bench seats. The smell of oranges filled the cab. Sweet after sour. She was sweet after sour. Her hair was pulled up in that bun he wanted to mess up. She was wearing her I LIKE TO PARTY, AND BY PARTY I MEAN READ BOOKS shirt. It was tighter than most of her shirts and hugged her breasts. He could see the delicate curves of her collarbones at the base of her neck.

She put a hand up. "Ox, what are you doing?"

Ox held his hand over hers, pressing it to his chest. He needed to take his time with Emmie. She was going to freak out. It both amused him and scared him a little.

"I need this to work," he murmured.

He was not talking about the shop.

"I know," she said.

Slow down, you idiot.

"Emmie." He clicked a button and released her seat belt. "Emmie Elliot, as a friend and a work associate, I am very respectfully asking you to sexually harass the hell out of me."

CHAPTER TWENTY-THREE

WHAT WAS HAPPENING? One minute she'd been mad as hell and tired of his vague comments, possessive attitude, and mixed messages, and the next she was sitting so close to him she could feel the heat from his chest and Ox was asking her to sexually harass him.

"You don't work for me," she said. "I can't sexually harass you."

"You're right." He leaned closer. His lips were so close she could feel his breath against her lips. "I don't work for you. You don't work for me. We're partners and we're grown-ups and Emmie, for fuck's sake, you have to kiss me because I can't do it and I'm dying here."

Emmie closed the space between them, pressing her lips to his.

Ox made a low growling sound, scooting to her side of the truck as he untangled Emmie from the seat belt and lifted her onto his lap so she straddled him. He hooked her leg over his lap, gripping her thigh as his other hand dug into the small of her back, plastering her to his chest. In the next second, his hand was at her neck, angling her mouth to his kiss. His teeth nipped at her lips, making her gasp, and he let his tongue slip in to tease her own. He tasted like the peppermint ice cream his mom had served after dinner.

Emmie's head was spinning. *Yes. No. Yes yes yes.*

Her body decided to tell her head to mind its own business.

Kissing Miles Oxford was a full-body experience. She pulled away and gasped only to have Ox capture her mouth again. His large palm fell to her bottom, caressing and squeezing. She squirmed on his lap and felt his erection between them.

He groaned and brought his hands up, cradling her face between his palms as he kissed her over and over.

"I"—*kiss*—"have been wanting to do this"—*kiss*—"for weeks."

"Me too," she managed to gasp. "You're a good kisser."

"Thanks." His teeth scraped over her jaw. "You too."

"I am?" Emmie hadn't heard that before.

"Your mouth." Ox left her neck and captured her in a sweet, lingering press of lips followed by another nip on her lower lip. "Your mouth drives me crazy."

The kiss moved from frantic to leisurely. Ox took the hands cradling her cheeks and ran them over her shoulders, tracing little circles on her bare skin before he slipped her cardigan down her shoulders and swept his arms up her back.

"I want to kiss your back," he whispered. "I've been dreaming about those butterflies."

"I've been dreaming about your chest."

"Yeah?" He reached for her hand and put it on his chest. "What about it?"

"The anchor over your heart," she whispered. "It's beautiful."

He trailed his lips to her ear as his fingers slipped under her shirt at the small of her back. "What do you want to do to it?"

"I want—" Emmie gasped when Ox's warm hands unsnapped her bra in a single move. "I want to lick it."

"Sounds good to me." His hands moved over her back, unencumbered by her bra. They moved up and down, teasing her skin until she wanted to weep and beg him to strip her bare. He was kissing her neck again.

"The letters on your left bicep?"

"Yeah?"

"I want to bite those."

He nipped her neck. "That can be arranged."

Emmie squirmed some more and Ox groaned.

"Buttons, I am trying really hard to not strip you naked and fuck you in my truck in the middle of Cary's orange grove, so we probably better stop."

"You started it." She arched her back and caressed his shoulders, enjoying the hard feel of him between her thighs. It had been a while—a long while—since she'd wanted anyone like this. She might not have ever wanted anyone like this. The tension had been building for weeks. "And stop calling me Buttons."

His hand moved between her thighs and cupped her. He stroked his thumb and pressed in, holding her just like that as he pulled away from her mouth and put his hand back on her nape to angle her eyes to his.

Emmie couldn't breathe. If he moved his thumb just a little, she would explode. She'd never been more turned on in her life.

The corner of Ox's mouth inched up; he knew exactly what he was doing to her. "Emmie."

"Yeah?" She was panting and near tears. Her skin felt like it was alive, every inch of it, but especially that inch.

"I'm always going to call you Buttons." His thumb moved, pressed in, and flipped her into a sharp orgasm. She shuddered when she came, falling against his chest and panting into his neck as she held on to him.

It was barely enough to take the edge off. A taste of pleasure when she wanted to indulge.

Ox smelled like cedar and salt. The air smelled like oranges. Emmie licked his neck, tasting his skin as she snuggled into him and slid her hands around his waist. Her head was buzzing and she barely noticed when Ox unclipped her hair.

He whispered against her cheek, "That was the hottest fucking thing I've ever seen."

"Really?"

He combed his fingers through her hair, smoothing it down her back. "And I'm staying at your place."

"Okay."

"On the couch."

"Why?" She frowned. He didn't want to sleep with her? The physical evidence was calling him a liar.

Ox ran a hand up her shoulder and pulled her away from his neck, cradling her head in his hand. "I like to take my time. And not just in bed."

Oh yeah. He was good.

Emmie nodded, and Ox drew her into a lingering, sweet kiss. Her head was spinning by the time he drew back, stroking her cheek as he opened the truck door.

"What are you doing?"

Ox slid out of the car and hopped up and down a few times. "Cold air. Kind of necessary right now."

She stifled a grin and buckled her seat belt. "Get back in the truck. I'll keep my hands to myself."

"That's not necessary. For future reference."

"It is when you're driving."

"Now you're just giving me ideas." His half smile turned into a grin. "Is your imagination really as good as Tayla said?"

"Guess you're going to have to wait and find out." Emmie closed the door and covered her head with her sweater when she heard Ox laugh.

What had she done?

———

EMMIE WOKE to the smell of coffee and man. The coffee was in the kitchen, but the man was beside her. She cracked open one of her eyes and saw Ox watching her.

"Hey," he said. "I believe you said morning cuddling was required as rent for the couch."

"Yes, it is." She scooted over and he moved closer. "Though I'm more a fan of naked cuddling."

His shoulders shook as he opened his arms and she put her head on his shoulder. He closed his arms around her, and Emmie luxuriated in the weight of his hug, the thud of his heart beating under her ear.

Oh, this was good.

"I'm also a fan of naked cuddling," he said. "But as I said, I like to take my time."

"I would have pegged you for a more... impatient approach."

"Hmmm." He played with her hair, spreading it over her shoulders. "Not this time. Anticipation is fun. Teasing is fun. The best things come to those who wait."

"Umm... but the early bird gets the worm?"

"Am I the worm?"

"Maybe? I hadn't really thought that analogy through. It's early and I haven't had coffee."

"I started the pot before I came in. Warning—Tayla has already spotted me and has a list of questions."

Emmie groaned. "Did she show you the list?"

"Wait, there's an actual list?" Ox tipped her chin up to meet his eyes. "There's an actual list of questions?"

"Yes, we put it together several years ago after her last disastrous relationship and promised to use it on any man who looked serious. It's very intrusive and thorough. I'm hoping you can laugh your way through it because I don't think she's going to let me get out of it."

His eyebrows lifted. "So this is serious?"

"The list? Yes, she takes it very seriously."

"I'm not talking about the list. I'm talking about you and me."

Emmie propped herself up on her elbows. "Ox, this was only ever going to be serious. Do you think I'd take a risk like this if I wasn't serious?"

He smiled a little. "Just checking." He leaned closer. "In exchange for morning cuddles, I demand payment by morning kisses."

She slapped a hand over her mouth. "Morning breath."

"Don't care." His kiss was long and thorough. He pulled her up until she was splayed across his massive chest.

"You really are kind of an ox, aren't you?"

He hitched her leg up and arched into her. "I don't know how much you know about cattle, but oxen are usually castrated."

"Well… that doesn't really apply then, does it?" She muffled her laugh in his chest.

"No. But I am a big guy." He tugged on her hair. "Does it bother you?"

"What?"

"That I'm overgrown. I think that's what you said, right?"

"Does it bother you I'm a little thing?"

"No." He lifted her and brought her close enough to kiss. "Just keeps things interesting, right?"

"Right." Coffee was suddenly the last thing on her mind. "Miles—"

"My mom calls me Miles. Please do not ever call me Miles in bed. Ever."

She smiled. "Ox."

"Emmie."

"Should we talk about this?"

"Yes, we should. At dinner tonight. Wait." He frowned. "I have a client tonight. That won't work."

"Tomorrow night?"

"Tomorrow too. And you have your first book club meeting the night after that."

"Nights are complicated. Lunch?"

"You don't think you're going to be busy during lunch? Lots of people run errands on their lunch break."

"True." She sighed. "Why is this so impossible?"

"We'll figure it out." He kissed her nose. "Maybe—"

Tayla banged on the door. "Hey, sexy time's over. Shop opens in an hour, and we have an order that came in yesterday. Put some clothes on, you hussy."

Ox yelled, "I told you to stop calling me a hussy. It hurts my feelings."

"Stop being such a delicate flower, Ox!"

He smiled. "Men have feelings too, you know."

I love you. It almost slipped out, which was ridiculous. Emmie couldn't love him. They were just...

She didn't know what they were. They hadn't even gone on a date yet. They spent all day together, but they didn't have time to go on a date. What was that? What kind of relationship could they possibly have when they were both starting brand-new businesses? It wasn't love. It couldn't be love. Not yet. She'd only known him a couple of months. There were all sorts of experiences they had to go through before she could really know if she—

"Stop." Ox grabbed her chin. "You're overthinking it."

Emmie blinked. "I am?"

"You have that look you get right before you freak the fuck out. Chill."

She nodded.

"It's still there." He rolled her to the side and kissed her forehead before he got out of bed. "Get dressed. Get some coffee. I have errands to run this morning, but I'll see you later."

"Okay."

"And don't freak out."

"I'm not freaking out."

Ox turned as he got to the door. "You're lying, but we'll work on that. Have a good morning. I'll see you later." He paused, then walked back and gave her one more kiss. "And I look forward to much more sexual harassment in our future."

Emmie waited until he shut the door to pull the covers over her head and groan.

She didn't know what she was doing! She'd had the man in her bed, and instead of screwing his brains out, she'd been mentally declaring her love for him. She was a cliché. A horrible, horrible romantic cliché.

Glancing at her phone, Emmie decided she was allowed to wallow in confusion for precisely five minutes and then she had to get dressed.

Five minutes. Then it was time to work.

CHAPTER TWENTY-FOUR

HE'D BEEN RIGHT. Lunch was as busy as Ox had predicted. Which was good! But not when she wanted desperately to get a little more alone time with a certain tattoo artist who was currently inking a baby name on a guy's shoulder.

"Number five, huh?" Ox murmured. "You must be a busy guy."

"My wife's busier." The man laughed. "But yeah. We have fun. Ten years, five kids."

Emmie glanced over at Ox's corner. His client had his shirt off and his hairy chest and belly were attracting a few glances from her customers, but no one seemed offended. Ox had offered to put up the privacy screen, but the man said it wasn't necessary. It was one of those things that Emmie hadn't thought about before they started. She wasn't concerned about men taking their shirts off in the bookstore, but she'd forgotten some of her customers might not feel the same way.

Luckily the general mood seemed to be curiosity and not disapproval. Two of her grandmother's old customers had wandered over and were watching the tattoo.

"Ladies," Ox said with a nod.

"Does it hurt?" one asked.

"A little," the client said. "I'm used to it now."

"Doris, you should get your granddaughter's name on your arm like this man." The older lady leaned toward Ox and his client. "She's much more daring than I am."

Ox looked up and caught Emmie's eye, winking at her before he turned back to his client and wiped off his shoulder. "Luis, you're done. I'll see you again in a couple of years."

"I hope not!" the man said while Ox smeared some gel over the new ink and covered it with a light bandage, giving the man the basic spiel about aftercare.

Emmie scanned the shop and the sidewalk outside. Guessing she'd have at least a few minutes of quiet, she went to check what Tayla was up to. She was back in the office, her glasses on and a bright red pencil stuck in her hair as she scanned the computer and made notes with a different red pencil on a notepad. "Hey, hussy."

Emmie leaned against the doorjamb. "Will you stop?"

"What was he doing on the couch? You still haven't answered me. If that man gave me a hickey on my neck, he would not be sleeping on the couch."

Emmie adjusted the collar of her shirt. It was a very faint bruise, but it was there. She hadn't noticed the night before. "He said he likes to take his time. Something about anticipation and teasing making things better."

"So he's cock-blocking himself?" Tayla's head fell back. "Why is that so hot?"

Emmie had to agree. It was hot. And frustrating. She'd been thinking about him all morning, which wasn't making work easier. She'd mis-shelved an entire shipment of adult romance in the YA fantasy section.

"I can't stop thinking about him," she whispered, sitting in the chair across from the desk. "This is nuts. I'm nuts. I'm being stupid. We both are, and this is going to mess everything up. I should just tell him to forget last night even happened."

Tayla narrowed her eyes. "You don't want to do that."

"Of course I don't! But how can this end well?"

Tayla pursed her lips. "You were the one talking about marriage and babies and all that the other night. Maybe this guy is the one. The real deal. Your one true love. The happily-ever-after in your own personal romance novel, baby."

Emmie rolled her eyes. "It is way too soon to talk about that."

"And it's way too soon to talk about breaking up with a guy that you're just starting out with," Tayla said. "You've been dancing around each other for weeks. You've gone through a store renovation together. You work well together professionally. Just give it a chance, Em. You don't know what might happen. Besides, as much as you work, where else were you going to meet anyone?" Tayla snorted. "Or were you going to give in to the predictable and go on a date with Adrian Saroyan?"

Adrian Saroyan. Emmie's eyes went wide. "Shit."

Tayla shrugged. "Who says he's even going to finish that book? It's been what? Three weeks or something?"

"Not everyone binge-reads like we do."

"Three weeks, Emmie. If he was motivated, he'd already have read it. Ox would have read it by now."

Heavy footsteps sounded in the hall. Ox poked his head in. "Did I hear my name? Emmie, you've got a customer in front."

Tayla asked, "How long would it take you to read a three-hundred-page book?"

"Three hundred pages of what?"

"Jane Austen."

Ox shrugged. "I don't know. A couple days? I've already read them all though. My mom made me."

"*Sense and Sensibility*?" Emmie asked.

"Colonel Brandon's the man," Ox said. "But Edward is boring as shit." He nodded toward the door. "Customer."

Emmie hopped up and slipped out the door, but Ox grabbed her hand before she could make it down the hall. He pulled her back, tilted her chin up, and kissed her quickly before he let her go.

"Been wanting to do that all day," he said quietly.

The kiss sent a buzz of energy through her, but Emmie turned and walked down the hallway without a word. She had a customer. Ox wasn't her boyfriend. Was he?

If he wasn't her boyfriend, what was he?

She had no idea. Was this just a hookup for him? They hadn't defined anything. Did he even believe in monogamy? That wasn't something she'd been able to assume in San Francisco. Of course, this was Metlin, which was still pretty traditional.

But Metlin had changed! Maybe monogamy wasn't a given anymore.

Was there an alternative-relationship scene in Metlin?

Is this what Ox would classify as "freaking the fuck out?"

The young woman standing in the shop had a clutch of mysteries under her arm and was staring at the biography section.

"Hi," Emmie said. "Did you have any questions about a book?"

"A couple, actually."

"Thank God."

———

SHE CLOSED up her side of INK at seven p.m., leaving Ox with two clients, one in the chair and the other waiting. She ate dinner in front of her iPad, watched reruns of *Doctor Who*, and ignored the voices below her. Sometime around eleven, she nodded off on the couch only to wake to a sharp rap on her door.

Emmie sat up, rubbing her eyes and wondering why Tayla was knocking. She must have forgotten her key again.

"Who is rapping, rapping on my chamber door?" Emmie unpinned the crooked bun on top of her head as she pulled open the door. "Tayla, you've got to stop..." Emmie's eyes went wide. "Hi."

It was Ox. "Caw." He tilted his head and stepped into her apartment, putting a hand on her hip. "I should put a raven on you somewhere. Maybe here?" He squeezed her hip. "That would be hot."

Good God, he understood Poe references and was talking about putting a tattoo needle on her hip.

Marry me. "Or kiss me." Emmie blinked. "I said that aloud."

Ox smiled. "Yes, you did." He walked her backward to the living area and spun around, sitting on the couch and pulling Emmie into his lap. "This is my new favorite make-out position."

"Oh?"

"Yeah, this way I don't get an ache in my neck when I kiss you." He leaned in and demonstrated. "See?"

She saw. She saw a little cross-eyed, but she saw. "It's late. Are you heading home?"

"Yeah, but I just finished and I wanted to say good night. Were you sleeping?"

She nodded. "I'm an old lady."

"We had a late night yesterday." He played with the ends of her hair. "This is nice."

"What?"

"Your hair down. You don't wear it down very much."

"It's gotten really long. I've been thinking about cutting it."

"Don't." He smoothed the red-brown waves down her back, playing with the ends that fell just at the small of her back. "It's sexy as fuck." Ox nosed under her chin and played his lips over her neck. "You smell good."

"I smell like dust and paper. I was sorting the used section."

"Whatever." He scraped his teeth along her collarbone. "It smells good."

Emmie shivered. "Are you trying to drive me crazy?"

"Yes." He kissed her, sucking on her bottom lip. "Were you freaking out today?"

"A little."

"Where are we going on our first date?"

"I don't know." Emmie could barely think. He was doing it again. Distracting her. Seducing her. His warm hands were playing with her hair, twisting the weight of it in his hand and pulling her head back to expose her throat. "We could... could go to dinner."

"Boring. No movies either unless we watch them here and I can kiss you during the boring parts."

Emmie smiled and put her hands on his cheeks, pulling his face up to meet his eyes. "So what do you want to do?"

"I want... to go for a hike. Or go riding. Do you ride?"

"Horses or motorcycles?"

"Horses."

Emmie shook her head. "I don't hike either."

Ox frowned. "Do you walk?"

"Not often in a straight line. Hence no hiking."

He rolled his eyes. "I'll hold your hand. Come hiking with me. We can do something simple."

"It's cold in the mountains."

He hitched her closer and pressed their bodies together. "Don't you trust me to keep you warm?"

Emmie could barely talk. She nodded and Ox kissed her again. He stroked her lips with leisurely attention, his kiss lazy and indulgent. She could hear him humming in the back of his throat, and her thighs clenched around his hips.

"Hiking it is. Your next day off. If I have any clients, I'll reschedule them." Ox slipped his large hands in the back pockets of her jeans and squeezed. "I like your ass."

Emmie smiled. "It's big."

"It's not."

"I just mean in proportion to the rest of me, it's kind of—"

"Emmie." Ox pulled away and looked at her with deadly serious eyes. "There is no such thing as an ass too big. It's very important you understand that." He squeezed again for emphasis.

She pressed her lips together so she wouldn't laugh. "I understand."

"Good." He slapped her butt teasingly. "I'd hate to have to repeat this discussion."

"Liar." Emmie draped her arms over his shoulders, relaxing against him. "You'd love to repeat this discussion."

"Caught me." One hand stayed on her ass while the other slid up the side of her body, cupping her breast in his hand. "We could always try variations." His thumb swept over her nipple.

Emmie's mouth fell open. "I'd hate for you to get bored."

"Not possible." He pulled back, and Emmie opened her eyes.

The look in his gaze told her too much. It was raw and a little confused. The confidence had fallen away, and Ox looked at her with a focused intensity that scared Emmie to death.

He blinked. "Tell me you're staying in Metlin."

"I reopened the shop, didn't I?"

"That's not a yes."

A tiny part of her hesitated. In the back of her mind, Adrian's offer still hung. He could rent out the building, find her solid tenants that would allow her to choose a different line of work. She could sell the building and move anywhere she wanted. Did she really want to stay in Metlin for the rest of her life?

Ox rested a hand at the base of her throat. "Are you staying?"

"Yes." Had she said that out loud?

"Good." He fell on her mouth with a hunger so intense it took her breath away.

Emmie pulled at his T-shirt, yanking it up and over his head so she could put her hands on him. Her fingers skimmed over his shoulders, down his chest, scratching at the hard points of his nipples before her fingernails trailed down his abdomen. Ox didn't let her up to breathe. He shifted until her hand fell on the swell of his erection beneath his jeans. She stroked over the button fly and he hissed, grabbing her wrist and holding it there as he arched into her hand.

He groaned and fisted his hand in her hair, yanking her head back as he scraped his teeth along her jaw. "Sweet," he muttered. "You're so fucking sweet."

"Ox."

He arched into her hand again, holding her palm pressed to his jeans for a searing moment before he brushed her hand away and cupped her cheeks in his hands. "You know it's killing me to wait."

"So don't." Emmie's need was as raging as his even if it wasn't as evident.

"But it's gonna be so good," he whispered, biting her earlobe. "Want to know why?"

Emmie dug her fingers into his chest and gripped his thighs between her own. "Why?"

"Because you have a very good imagination."

CHAPTER TWENTY-FIVE

HE WAS CURSING his sister as he and Emmie made their way up the gently sloping trail on Monday morning. He'd had days and days of teasing Emmie with no relief for him or her. He was trying to follow his big sister's advice for once, and it was damn near killing him as he watched Emmie's excellent ass sway in front of him. She was wearing jeans that hugged her hips, a long-sleeved thermal, and a heavy padded vest to ward off the bite of winter that was already descending in the mountains.

"Just do me a favor," Melissa said. *"Don't sleep with this one right away. Just try it for once and see what happens."*

"Sexual chemistry is important. If we're not compatible—"

"Be honest. Do you really think you and Emmie might not have chemistry?"

He hadn't had an answer to that one. It was pretty obvious to everyone around them that they did.

"Just take your time and get to know her first. Sex is awesome, but it can cloud everything up. If you really like this woman, then spend some time getting to know her outside of bed, Ox. Trust me, it'll be worth it."

It better be fucking worth it. He wanted to pull Emmie off the trail, shove her against a tree, drag her jeans down her legs and—

"What is that?" Emmie pointed at something off the deserted trail.

Ox paused at her side. "The pinecone?"

"It's as big as my arm!"

Ox grabbed it from the bushes. "It's a sugar pine cone." He held it up. It *was* a giant cone and nearly perfect. Ox placed it on a fallen log on the side of the path. "The squirrels need it. Winter'll be here soon."

"Is that why most of them are all torn up?" Emmie kicked a shredded cone with her foot. "Squirrels?"

"Yep. They eat the seeds."

"I've never seen a pinecone that big." Emmie took it and held it up. "Are sequoia pinecones huge like that?"

Ox smothered a smile. "Well, sequoias aren't pines. So they're called sequoia cones, not pinecones. And you really didn't spend any time in the mountains as a kid, did you?"

Emmie shook her head and put the cone back on the log, brushing her hand off on her jeans. "Bookworm. I didn't like the outdoors, and my mom was always playing gigs. My grandma was running the shop. We didn't do mountains."

"Tragic." He grabbed her hand. "But we will remedy that."

"My thighs are killing me."

"You're doing great." He squeezed her hand. "You're a natural. Once I got you looking up from the book, you haven't tripped once."

"That guide book was really good. It had all sorts of stuff about the history of the national park and the conservation efforts that—"

"But you would have missed that sugar pine cone the size of your arm if you hadn't been looking." He shook her arm. "Right?"

She sighed and kept walking. "I'll read more later. I need to expand the outdoor section of the shop. I had a tourist in last week asking about hiking maps for the national park."

They walked along the wide path for a few hundred yards,

enjoying the silence and occasionally passing a fellow hiker, but for the most part the trail was deserted. Summer in the Sierras was crowded with tourists from all over the world, but in the fall and winter, most traffic died off. If they were lucky, the rain and snow would come early, and cut off much of the Sierra Nevada from casual visitors. The valley below depended on heavy falls of snow in the mountains to feed the lakes and rivers the farmers and ranchers would need for the hot, dry summers. It was a cycle Ox had grown up watching even if he had no desire to follow in his grandfather's footsteps.

The rhythm of their footfalls was muffled by the thick layer of pine needles on the trail. Ferns and underbrush burst from the forest floor as they approached a grove of giant sequoias. It was one of Ox's favorites. Far from the paved trails of the national park, this area was visited by locals more than outsiders.

He watched Emmie as they approached. Her face turned from interest to wonder as they grew nearer.

"Are those...?" Her smile grew. "Wow." Her eyes went up. And up. And up. "Wow!"

Ox drew her into the center of the sequoia grove where a fire-scarred monarch dominated the clearing, surrounded by other mature sequoias. Light filtered through the tall branches above as Emmie wandered through the clearing, and Ox spread a blanket at the base of the monarch, kicking away a few of the rocks so they could eat lunch at the foot of the tree. He set down his backpack and walked around the massive trunk to find Emmie leaning against the thick bark on the other side, looking up at the giant trees. Utter and complete wonder was written all over her face.

"I'm in Narnia," she whispered as he approached. "Middle Earth."

Ox didn't say a word, but he sat at the base of the tree and drew Emmie down to sit between his legs. She rested her head on his chest and looked up, her eyes still locked on the giant trees surrounding them.

They sat in silence as the sun warmed the bark at his back and Emmie warmed his chest. His arms were around her, her fingers knit with his. Neither of them broke the silence. They listened to the birds and the creaking of the branches above as they moved with the wind. A profound sense of peace fell over Ox, a peace that had eluded him since his grandfather's death.

I could stay here—right here, with this girl—for the rest of my life if I had a chance of putting that look on her face.

His breath felt heavy in his chest as he bent down, placing a kiss on the top of Emmie's head. She turned her face to the sun and laid her cheek over his heart, closing her eyes and letting the warmth kiss her skin. There were colors in her hair that reminded Ox of a campfire, red and gold threads that weren't visible until the light hit them. She was little but sturdy, and the weight of her body against him was... satisfying. That was the word. He wrapped his arms around her more securely as she snuggled closer.

This is what it feels like to fall in love.

The realization was quiet and sure. This was what it felt like to fall in love. It wasn't the lightning strike he'd been expecting. It wasn't the big dramatic moment. It was this. This... solid feeling that crept into his chest like a root. Ox looked at the trees around him, thinking about the giant trees around them secured by such shallow roots. Sequoias grew on granite bedrock. Their roots couldn't sink deep, so they spread wide. They couldn't exist on their own. They grew in groves so their roots could spread out and tangle together, holding the whole grove up through centuries of fire and snow and wind and flood.

Groves were family.

He had family. He had a great family even if the responsibility for them weighed heavy at times.

Emmie didn't have family though. How many years had she been standing alone? For most of her childhood, she was the responsible one holding her family together. Her idealistic grandmother. Her loving but flighty mother. Was it any wonder she looked for respect and dependability and routine? Was it a surprise she had a tendency to freak out at the unexpected?

The trust she'd placed in him—and his business—humbled him.

He ran a finger over her cheek until Emmie's eyes fluttered open. Without a word, he bent down and took her mouth in a soft kiss. Emmie turned and put her arms around his neck, drawing him closer. He sank into it, tasting the sweet peppermint gum she'd offered him earlier. He unbraided her hair and ran his fingers through the waves while her mouth drove him crazy.

He trailed his fingers down her spine until his hand landed in his favorite spot. He palmed the curve of her ass, pressing her closer as he made love to her mouth.

Fuck yes, this was why his sister had told him to wait. He wouldn't have missed the thrill of this slow fall for all the money in the world.

Emmie seduced him with her silence. He was intoxicated by her. He wanted to learn all her secrets and knew he never would. She drove him crazy and she didn't even try. It was beautiful and addicting, and he couldn't imagine ever getting enough.

Ox wrapped his arms around her, picked her up, and walked back to the blanket he'd spread out.

Maybe he wanted to wait for the full meal, but they both needed a little taste.

CHAPTER TWENTY-SIX

OX ROLLED the stool from his corner, pushing across the room, and spun behind her counter. The only customer had just walked out of the shop when he lifted Emmie's shirt, stuck his head under it, and nipped at her belly.

Emmie muffled a laugh and shoved him back. "Stop!"

"No." He wrapped an arm around her waist. "You know, sex in the forest is on my to-do list."

Her face heated up. "We did not have sex in the forest."

"But what we did do gave me hope. I'm holding on to it." He pushed away and rolled back to his corner just as another customer walked past, paused at her display window for holiday cookbooks, and reached for the door.

"Hi!" Emmie said. "Can I help you?"

She'd collaborated with Pacific Kitchen Supply a block down Main Street to showcase some of their brightly colored enamel kitchenware in the window with some of the new cookbooks she'd ordered. So far the display had been successful for both shops. The window drew a lot of customers into the bookstore, many of whom asked where Pacific Kitchen Supply was after they noticed the shop's sign in Emmie's window.

The customer said, "I was looking at that new vegetarian holiday cookbook in the window. Do you have other copies of it?"

"I sure do. Let me show you our vegetarian section."

Emmie had sold three cookbooks after story hour that morning. Daisy had walked down from Café Maya to do a reading of *Too Many Tamales* by Gary Soto and invite the parents and kids to the tamale-making workshop she was hosting in the café the Saturday after Thanksgiving. Emmie had sold more than a few copies of *Too Many Tamales* too.

"You want to try for a late lunch?" Ox asked after the customer left. "I don't have a client today until three."

"Let me check with Tayla." Emmie texted Tayla, who was helping Daisy with her books that morning. Most days there wasn't enough for Tayla to do at INK, so she'd started helping Daisy and Ethan with their bookkeeping. Emmie was hoping it would turn into a full-time gig for Tayla so her friend would find more reasons to stay in Metlin. In their first month, INK had shown a small profit for both Emmie and Ox. Ox had looked disappointed, but Emmie was fine with it. Small profit was fine as long as it was growing profit. They were just heading into the holiday season too. In the retail world, there was no better time to sell.

She glanced over at Ox, who was sketching while she waited to hear back from Tayla. "Holidays are best for retail. Are there best times for tattooing too?"

He shrugged. "I've only worked in Metlin. And in Metlin, it's usually fall when all the college kids come back to town."

"That makes sense."

"And I usually get a spike in the early summer. People get anniversary tattoos."

Emmie smiled. "Really?"

He nodded. "But I refuse to do names. Designs are fine. Hearts. Flowers. Symbols or verses. But no names."

"Why?"

"Kiss of death for any relationship."

She cocked her head. "Fifty-year anniversary?"

"Nope. Not even then."

Emmie frowned. "But I've seen you do names."

"Kid names. Mom names. Dad names. All those are fine. Significant others? Not a chance." He glanced up and smiled. "So if you ever ask me to write my name on your ass, I'll be tempted but I won't do it."

Her mouth twitched. "I was going to ask for that for my birthday."

"No, you weren't." He held up his hand. "My handprint though..."

Emmie balled up a piece of paper and threw it at him. Ox laughed just as her phone chimed.

"It's Tayla. She can watch the shop from one to two."

"Cool. Tacos?"

"Sounds good to me."

Emmie tried to keep the smile from breaking through. So far working next to Ox and dating him wasn't hard at all. In fact, it was easy. Most mornings he stayed out at the ranch helping his sister and mom with something or another. He rolled in around noon and got ready for work. He'd sketch custom pieces or do the small amount of bookkeeping his shop generated. As long as he didn't work too late, he'd come up after he was finished and hang out at her place for a while. Sometimes he fell asleep on the couch, making her wonder just how early he was waking up at the ranch.

Emmie estimated Ox was working an average of three hours a day tattooing. At one hundred dollars for a one-hour tattoo, it seemed like a sweet income, but every client took at least an hour of preparation, so it was really more like fifty dollars an hour for six hours of work. She didn't know all his expenses, but he probably needed to get more customers to make a solid profit.

She tried to keep her mind on her own accounts. Ox's business was Ox's business. She just wanted him to be successful because she could tell how much he loved his work.

His favorites were the custom pieces he sketched himself. Emmie could see how much he enjoyed them, and he put a lot more time into perfecting them than his clients probably realized. He would fiddle with a single sketch for hours, trying to imagine how his art would look on the natural curve of a back or shoulder or hip and how it needed to change when it was translated onto skin. He'd often sketch something out and then ask her or Tayla to come over so he could see the piece against a body. But Ox didn't care about the extra time because his custom clients were his best clients.

The worst were the kids who wandered in and didn't know what they wanted. Sometimes they'd find a design they liked on his wall. More often he'd spend a half hour talking with them and they'd wander out, promising to come back later. They usually didn't.

She saw him nodding off as lunch rolled closer.

"Ox."

He blinked and sat up straighter. "Hmm?"

"I'll be here another hour," she said. "Why don't you go upstairs to my room and take a nap?"

He yawned and shook his head. "I'm fine."

She walked to him and ran a hand over his fine buzz cut, glancing at the customers on the other side of the shop who were looking at them. She'd been shy about public displays of affection so far. She didn't want people talking too much.

Of course, in Metlin that was almost impossible.

She could tell Ox was pleased. He grabbed her hand and kissed the palm. "Hi."

"Go take a nap. You hiked all day on Monday. You worked until midnight last night. And how early were you up this morning at the ranch?"

He bit the tips of her fingers. "Are you trying to take care of me, Emmie Elliot?"

She shrugged.

He rose and pulled her closer. He was really taking advantage of the public display thing.

Give him an inch...

Ox took the mile. He bent down and kissed her before she could stop him.

"Since you're trying to take care of me, I'll let you. Is the apartment open?"

She handed him her keys. "For you? Yes. I'll let Tayla know you're up there if she comes back early."

"Sweet, sweet, sweet," he muttered. "Thank you. Wake me up for lunch, yeah?"

"I will."

But she couldn't. By the time lunch rolled around, Tayla came back for the afternoon, and Emmie walked upstairs, the sight of Ox lying in her bed sprawled in a sunbeam was too tempting. She set the alarm on her phone, crawled in next to him, and cuddled close. Eating could wait.

———

"EMMIE?"

A sunbeam shone across her closed eyes.

"Em?"

Something tickled her nose. She turned her head and smacked her face into a hard chest, startling her awake. Emmie reared back, suddenly remembering where she was. She was in her own bed next to Ox.

"How much time do we have?" she mumbled. "Why is your shirt on?"

A low laugh rumbled in his chest, and she forced her eyes up.

"Hey," Ox said. "I wish we could skip lunch to fool around, but I have to drive out to the ranch."

Emmie blinked and tried to clear her head. She grabbed for her phone and checked the clock. "You don't have time. You have a client at three."

"I already called him." Ox rubbed a strand of hair between her fingers. "He can reschedule. And Melissa had a minor emergency with a picking crew that she needs some help with."

"Shoot."

"So I have to cancel lunch." He kissed her forehead. "Sorry."

Emmie shook her head. "It's fine. Are you coming back later?"

"Depends on how long it takes. I might just stay out there for dinner. I haven't been spending enough time with Abby the past few weeks."

He didn't say it, but Emmie heard it. *Because I've been spending time with you.*

"It's fine. I'll let everyone know you had to take off."

"Thank you." He bent down and took her lips, kissing her so long and slow that her body forgot they didn't have time for more. She was aching by the time he rolled away and stood up. Ox walked out the door and closed it softly a moment before the alarm on her phone went off.

Emmie sighed and decided to walk back down to INK. She wasn't all that hungry for lunch.

———

BY THE TIME dinner rolled around and she still hadn't heard from Ox, she decided to turn the CLOSED sign around in his window and start cleaning up.

"What's up with your inked mountain man?" Tayla asked.

"Some kind of problem on the ranch," Emmie said. "He told me he might not come back tonight."

Tayla pursed her lips.

"What?" Emmie asked. She could tell when Tayla had something to say.

"He spends a lot of time out there. That's all I was thinking."

"Well, he lives out there and it's his family's place."

"Does he get paid?"

"Tayla, that's none of my business."

Emmie had tried to forget it, but Ginger's first visit to the shop sprang back into her mind, and a thread of doubt began to twist. *"He'll always pick them over you. You know that, right?"*

EMMIE TRIED NOT to let Ginger's voice in her head, but it was hard not to the following week when Ox once again canceled a client and dinner plans to help his sister out with a broken fence.

She and Tayla had been closing up the shop the night before, after Emmie had been forced to turn away two walk-ins at Ox's shop. She handed them a card but didn't know what else to do.

"Did you ask him if he's getting paid to work out there?" Tayla asked.

"I can't do that! It's none of my business. It's his family, and I'm sure his sister wouldn't call if it wasn't an emergency."

Tayla was straightening up the lounge area. "I know what you're saying, but he's missing work right now so he can help with something that he's probably not getting paid for. Those were two new customers that—let's be honest—aren't likely to come back."

"I don't know. They took his cards." Emily turned the Main Street sign to Closed. "It's different with a family business. Do you think I got paid every time I watched the shop for my grandma?"

"Of course not, but you also weren't trying to get a new business off the ground." Tayla walked to the coffee station and unplugged the machine, putting the carafe into the sink and tossing in spoons and mugs beside it. "I'm a little worried that his sister doesn't realize how important this is to him."

"...at some point they will make him choose, and he will choose them."

"You mean you're worried Ox's sister doesn't know what the shop means to *me*."

"Yeah." Tayla turned. "To you too. I know technically he's just a renter and you don't have a legal partnership, but the two of you planned this place together, and you've invested a lot. I just want to make sure he's still in this. We've passed the exciting new stage, and now it's time to buckle down and work. I know you're all in. I just want to make sure his priorities are in line. He still hasn't answered my questions, by the way."

"I think you need to let the questions go." Emmie shook her head and plugged the register in to the wall charger. "I'm not his boss. We wouldn't have any relationship at all if I were his boss."

"I know. But you deserve to—" Tayla stopped when someone tapped on the door. "Well, shit."

Emmie turned to see who had... "Ohhhh, shit." She forced a smile to her face and waved.

Adrian Saroyan was standing at the Main Street door, his tie loose, holding up the copy of *Sense and Sensibility* he'd bought from Emmie.

"I have to let him in," Emmie whispered.

"Why?" Tayla hissed.

"Because it would be rude not to!" Emmie kept the smile on her face and went to unlock the door. "Hey! How are you doing, Adrian?"

"Better now that I caught you," he said. "The past couple of weeks have been insane at work, but I finally finished the book and I was walking home, so I thought I'd swing by."

Shit. "How did you like it?"

"I was way off about Willoughby." Adrian smiled. "No wonder you got that look on your face when I mentioned him."

Emmie laughed. "Yeah, he's definitely not the hero."

"Not in the least. But I don't want to say more." He held up the book. "I'd rather talk about it at dinner with you."

Shit shit shit. "I'm not sure what my schedule is this weekend. Can I text you?"

Adrian smiled. "Absolutely. I know what it's like working for yourself, so I get it. Maybe Sunday or Monday night? Monday's your day off, right?"

Emmie nodded. "I'll text you."

"Great." Adrian backed toward the door, holding the book up. "I'm so glad I read this. It was not what I was expecting. Really funny. I can't wait to read more Austen."

Emmie's bookseller brain was thrilled at the prospect of anyone reading more Austen while her introvert brain had already checked out to hide in a closet somewhere, far away from any interpersonal drama.

Adrian nodded at Tayla and Emmie. "Ladies, I'll see you later. Have a great night. Emmie, can't wait to talk more."

"Bye," Tayla said. "So nice to see you again." She locked the door behind Adrian and turned, her eyes as big as saucers. "Why didn't you tell him you're with Ox?"

"I don't know!" Because she wasn't sure she was?

They weren't sleeping together. They kissed a lot, but their dates were pretty casual. Ox wasn't calling her his girlfriend or anything. She felt the knot of anxiety she kept locked down during her workday begin to tangle even more, and there was no Ox there to distract her or put her at ease. Just her old neuroses welcoming the new neuroses that had walked in the door with Adrian Saroyan and a finished copy of *Sense and Sensibility*.

"Are you going to go out with him?" Tayla asked. "I mean, I would, but I'm not you. You're more of a one-dude-at-a-time person."

Emmie put her phone in her purse and shut off the lights in the shop. She walked down to the office.

"Emmie, what are you doing to do?" Tayla followed her. "Did you already say yes to the date?"

Yes. Yes, she had.

"Talk to me." Tayla grabbed her shoulder and turned her. "Don't freak out. Talk to me."

"I don't know what I'm going to do," Emmie said. "I did agree to go out with him. And it's not as if he tricked me into a date or any shit like that. He asked. I said yes."

"What about Ox?"

"I don't know!" Emmie threw up her hands. "Are we exclusive? Should I go out with Adrian and tell him that I'm falling for another guy? That seems shitty. Do I tell him ahead of time and cancel? I don't know how this works. I've never had two men actually interested in dating me at the same time. How do you do this?"

Tayla shrugged. "I keep all things casual, but you're not me. Okay, calm down." She walked to the desk and turned off the computer. She switched off the copy machine and the lights before she herded Emmie out the door and toward the stairs. "Chill out. Take a breath."

Emmie breathed. She took multiple breaths. Deep breaths. Breaths her yoga instructor would be very proud of. It didn't help the fact that she was actively lusting after one guy and pretty sure she was falling in love with him while she'd already agreed to a date with another guy.

And to complicate things more, the guy she was lusting after was being oddly reticent about taking things further than heated kisses. He spent more time at his family ranch than at their shop and hadn't asked her to be exclusive. In fact, up until a couple of weeks ago, she'd been firmly in the "do not get involved with" category for Ox.

And it wasn't as if Adrian was a bad guy! He was a nice guy. A really nice guy. He'd made a bad first impression and then set about correcting it. He'd actively pursued something that was important to her so he could get to know her better. He took flowers to his mom and had offered to read a math picture book at story hour in the shop. She admired Adrian. He was a good person.

Tayla heated up the lasagna she'd made the night before and served two pieces while Emmie's mind whirled.

Ox and Adrian. She couldn't imagine two men more opposite. Both were great in their own way. Both were interested.

But only one kept her up until midnight worrying that she hadn't heard from him.

200

CHAPTER TWENTY-SEVEN

OX HAD LEFT ON A WEDNESDAY. By Friday, Emmie still hadn't heard from him. She'd had a quick text on Thursday, but that was all.

Rockslide in one of the pastures.

Need to take Thursday off too.

I've called my clients.

Sorry, Buttons.

Ox might have called his own clients, but Emmie had to explain to three customers that morning that she didn't know when he'd be available for a consultation. Ox had more than a few walk-ins, even with his sign turned to CLOSED. Emmie could do little besides smile and give out his business card.

Added to Ox's noncommunication was the fact that Adrian had texted her three times, hoping to make a dinner date for Sunday night. Emmie still didn't know what to do.

Luckily she had work.

Tayla leaned over the coffee table, looking at the sketch Emmie had shown her while they drank their morning coffee. Ethan had joined them that morning, walking over from the hardware store with a few "props" Emmie had asked to borrow.

"I like this," Tayla said. "You said the time between Thanksgiving and Christmas is really that busy for home-improvement stuff?"

"Earlier," he said. "Right about now, in fact."

"That surprises me," Emmie said.

"Me too."

"I know it seems crazy with how busy things are around the holidays, but there are a lot of people who want to get that room painted before the Christmas party or finish the guest room before the parents visit, you know?"

"That makes sense," Emmie said. "And if it's starting now, that gives us a good second theme window before Thanksgiving." She'd started changing the windows to have a new window a week, alternating between the west and east windows. So each theme was highlighted for two weeks, but there was something new to see every week. So far foot traffic, especially on weekends, had been their most successful local advertising. The windows drew people in. The uniqueness of the shop kept them browsing and buying.

If only the other half of INK were present.

She tapped the sketch. "So if you can help me with this background—"

"Easy," Ethan said. "All you'll need is a mounted pegboard and some hooks. I can even put a couple of display shelves on the pegboard if you want. Mix up the tools and the books."

"Perfect. And the sign I'll make up will direct them next door. Did you want to do the coupon thing?"

Ethan nodded. "I'll do ten percent off for anyone bringing in a book receipt from INK. Certain conditions, blah blah blah. I'll talk it over with my dad, but the coupon is a great idea."

"That and the location should keep people out of the big box stores for their projects."

"Let's hope so." Ethan leaned back. "With gardening workshops and the farmers' market done for the season, things are getting slow downtown. Hard to compete with the chain stores for sales this time of year."

"You having Rickard's back for Christmas trees this season?"

He nodded.

Emmie smiled. "Do they still do the hot chocolate?"

"Better believe it. They even have peppermint syrup for the hot chocolate now. They're gettin' fancy."

Tayla rolled her eyes. "This town is a Hallmark card."

"You love it," Ethan said. "Don't lie."

"God help me, I do." Tayla curled her lip. "I've even stopped playing traffic noises at night to fall asleep."

"Traffic noises?"

Emmie rose. "Don't ask. Ethan, can you have this background finished by Sunday?"

"Yeah. Are you going out with Adrian Saroyan?"

Emmie's head shot up. "What?"

"He said something at Daisy's. But I thought you were going out with Ox."

"How did you know I was going out with Ox?" Emmie's mouth dropped open. "I haven't… we haven't—"

"I was down at Supreme getting my tires rotated. Sergio said you and Ox were a thing now."

Tayla settled back on the couch and grabbed her coffee. "I love how gossipy the men in this town are."

"We don't gossip."

"You totally gossip."

"Yeah?" Ethan asked. "Is that why I hear you're suddenly interested in comics?"

Emmie muttered, "Jeremy's a gossip too."

"Apparently." Tayla stood up and walked back to the office. "I have to work."

"Are you helping my dad with the books later?" Ethan asked. "He has all the receipts organized now."

"I'm charging you this time!" she yelled.

"Fine!" Ethan smiled at Emmie. "We've been trying to pay her for two weeks. She's a godsend. My dad and computers do not get along."

"I'm hoping she'll stay," Emmie whispered. "If she gets enough bookkeeping clients, she might."

"Between me and you, Daisy and Jeremy and all the rest of the shops around here, I don't think she'd have a problem keeping busy if she wants to."

Emmie's phone dinged. It was a text from Ox.

Is the shop busy? Call me.

The sinking feeling in her belly told Emmie that Ox wouldn't be coming in that day. Dammit. Just as she was about to call, the bell above the door chimed and three women walked in with strollers. Friday morning. Story hour.

Emmie plastered on her smile and tucked her phone behind the register before she reached for her battered copy of *Strega Nona*. The moms began to browse the Tomie dePaola table set up in the children's section.

She didn't have time to call Ox. He'd come in when he came in. Emmie had a shop to run.

———

SHE WAS STANDING in line for her post-story-hour coffee break at Daisy's when she felt a soft tug on her braid. She turned to see Adrian standing behind her.

"Hey!" She couldn't stop the smile. "Tugging on my braids? We back in grade school?"

"I did actually try to get your attention, but you were off in your own world."

"Sorry. Busy morning."

"Don't apologize. I know how life gets. Did you know Metlin Lumber Yard is selling?"

"I didn't. Did they hire you?"

He nodded. "They did."

"Congratulations!"

"I'd love to celebrate." He leaned closer. "With dinner maybe? You haven't called me back."

Emmie opened her mouth, but the words didn't come out.

Adrian's smile fell a little. "There's someone else."

"I think so?"

He nodded slowly, urging her forward with a hand on her elbow. "Your turn."

Emmie ordered a cinnamon roll while Daisy shot glances between her and Adrian with wide eyes.

I don't know, she mouthed silently. Adrian caught her arm before she moved away.

"Grab a table," he said. "At least have a cup of coffee with me."

Emmie hesitated.

"Please?"

"Okay." Emmie grabbed a table in the corner and waited while Adrian took a cup and her cinnamon roll from the girl at the counter. He set both down at the table before he went back to grab her a napkin and a fork.

"So"—he sipped his drink—"someone else moved faster. Fair enough. I couldn't exactly expect the entire town to ignore a beautiful woman moving back to town and opening a fantastically cool bookshop, could I? It's my own fault. If I hadn't come across as such an ass at the beginning, I might have convinced you without the book."

"Listen, Adrian—"

"Give me a shot," he said simply. "Are you and this guy exclusive?"

"I don't know. But I have strong feelings for him. I don't want to mislead you about that."

"I appreciate that," he said. "But even knowing that, I still want a shot. And if he hasn't made it clear to you that he only wants to date you and he doesn't want you dating anyone else, then that's on him."

"Adrian—"

"One dinner. If we get halfway through and there's nothing there, then it's just a dinner between old friends, right?" Adrian leaned across the table. "I do want to be friends with you. I like you. I've always liked you. If this ends up being just dinner between friends, that's okay with me. But I'm not going to lie. I want it to be more." He sat back. "I also need to talk to someone about this book, because I'm not too sure about Marianne and Colonel Brandon. I feel like there's some odd, paternalistic thing going on there, right?"

Emmie smiled. "Maybe."

"It can't just be me that's weirded out by that."

"Fine!" She folded her hands. "I will have dinner with you—as friends—but I think that's all it's going to be. And I want to pay for my half. It's not a date, Adrian. I'm not that nimble. Whatever is going on with me and Ox—"

"So it is Ox." Adrian had a wry smile on his face. "The hovering makes sense now."

"What?"

"At the opening. He was practically hovering over you the entire night. I wanted to talk to you, but—"

"He knew I was nervous."

"You didn't look nervous. You looked amazing." Adrian cocked his head. "I don't really know the guy, but it surprises me you want to be with someone who's so overprotective."

"He's not overprotective." Was he?

Adrian lifted his hands. "Like I said, I don't know him. I'm sure he's great."

He was great. Ox was great. And Adrian was right; he didn't know Ox. Emmie did.

Didn't she?

"Sunday night," Adrian said. "Dinner as *friends* at Marley's. We talk about Jane Austen. I flirt with you as you try to resist my charms. It's a date." He swiped a finger through the icing that had dripped over the side of her plate. "And I have to get back to work." He licked the icing off his finger. "Damn, that's good."

"It's not a date."

Adrian backed away, still licking his lips. "It's a friend date."

"Friend dates aren't a thing."

He nodded. "I'm pretty sure they are. Bye, Em."

"Not a thing!"

Seconds after Adrian was out the door, Daisy was at her table. "What are you doing?"

Emmie closed her eyes and covered her face. "I have no idea."

CHAPTER TWENTY-EIGHT

OX SLID his phone back in his pocket. Four texts to Emmie. No calls back.

Dammit.

She was probably busy. And she hated talking on the phone. Friday was one of her busiest days, and it wasn't as if she ever sat around. If she wasn't talking to customers, she was ordering books or contacting other local businesses or organizing book clubs or writing newsletters. Friday morning was story hour. The store was probably packed. He loved seeing her read with the little kids and usually made an excuse to be there even if it was before his normal hours. This rockslide was kicking his ass.

Cary backed up the loader with another bucketful. A sudden rainstorm in the mountains had brought a rush of mud and rocks down in the upper pasture, killing one of the steers while also taking out a good forty yards of fencing. They couldn't fix it without clearing out the rocks and also shoring up the hillside. Melissa and Cary had taken the lead on the project, leaving Ox to juggle the rest of the ranch with his mom.

It was hard to remember his mother was in her late sixties when she still worked a ten-hour day. He'd been nearly out the door to Metlin that morning when she'd had a dizzy spell. His mom claimed she was fine, but Ox wanted her to go to the doctor. She'd refused so far, so Ox was trying to get his sister on board. He'd ridden Melissa's horse out to the pasture since Melissa had taken the truck and the trailer with supplies to repair the fence.

Ox stood next to his sister as they watched their neighbor work the tractor. "Has Mom had dizzy spells before?"

Melissa frowned. "Every now and then, but you know mom. She's always going ninety miles an hour. It's probably just age. I need to hire someone to help around the farm."

"I can help more."

"You have your own business." She glanced at him, wiping a smear of mud across her cheek. "Speaking of, why aren't you there?"

"'Cause Mom practically fell over in the kitchen?"

"She says she's iron deficient."

"Bullshit, Lissa. The woman eats red meat five times a week."

Cary yelled for Melissa, who went running across the field to find out why he'd stopped.

A few more minutes and they'd cleared enough of the rocks to repair the fence. Cary and Melissa started working, forgetting all about Ox, who mounted Melissa's mare, Moxie, and headed back to the house.

His mom was taking a nap when he arrived. He checked in on her and closed the door to her bedroom before he went to put Moxie in the stable and collect the eggs his mom hadn't had time to grab that morning. Melissa needed to put her foot down with Abby. When he was Abby's age, he was doing twice as many chores.

Not your kid, Ox.

He had a sudden vision of Emmie cuddled under a blanket with a book and a little girl with red-brown hair, whispering as she read a story.

Fuck him, he was so gone for the chick. And he was

completely fucking it up. He really wanted her to call him back. He didn't want to text her that something was going on with his mom. He wanted to hear her voice. He'd been going to call the night before, but he was asleep as soon as his head hit the pillow. Then this morning, he'd been rushing to finish chores and get out of the house. Then his mom had fallen and he'd freaked out.

He was fucking it up. His clients would be cool, but Emmie?

She liked schedules and spreadsheets. She kept a damn time card for herself and didn't close the shop until precisely eight on the dot. It was fucking adorable until he had to think about the ranch. Cows didn't keep time cards. The weather didn't shut down. Ranch life would drive Emmie crazy.

You're not a rancher, remember?

He kicked the mud off his boots before he entered the barn. He sure felt like a rancher that morning. And four unanswered texts were taunting him.

Maybe he should back off. They were only starting out, after all. They'd gone on a couple of dates and they'd been amazing, but Emmie was a cautious girl, and he was supposed to be taking his time, right? As for the business, he was her tenant, not her partner. It was one of the reasons he wanted to work for himself. So that he could make his own schedule.

He'd wait for Emmie to text him. He'd be able to make it into INK tomorrow, and then he'd fill her in. If she called, she called, but he didn't want to assume she was spending all day thinking about him. Not when she had a life. He wasn't some inconsiderate fuck who expected his girl's world to revolve around him.

Ox glanced at his phone again. He tried to convince himself that the unanswered texts didn't mean anything. He and Emmie were fine. The shop was fine.

His mom... was not fine.

———

OX PACED in the emergency room of Metlin General Hospital with Abby sleeping on his shoulder, his adrenaline still racing from the drive into town. It was a fucking miracle he hadn't been pulled over.

"Mr. Oxford, can you tell me when her symptoms started?"

He rubbed his eyes. "Uh... this morning?"

"Was that the first nosebleed?"

"I don't... I don't know. She didn't have a nosebleed this morning. Her nose started bleeding at the dinner table. She had other symptoms earlier in the day. She was dizzy. Had a headache. Is that what you're talking about?"

"Yes. You're very lucky," the nurse said. "I know it might not seem like that right now, but you are. Your mother had symptoms that brought her into the hospital to get checked out. Many people with high blood pressure have no symptoms at all."

"Right." He didn't feel lucky. He felt fucking panicked. Melissa was back with his mom while he was out talking with the nurse and taking care of Abby. His mom's nose had started bleeding at the dinner table. Her eyes had rolled back and she'd slumped forward. Abby had started crying, and Melissa had immediately jumped into action. They'd driven their mom into town in the truck, breaking every speed limit in the county while Melissa was on the phone with the hospital. Ox and Melissa both knew waiting for an ambulance to get to the ranch would take too long.

"Is there any news yet?" Ox asked. "Has her blood pressure stabilized?"

"I believe so, but this kind of attack spurs a number of different tests to check for related conditions. The doctors are going to want to check her heart especially and make sure there are no cardiac problems related to her blood pressure. She'll be here for a while. Do you know when her last cardiac stress test was?"

"I don't know."

"Her last physical?"

"She never tells me about her doctor's appointments." He rubbed Abby's back. "You might have better luck asking my sister."

"Okay."

Ox took a seat, giving his arms a rest. Abby was a little thing, but carrying her for hours hadn't been easy. The little girl must have remembered more about her father's death than they realized. She was shaking as soon as they entered the emergency room and hadn't said a word since. Melissa was taking care of their mom, so Ox did the only thing he could think of. He held his niece like he had when she'd been a tiny girl and Calvin had been the one in emergency surgery.

Not the same. Not the same. His mom was going to be fine.

High blood pressure was common, right? Treatable. Hell, Cary had high blood pressure, and he wasn't even fifty. It was genetic. His mom probably just needed to eat less eggs and stop using lard in her pie crusts.

Abby let out a huge sigh, and Ox felt his phone buzzing in his pocket. He couldn't reach it without disturbing Abby, so he ignored it. Cary would call Melissa. Ox wanted to call Emmie, but what could she do? He'd just be dumping a whole ton of worries on her when she had plenty of her own to deal with. She'd lost her grandmother less than a year ago. She didn't need to worry about Ox's mom. He'd explain later and she'd understand.

He was tempted to call and see if Abby could sleep at the shop, but it was after midnight. He didn't want Abby waking somewhere where Ox wasn't, and he didn't want to leave Melissa and his mom. So he leaned against the wall, held Abby, and closed his eyes, hoping he could get a little sleep.

It was going to be okay. It was all going to be okay. He'd make sure of it.

CHAPTER TWENTY-NINE

FOUR DAYS. Did four days with nothing more than cryptic texts qualify as ghosting? Emmie could tell something was going on, but Ox wasn't sharing, nor had he shown up for work in four days. The longer it dragged on, the more resentful she grew. The more her mind went in circles.

This was it. This was what Ginger had been talking about. Ox was going to get pulled back to the ranch, and she was going to be out a tattoo artist a month after she started the bookshop, right at the busiest part of the retail year. And whatever had been between them... that was probably history too.

"I feel like you're not really here," Adrian said from across the table. "Everything okay?"

Emmie forced a smile. "Fine. I'm fine. Sorry, thinking about work. And rain. I'm so glad it's raining, aren't you? We really need the rain." She picked at the bread on her plate. They'd ordered wine, but she hadn't decided on a meal.

"We do." Adrian glanced out the window of Marley's. It was the newest restaurant downtown, started by a chef who'd moved from Chicago. It was small plates and wine and great cheese.

ELIZABETH HUNTER

Emmie had been excited to go when she and Tayla talked about it. Going with Adrian was less exciting and more confusing.

"We're talking about the weather." Adrian smiled slowly. "Surely we can do better than that."

"Work?" She shook her head. "We shouldn't talk about work."

"I know how you feel. I'm the same way, but you have to pull back. It's one of the hardest things about working for yourself."

"Oh no," Emmie said. "I was preoccupied when I worked for other people too. I just really love my job."

"That's awesome," Adrian said. "You're really lucky."

"It's not all luck."

"Of course not." He poured more wine from the bucket the waiter had set by the table. "I've seen how hard you work. You're there every day. How is it working to have just Monday off?"

Switching her brain from Ox mode to work mode was a relief. "It's fine for now. I might hire someone down the line. Depends on my hours and what my busiest traffic days are."

Adrian leaned forward. "Do you really want to talk about work?"

Yes, please. "Did you want to talk about *Sense and Sensibility*? If you want to read more Austen, I'd recommend *Pride and Prejudice*. It's her most popular for a reason. Or *Emma*. Both are pretty funny."

"I want to talk about you." Adrian sipped his wine. "What do you like besides reading?"

Emmie swallowed. She hated these types of conversations. Wasn't reading enough? There were enough books to keep her occupied for the rest of her life. Books about everything! What else could she talk about? "I went hiking recently. That was fun."

And now she was thinking about Ox again.

Adrian lit up. "Nice! I like going to the coast. I love hiking at the beach."

Emmie hated the beach. Well, she liked the ocean from a

distance, but not lying in the sand. Sand got everywhere. "We went hiking in the mountains. Up to the sequoias."

"We?" Adrian's smile was tight. "Did you go with Ox?"

"Yeah."

He nodded slowly. "Maybe I can take you to the coast for a wine-tasting trip or something like that."

"That sounds fun." It did sound fun, so why was Emmie feeling so guilty? Ox hadn't talked to her in days. He'd all but disappeared by Saturday morning. He wasn't answering texts. He didn't call. He wasn't even calling his clients because two had shown up at the shop for their appointments, and Emmie had been at a loss making excuses for him.

And now she was on a date with Adrian Saroyan.

Ox had never called her his girlfriend. She wasn't cheating on him. Besides, this was a friend dinner. That's what she'd told Adrian. They were friends and he was talking about taking her on a friendly wine-tasting trip to the coast. As friends.

Emmie, you are so full of shit.

Adrian was not looking at her like a friend. He was looking at her like he wanted to get in her pants. Not that she was wearing pants. She was wearing a pretty skirt and shirt, not jeans and a goofy T-shirt like she would if she went out with Tayla or Ethan or Jeremy.

She fidgeted in her seat. "Adrian, I'm sorry."

He set down his wine. "Why?"

"I shouldn't be here. It's not fair to you. And—"

"Where's Ox?" he asked. "He wasn't working when I picked you up. Doesn't he usually work on Sunday?"

"I don't know."

"You don't know when he works?"

Emmie's eyes flashed. "Why the third degree?"

"I'm trying to figure out why you're sorry to be with me when the other man you're involved with isn't around. In fact, he hasn't been around in a few days, has he?"

"You've been keeping track? So those times you stopped by the shop to chat weren't friendly, I guess. Were you spying on me? On him?"

"Where is he, Emmie?"

"Why is that your business?" A gust from the door touched her neck and Emmie shivered.

"Because I like you." His voice rose a little. Not too much, but enough that their neighbor turned his head. "I like you very much. I'm attracted to you, Marianne Elliot, and I think if you gave me a chance—"

"Who's Marianne?"

Emmie's eyes went wide when she heard his voice. She turned and saw Ox standing in the foyer of the restaurant, staring at her and Adrian. "Ox?"

He was dripping wet from the rain. He strode toward them, his eyes blazing. "Who's Marianne?"

Emmie turned around and crossed her arms. Of course he'd chosen the middle of her... non-date to turn back up. Of course he did.

"Marianne is her name," Adrian said. "Her actual name, not her nickname."

"Emmie?"

Her cheeks heated. "I don't like Marianne. Don't call me Marianne."

"Is that your name?"

"Marianne Elliot. M.E. I've gone by Emmie since high school. It's not a big deal, *Miles*."

"How about that?" Ox was dripping on the carpet, his thumbs hooked in his pockets, the bottom foot of his jeans covered in mud, and everyone was staring at them. He did not look amused by her nickname. "So I'm gone four days and you're out with someone else?"

"It's not like that," she whispered. "Can we talk about this—"

"If you'd called me two days ago when I asked you to, we could have talked about this." Ox glanced at Adrian. "But I guess I know why you were so busy. Good to know where I stand."

"It is not like that!" Emmie glanced around the restaurant, mortified by the public scene.

"Four days, Em. What the hell?"

"Where have you been?" she hissed. "I don't even know where you've been."

"My mom was in the hospital."

"How's she feeling, Miles?" a voice called from the other side of the dining room.

"Much better, Mr. Howard. She's home now. Thanks for asking."

Emmie stood up, her napkin falling to the ground. "Your mom was in the hospital and you didn't call me?"

"I didn't know what was going on, and I didn't want to bother —" Ox suddenly stopped and looked around, realizing that every eye in the restaurant was on them. He leaned down to Emmie. "I'm not doing this here. Him or me?" he whispered. "Who do you want?"

"You, you idiot! Why didn't you call me?"

Ox grabbed her chin, kissed her hard, and reached for her hand. "Get your coat, Buttons. You're not having dinner with Adrian Saroyan."

Emmie picked up her napkin and set it on the table. "Adrian, I'm—"

"You're not sorry," Adrian muttered, "so don't say you're sorry. See you later, Emmie."

Ox muttered something she couldn't hear under his breath, then he grabbed Emmie's coat while she grabbed her purse. He walked to the door, taking a second to drape Emmie's coat over her shoulders before he strode into the pouring rain, Emmie's hand still clutched in his.

She put up with it for five long strides before she yanked her hand away.

Ox spun around. "What?"

"I am not finished being mad at you for disappearing, and also I am not impressed by the caveman deal back there." She marched past him. Her feet were squishing in her heels it was raining so hard. But she was only three blocks from her house. At this point she just wanted to go home. Tayla was in San Francisco visiting some friends, and Emmie decided she should have gone with her even if she had to take the train. She wanted to go home and eat ice cream and read a book she knew the ending to. It was going to be a happy ending where heroes weren't assholes who disappeared for days on end and didn't call you when their mom was sick.

"Where are you going?" Ox yelled.

"Home! I'm freezing cold and soaked and I don't want to talk to you."

"So you're mad at me? Is that what's happening? I'm the one who found you on a date with Adrian Saroyan, and you're mad at *me*? What the hell?"

It was eight o'clock and no one else was on the sidewalk, but Emmie was still allergic to public displays. She kept walking.

Ox yelled, "What if it was me and Ginger, huh? Would you like that?"

Emmie stopped in her tracks and spun around. "It wasn't like that. I promised him weeks ago—way before we started... whatever it is we're doing—that I'd go out to dinner with him and discuss a book he was reading."

"Whatever it is we're doing?" Ox asked. "What do you think we're doing?"

"I don't know!"

"I'm fucking falling in love with you and you don't know?"

Emmie's jaw dropped open. She could feel rain falling on her lips. Down her cheeks. It was pouring, but all she heard was Ox.

"You're falling in love with me?"

Ox didn't say anything. He walked toward her, grabbed her hand, and started dragging her toward the shop.

"Ox?"

"It's fucking pouring out here. You need to get inside."

Had he meant it? Was it said in the heat of the moment? She thought he'd been playing. She'd been convinced he was ghosting her.

Emmie stumbled, and he caught her before she fell. Ox bent down, pulled off her soaking-wet shoes, then handed them to her before he picked her up and carried her down the sidewalk cradled in his arms.

Emmie was speechless for a block.

"Total romance-hero move," she said. "If I were writing a romance novel, I'd want to put that in, but I couldn't because it would be considered too cliché."

He barely cracked a smile. "Buttons, you kill me."

"Is your mom going to be okay? Are you?"

"They put her on a couple different blood pressure medications. She should be fine once they figure out what the right combination is."

"When did it happen?"

"Saturday morning. I was on my way here when she had a dizzy spell. Her nose started bleeding and she passed out at dinner. The hospital just let her out this afternoon."

"That's why you didn't call."

He gave a short nod and set her down when he reached the door. Digging into his pocket, he unlocked the door and pushed it open. The shop was warm and dry and utterly silent. All she could hear was the rain falling outside and low thunder in the distance. Emmie dropped her shoes by the door and peeled off the soaking-wet coat, hanging it on the coat tree by the door.

"I left my umbrella at Marley's."

Ox had his hands in his pockets again. "And I left my truck there. I'll grab your umbrella when I get it."

"How did you know we were—"

"I didn't. I was driving here to see you when I passed the restaurant. I could see you right in the window."

Emmie tried to imagine what she'd feel like if she'd seen him having dinner with Ginger. She'd have been devastated.

Ox was staring at her. "You look beautiful."

She looked down at her dripping outfit. "I look ridiculous."

"No, you don't. You're beautiful."

She shook her head. "I told him dinner was just as friends. But then he wanted to go to Marley's, so I wanted to dress up. It's not... When I told him we could go for dinner when he finished *Sense and Sensibility*, it was before... us. And then when he finished the book and called me—"

"He read a book so you'd go out with him?"

"I know." She desperately wanted to get into dry clothes. "Stupid, right?"

"Smart." He took a step closer. "He knows you."

"Not as well as you do."

"Yeah? I didn't even know your real name."

"I hate my real name."

Ox put a hand on her cheek, rubbing away the drips that were falling from her hair. "You should get upstairs. Get dry."

Emmie caught his hand before he could pull it away. "You said you were falling in love with me."

CHAPTER THIRTY

OX FROZE.

"You said it, and it's just hanging there now," Emmie whispered. "I can't pretend I didn't hear it. I don't want to pretend I didn't hear it. But I don't want to say the same thing back to you right now because then what if you think I'm just saying it because you did? I don't want you to think that, because... because it's not. That's not why I'd be saying it, but I can't say it now."

His voice was rough. "Why not?"

"Because you scare me to death." She fisted a hand over her heart. "I almost said it the first morning after you kissed me. You were joking with Tayla through the door, and you two were making each other laugh and I thought it, which is crazy because that's way too soon, right? It's crazy soon, and that's not who I am, Ox. I need time and I need to know I can depend—"

"Stop." Ox put a finger on her lips. "You're freaking out again, and I'm done being patient." He didn't say another word. He bent down, picked her up, and lifted her to his mouth. Emmie wrapped her legs around his waist held on while he kissed the hell out of her. She went from frozen to boneless in seconds. Ox turned the deadbolt in the door and strode toward the stairs, his mouth never leaving hers.

Emmie dug her fingers into his shoulders and gripped the thick muscles that tensed under her hands. Ox stopped at the base of the stairs and set her down.

"My shoes are muddy," he said.

"So take them off." She started unbuttoning the quilted flannel shirt he wore over his T-shirt.

Ox bent down and tugged off his boots and socks, leaving them in a pile at the base of the stairs. He looked at her fingers unbuttoning his shirt.

"What are you doing?"

"You're soaking wet."

"So are you." He fingered the tiny buttons on her black cardigan. "Buttons."

She shoved his wet flannel off his shoulders. "And your jeans are muddy."

"I'm filthy."

"You should take them off."

"I should."

Her heart started to race as soon as his fingers flipped open the buttons on his fly. He peeled down his wet jeans, leaving himself clad only in a soaking-wet pair of boxer briefs and a T-shirt.

Emmie backed up the stairs, her fingers hooked in the hem of his shirt.

"Your clothes are all wet." Ox gripped her black cardigan at the waist and pulled it up and over her head. "That's better."

She kept walking backward up the stairs, pulling him with her. "Are you cold?"

"Freezing." He peeled off his T-shirt, exposing every delicious inch of his black-and-grey-inked chest. "But I'm getting warmer all the time."

"Tayla's out of town."

"Don't care."

Ox kept up with her on the stairs, knitting their fingers together and pulling her close for a kiss. His lips were chilled but heated on hers. Steam had to be coming off her skin. Ox reached behind her and opened the door at the top of the stairs, but they didn't make it inside. Emmie lost her footing and sat down hard on the top step. Ox crawled up to her, fumbling with her skirt as he tried to pull it off.

"You okay?"

"Fine."

"Where's the…?"

"Here."

"Is it a zip— Got it." He pulled the skirt down her legs, exposing her legs to the dim light in the stairwell. The hardwood floor was cold, but she barely noticed as Ox reached for her shirt and rolled it up her torso. Emmie lifted her arms and let him undress her.

She was freezing cold and hot at the same time. The air chilled her skin, but Ox heated it. He nipped at her neck as he threw her shirt over his shoulder and down the stairs. He crawled between her legs, knees on the steps beneath the landing, and pushed her back, coming down on top of her and covering her torso with his body.

"Are you cold?" he asked, his lips hovering over hers.

"Not anymore."

He flashed a smile before he kissed her again. His tongue teased her lips until she opened for him. Her thighs cradled his hips, and she could feel the delicious weight of his body pressing hers into the floor. They were at the top of the stairs, only a few feet from her door, but she couldn't seem to pull away. Ox was ravenous, biting her lips and squeezing her breasts before he ran his hands down the side of her body.

"Sex on stairs," he whispered against her lips, "is highly over-rated. Except for one particular thing." Kissing down her body, he rolled her panties down her legs and tossed those over his shoulder too. Spreading her legs, he settled between them, kneeling and bringing his mouth down to the juncture of her thighs.

"Oh my—" Emmie gasped and clutched at his arms as Ox feasted on her.

She writhed on the floor, the cold hardwood at her back and the heat of Ox's mouth between her thighs. Lights flashed behind her closed eyes as she climaxed in a sharp crescendo of pleasure. His lips and tongue stayed on her, driving her out of her mind. She couldn't remember what it felt like to be cold. There was only heat and pleasure and Ox. His kisses turned softer, savoring her, easing her down from the high. She watched him as he sat up. He licked his lips and held his hand out, helping Emmie to her feet on nearly boneless legs.

"Bed."

Emmie nodded wordlessly but didn't move. Ox picked her up and she clung to his shoulders as he unhooked her bra and dropped it in the middle of the living room. She was completely naked as he carried her through the apartment. Rain pounded on the roof, running down the windows and turning Main Street into an oily blur. He found his way to her room in the darkness, tossing her on the bed and stripping down to his skin. The room was lit by streetlamps outside, awash in blacks and greys, lending her familiar surroundings a surreal air as rain smeared the windows and beat against the roof.

Ox put a fist around his erection and watched Emmie scoot up the bed in the dim light. "Condoms?"

"Bottom drawer in the bathroom."

He nodded and walked out the door, returning in moments with a box he tore open with his teeth. He rolled on a condom and fell on the bed, grabbing Emmie and searching for her mouth again.

"Wanted you...," he murmured against her lips. "I've wanted you since the first day we met."

"Even though— Oh my…" Emmie gasped as Ox shoved her up to the pillows and latched his mouth around one breast. "Ox, stop teasing."

"Never." He rolled to his back and dragged her over his chest. Then he sat up and scooted against the headboard, bracing Emmie on his lap with his hands gripping her hips. "I like teasing you. I like handling you."

Emmie had never felt more handled. Or turned on. Ox was strong. He lifted her and brought her down over his lap, easing himself into her body as he captured her lips. He groaned out her name as she sank onto him, pressing their bodies together. He moved them together, surging into her as she braced herself on his shoulders.

His name was on her lips when he captured them again, swallowing her cries as they moved together. He surrounded her. Consumed her.

I love you. Forget falling. I fell.

"You caught me," Emmie whispered.

Ox blinked and cupped her face in his palm. "What?" Red rode high on his cheekbones, and his lips were swollen and dark.

"You caught me. I fell and you caught me."

She didn't say it, but the look in his eyes told Emmie he knew. The hand that gripped her hip turned soft, and his lips were tender when he kissed her again. "I'll always catch you."

Ox rolled her to her back and braced himself over her, moving more slowly as he made love to her. Emmie spread her hands over his chest, stroking his skin and smoothing her hands over the hard planes of his abdomen. She lifted her hips and moved with him, meeting his thrusts with her hips.

"Emmie." His breath caught. "Are you—?"

"Close." She could feel it building again, the slow steady thrum of pleasure that coiled and gripped her. He didn't stop. He didn't pause. He didn't lose a single beat.

"Fucking come," he hissed between gritted teeth. "Emmie—"

"Yes!" She arched her back, gripping his shoulders as she lost control and heard him shout her name. He gripped her thigh and spread her legs wider, driving impossibly deeper as he came. Ox fell over her, kissing her mouth. Her cheeks. Her chin. Her eyelids. He rolled to the side and gathered her close, keeping them linked as he caught his breath.

His chest rose and fell. He pulled out and rolled to the side to get rid of the condom, then came back to her and buried his face in her neck, inhaling deeply against her skin and peppering kisses over her neck and shoulder.

"Oh fuck," he breathed out. "Best thing ever."

Emmie smiled and kissed his temple. She could already feel his body relaxing against hers. He scooted up the bed and shoved pillows underneath his head, tucking Emmie against his shoulder as his eyes began to droop.

"Gonna fall asleep," he muttered. "Been... up. For a while."

"Sleep," Emmie whispered. "Sleep as long as you need to."

He pressed her closer. "Stay."

"I'll stay."

Emmie fell asleep minutes after Ox did, listening to the storm roll around them.

———

SHE WOKE in the middle of the night. Ox was kissing her shoulder, tracing his tongue over the vines and flowers that covered her back, kissing each butterfly with soft lips. She reached down and knit her fingers with his, bringing his hand to palm her breast. He indulged with lazy strokes and lingering kisses, heating her blood to the boiling point as the rain spattered against the windows. The storm had turned and the rain fell soft and steady on the roof.

He was kissing her neck when he lifted her knee and slid into her from behind. Ox curled his arms around her and hugged her to his chest, whispering in her ear as he rocked her slowly.

His hands, his words, his heat eased her into a bone-melting orgasm. She turned her head, searching for his mouth. He met her kiss, holding her closer as he let himself come.

"Love you," he murmured, falling back into sleep.

Emmie clutched his arms around her. If this was a dream, she didn't want to wake up. If this would end in heartbreak, she didn't want to know. She felt a tear slip down her cheek as her heart clenched painfully.

I love you, Miles Oxford. I love you so much.

He scared her to death, but she couldn't bring herself to be cautious anymore. For once, Emmie wanted the dream.

"EMMIE." A tickling touch on her nose. A kiss on her lips. "Wake up, Buttons."

Emmie kept her eyes closed. "I can't believe you're still calling me that."

He slid a hand between her thighs. "Do you need a reminder?"

"Mmmm." She wiggled her bottom back into him and felt jeans. Emmie frowned and opened her eyes. "You're dressed."

"I have to head out to the ranch for a couple hours," he whispered. "I thought I'd go early so I could come back and we could spend your day off together. Did you have plans?"

She shook her head and reminded herself that she wasn't some needy child. Ox's mother had just had a health scare. He needed to help take care of her. She couldn't be selfish.

"What time will you be back?"

"I'm not sure." He kissed her. "The earlier I go, the earlier I can come back. I didn't want to leave without letting you know."

"Hmm." She grunted. "From now on, let's have a policy about responding to phone calls and text messages."

He squeezed her ass. "For both of us."

"Yes, for both of us."

"Good. Can this be an amendment to the employee manual right after the one about you sexually harassing me daily?"

"I am not your boss."

"But office sex is still an option, right?"

"Yes."

"How about my tattoo chair?"

She pinched the skin on the inside of his elbow and he yelped. "There are no curtains in that shop. Don't even think about it."

"Too late," he whispered. "I'm already thinking about it. Privacy screens? I can get another one. Think about you riding me in that chair. Fucking me while you—"

She slapped a hand over his mouth. "Stop unless you want me to strip you out of those clothes you just put on."

Ox took her hand off his mouth and tore the shirt over his head. "Smart girlfriends are the best."

Before Emmie could think about the word Ox had casually thrown out, he thoroughly—*very* thoroughly—distracted her, and she didn't think about anything for another hour. Or so.

CHAPTER THIRTY-ONE

OX WAS SINGING along to the radio as he drove through the country. The storm had washed the dust from the hills and water pooled on the roads. He splashed through deep puddles and bumped over potholes the farther he got toward the ranch. The front pasture would probably be flooded, but luckily Cary and another neighbor had finished the repair on the north pasture while his mom had been in the hospital. There were probably a million things to do, but Ox had a shit-eating grin on his face that would not leave.

He was in love and she loved him back.

The evening had started out the way the entire weekend had gone. He was exhausted and wrung out. He knew Emmie had to be mad at him for disappearing, but he'd figured he could apologize and hopefully talk his way onto her couch because he just needed to see her. He'd been driving down Main Street and glancing in the glowing windows of the restaurants downtown, thinking he should take Emmie out someplace nice instead of diner food or tacos. His truck jerked to a stop in the middle of Main Street when he saw them.

Emmie and some dude. It wasn't Ethan or Jeremy, one of her

friends. It was fucking Adrian Saroyan. He could tell by the slick hair and the suit.

A car had honked behind him and Ox didn't think. He pulled into the first parking spot he could find and marched into the restaurant where he'd seen her. He was a mess. He'd probably ruined the carpet. He didn't give a shit. He hauled Emmie out into the pouring rain and ended up having the hottest damn sex of his entire life.

And then he'd had to leave this morning.

Smart girlfriends are the best girlfriends.

When he'd left, Emmie was on her laptop, researching the best home remedies and natural diets to control high blood pressure. She'd given him a cookbook to take to Melissa and made him promise to text when he got to the ranch.

So fucking adorable.

He pulled up to the cattle gate and saw that, yes, the front pasture was flooded. Luckily the barn sat on a hillside, and so the corral by the house was fine, as were the animal pens near the barn. He drove through, closed the gate behind him, and saw Melissa and Cary talking on the porch.

Nope. Not talking. Arguing.

Cary threw up his hands and stomped to his truck. He drove down the road, stopping and rolling down his window when he passed Ox.

"Hey," the older man said. "Did you know your sister is the most stubborn damn woman on the planet?"

"Yeah. Do you know you're in love with her?"

"Shut the fuck up." Cary glared. "How's your girl?"

"She's okay. Pissed at me for not telling her what was going on, but I talked her around."

Cary grunted. "I'm trying to get Melissa to let my mom come over and stay with Joan. My mom would be happy to help, but they're both being stubborn and reminding me my mom is seventy-two. I fucking know my mom is seventy-two. She reminds me every day while she's kicking my ass in one way or another."

"Your mom is a badass." Ox glanced at the house. "Just tell her to come up. They can't say anything once she's here, and Melissa can use the help. I'm going to have to cut back at the tattoo shop and—"

"Why?"

"What?"

Cary frowned. "You can't cut back at the shop, man. You're just starting out. You don't have any employees. You need to get back to work."

Ox waved a hand out at the flooded pasture. "Between this storm and my mom having to cut back, there's no way Melissa—"

"Your sister can fucking ask for help when she needs it from people who are offering to help her and not from her brother who has his own damn life and his own damn business! Don't piss me off. Besides, you're good with cattle, but you know shit about trees." Cary rolled up his window and drove off without another word.

Ox couldn't stop the smile. The man was gone over his sister and had been for years. But talking Melissa around to anything was damn near impossible. She hated asking for help from anyone and only relented when it was family.

Melissa had her arms folded across her chest and was glaring at Cary's truck as it drove away.

"Hey," Ox said. "I see everyone is in a good mood here. How's Mom?"

Melissa turned her glare to him, looked him up and down. "Someone got laid," she muttered. "Is your shop still standing?"

"I am not talking about my sex life with my sister."

"Gross." She wrinkled her nose. "I was just asking if the business was okay, not if you and Emmie—" She put both hands over her eyes. "Brain bleach!"

Ox chuckled and wrapped his arms around his sister's tense

shoulders. "I'm fine. We're fine. I'm happy as shit actually, which is why I'm hugging you. You look like you need a hug. What do you need help with?"

Melissa sighed and unleashed the litany of things that needed to happen that day. Ox felt tired just hearing it, but he went inside, changed his clothes, and got to work.

———

HE RETURNED to Metlin with a duffel bag in the passenger seat and a sore back just in time to meet one of his clients who'd booked a session two weeks before. He left his client waiting in the shop while he ran upstairs and knocked on the door to the apartment.

Tayla answered. "Hey, ghost boy." She opened the door wider to let him in. "Emmie, Ox is here."

"Hey." He walked to her bedroom as she opened the door, pulled her inside, and sat on the bed, drawing Emmie between his legs. His cock immediately went to attention. It was as if it had some Emmie-bed radar. His cock would have to be patient.

"How's your mom?" she asked.

Ox smiled. "She's feeling better. Liked the cookbook."

"I'm glad." She put her hands on his shoulders. "I was thinking we could go out for dinner. Maybe—"

"I've got a client downstairs that I forgot about until he texted me this afternoon."

Emmie groaned. "Really?"

He let his head fall against her and inhaled. Her scent was some combination of her detergent and her shampoo and her soap and sometimes a little perfume, and it was all just Emmie and it was so damn good.

He wrapped his arms around her waist. "I promise it's only going to be an hour, hour and a half max. And then I'll kick him out and we can go out. Is that cool?"

"That's cool."

Emmie rubbed her hand over the nape of his neck, playing with the short hairs and making his cock even harder. It was impossible not to want her, but he really didn't want to walk downstairs to his client with a hard-on.

"Tell me more about distribution agreements and returns," he said.

Emmie pulled back. "You hate that stuff. Your eyes glaze over when I talk about distribution."

"I know, but I can't go meet Clyde with a hard-on. Talk."

Emmie laughed and shoved him away. "Stop. Why don't you think about the expanded list of questions Tayla has ready for you?"

"I bet." He could tell her best friend was pissed at him. That was a situation that would have to be remedied because if there was one thing you didn't fuck up, it was being in good standing with your girl's best friend.

Ox stood and rubbed his hand over his scalp. "Hair's getting long."

"Do you ever grow it?"

He shook his head. "It just annoys me. I'll shave it tomorrow." He bent down and kissed her quickly. "I'll try to be fast."

"Don't rush poor Clyde. You'll end up spelling his kid's name wrong or something, and no one wants that."

"Would I do that?" He walked out of Emmie's bedroom and saw Tayla sitting at the kitchen counter, looking through a magazine and giving him the stink-eye. "Fine," he said. "I'll be back later and you can interrogate me."

"I'm glad you've resigned yourself to your fate," Tayla muttered. "Later."

"Later." Ox kissed Emmie again at the door, still unable to wipe the smile off his face. "See you soon."

"You called me your girlfriend this morning."

"Yeah."

She looked to the side. "So you're my boyfriend now?"

"I better fucking be. You think I'm gonna let some other asshole have the job?" He laughed when her cheeks turned red. "So damn sweet."

"Go to work," she said. "You're violating the... clause in the employee manual."

She shut the door, and Ox walked downstairs to see Clyde paging through a design book Emmie had left out on the coffee table. It wouldn't have been notable except for the fact that Clyde was about sixty, had naked pinups on both biceps, and Ox was pretty sure he lived in a battered old trailer on the edge of town. Ox did not expect Clyde to be looking at *Tiny House Living*.

Clyde looked up. "Thinking about redoing the kitchen."

"Cool." He glanced at Clyde's hairy shoulder. "We still starting the cover-up on the ex-wife?"

"Yep."

"Let's get you shaved."

CHAPTER THIRTY-TWO

TWO WEEKS of relative peace passed before Ginger made her third visit to INK. This time she ignored Emmie completely and marched straight over to Ox, who was sketching before his first client came. Emmie saw him glance up then look down again.

"Go away," he said.

"Are you still doing the Celtic-knot-work stuff?" she asked without preamble.

"Yep." He didn't look up.

Emmie glanced around the shop. She was working on the online store on the computer and only had two browsers, one of whom seemed determined to read the newest thriller in one-hour chunks on his lunch break instead of buying the hardback. Of course, he also helped himself to the free coffee INK offered.

Grrrrrrr.

No one paid attention to Ginger and Ox except Emmie.

"You're the last person I want to give business to, but I have a client I like—

"That's exceptional," Ox said.

"Look who's using five-dollar words now. Aren't you precious?" Ginger said. "Anyway, my client's boyfriend wants like a shield thing on his shoulder, and I don't have anyone who does the knot-work stuff anymore. He says it's Irish, so I thought of you."

"A shield?" Ox looked up. "What—"

"Saint Patrick's shield or something."

Ox frowned. "I don't know what he's talking about. I wish I could help, but…"

"Probably Saint Patrick's breastplate," Emmie said from across the shop. "It's not really a shield; it's a prayer."

"Oh," Ox said. "I know what he's talking about if it's that. 'God's might to uphold me, God's wisdom to guide me, et cetera.'"

"It's a long prayer," Emmie said. "I don't think he'd want the whole thing. Maybe an excerpt."

Ox nodded. "I imagine he wants some scrollwork or design around it. Tell him to come in or you can give him my card." He looked at Emmie. "Thanks, Em."

Ginger sneered. "Yeah, thanks for eavesdropping, *Em*."

"You're welcome." Emmie decided to ignore Ginger. After all, she was giving Ox business, and she was mostly being civil.

Unfortunately, the interchange had attracted Mr. Read Not Buy's attention. "Is it really eavesdropping if it's her own shop?" he asked the room.

Emmie's other browser spoke from the self-help section. "I could hear her from the back corner, so it's not really eavesdropping at all."

Mr. Read Not Buy said, "I'm just saying. She was being helpful, so I don't understand the tone."

"Know what she'd probably find helpful?" Ginger asked. "If you bought the fucking book instead of walking your fancy ass down here every afternoon to read it for free, asshole."

"That's enough." Emmie's heart was in her throat, but she kept talking, pretending it was a rowdy customer in someone else's store and not Ox's ex-girlfriend. "You're welcome to speak to Ox, but you're not welcome to insult my customers. If you can't be polite, please leave."

Ginger turned back to Ox. "This uptight bitch is who you're fucking now?"

Ox stood and pointed at the door. "Out. Right now."

"I bet your mom loves her. She's as uptight as your sister."

Ox opened the 7th Avenue door and pointed outside. "I'll call the cops, Ginger. Don't think I wouldn't. I'm not doing this shit anymore."

Ginger brushed up against him as she walked out. "No, you're definitely not doing this *ever* again. Poor boy. I doubt she has you begging like I did."

Emmie's face was on fire. Ox gave Ginger one last shove out the door and closed it. He walked to Emmie and grabbed her hand, walking toward the hallway. "Tayla, can you watch the shop?"

Tayla stuck her newly red head out the office door. "What?"

"Watch the shop, please?"

Tayla glanced at them and must have seen something on Emmie's face. "Yeah sure."

Ox paused near Mr. Read Not Buy. "You really should buy the book. You don't even donate to the coffee jar when you come in. Not cool."

"It's fine," Emmie murmured. "Really it's—"

"It's not fine," Ox said. "She's just nicer than me."

Tayla brushed past them and walked to the counter just as Mr. Read Not Buy stood and put the book back on the coffee table before he slipped out the door.

"Why did you do that?" Emmie hissed once Ox had closed the office door. "Maybe he can't afford the hardback."

"Have you seen his shoes? He can afford the hardback, he's just cheap. If he wants free books, the library is four blocks away."

"The bookstore is my business, not yours. I don't interfere in your shop. Don't interfere with mine."

His mouth dropped open. "Seriously? I was sticking up for you."

"What you did was drive away a customer who didn't buy today but might have bought something else tomorrow. You think he's ever going to come back here now that you embarrassed him?"

Ox closed his mouth and crossed his arms over his chest. "That dude was never going to buy anything."

"Maybe not. But you still embarrassed him."

"I'm not his mom and neither are you. If the man can't handle someone confronting him about being an asshole, he shouldn't be—"

"He wasn't being an asshole!" Emmie said. "Maybe he just liked hanging out here. Maybe he likes reading some place with company instead of being alone. Yeah, maybe he should have donated to the coffee jar, but that wasn't your place to say. It's my shop."

"It's *your* shop now?"

"The whole shop is *ours*. But when it comes to the books? Yes, it's mine."

"Fine."

"Fine!" Emmie felt like crying. Things had been going so well, and now they were fighting. Pretty soon they'd have a real fight, then Ox would get fed up and leave, just like all her mom's boyfriends. Then Emmie would be out a boyfriend and a tenant. She'd have spent thousands of dollars redoing a building that—

"For fuck's sake, you're freaking out again," Ox said.

"I am not." She totally was. This was the beginning of the end.

"We're having a fight; it's not the end of the world. Fucking Ginger. I only snapped at that guy because she pissed me off."

"Why does she piss you off so much?"

"Because she was being rude to your customers."

"So you also decided to be rude to my customers?" Emmie blinked. "That makes no sense!"

"I know!" His lips twitched. "Tell me that guy wasn't irritating you."

"I nicknamed him Mister Read Not Buy in my head. Yes, he was irritating."

"So why are you mad at me?"

"Because that's just bookselling, Ox. Trust me, I'm going to get a lot of Mister Read Not Buys. And people who pull out books and put them back in the wrong spots. Why do you think I spend so much time reshelving books? There will be people who buy books and return them after they've read them. And people who don't like a book and think they should get their money back. And teenagers who think they can get away with getting naked in the self-help section."

His eyes went wide. "What?"

"Or whatever section is in the back corner. It doesn't have anything to do with self-help specifically. At Bay City it was Religion and Spirituality."

"Kinky." He narrowed his eyes. "People try to have sex in bookshops?"

"Uh, remember the thing you wanted to do last weekend?"

"But that's because my girlfriend actually *owns* a bookshop and the back bookshelves are not visible from the windows, so there is no reason we couldn't— You know, never mind." He huffed. "What you're saying is that you're going to have all kinds of asshole customers and I can't say anything to them."

"Just like I can't get irritated and tell off the next group of college girls who comes in here and flirts with you for an hour, trying to show you their boobs to get your professional opinion on where the little heart tattoo should go."

His lip twitched again. This time it was almost a smile. "You could tell them off if you wanted to. That would be hot."

"And then they'd never come back to you for a tattoo."

He shrugged. "Worth it."

"Ox, will you be serious?"

He hooked an arm around her waist. "Will you loosen up a little?" He played with the buttons on her sweater. "I like you buttoned-up so I can be the one to unbutton you, but we're both going to have bend a little to make this work."

She took a deep breath. "Okay. Agreed."

"So in the spirit of bending, I am not going to tell off your irritating customers or drink the last of the coffee without making a new pot. But I draw the line at anyone who's actually being threatening or harassing you. Don't ask me to not react to that shit because that's out of line."

"Fine. And how do I need to bend for you? Is there something I'm doing or some part of the bookshop that's interfering with your work?"

He fiddled with her buttons some more.

"Ox?"

"Honestly? No. You're fucking adorable, and I love hanging out with you all day. I do wish you'd let me pick the music on the radio a little more, and I also wish you'd pursue a liquor license. At least for wine and beer. It would be really good for evening events. I know it's expensive, but I think it's worth the money. And Metlin doesn't have anything like a wine bar downtown. It could pull in an entirely new clientele that would probably be good for both of us."

She nodded. "I will talk it over with Tayla and look into the liquor license thing."

"Also, you definitely need to get more jealous if girls try to show me their tits. Maybe fight a little. Tear your shirt while you wrestle—"

"That is never going to happen." She couldn't stop the smile. "Ever. And you hated it when Ginger got jealous about girls."

"I think I'd kinda like it with you."

"Ego?"

"Yeah." He was still fiddling with the buttons on her cardigan. "Hey Emmie?"

"Yes?"

"We just had a fight."

"Would you really classify it as a fight?" She took a deep breath and calculated the odds of a relationship succeeding when a couple fought in the first month. Was that bad? Good? Average?

Ox started to unbutton her sweater. "Oh, I'd definitely classify that as a fight."

"Why?"

He crowded her until Emmie stepped back. And back.

Emmie's back hit the door just as Ox finished unbuttoning her cardigan. He slipped it off her shoulders and slid a warm hand under her shirt.

Oh.

"Because if that was a fight"—he bent down to whisper—"then we get to have make-up sex."

"Right here?" She felt behind her for the doorknob. She turned the lock before Ox slipped her T-shirt up and over her head. "Right now?"

"Yes and yes." He bent down and took her mouth in a leisurely kiss. "But we have to be quiet," he whispered. "Can you be quiet?"

"I'm always quiet."

The corner of his mouth turned up. "Not always."

"You be quiet then." She reached for his belt and slid the worn leather through the loops.

She undressed him with silent efficiency while his lips covered hers, exploring her mouth and swallowing her moans when his hands began to roam. Ox reached down and slid his hand up the back of her thigh. He worked her panties down until Emmie felt them around her knees. She kicked them away while he lifted her skirt, cupping her bottom and picking her up until her back was pressed against the door, her legs around his waist and Ox's fingers teasing her.

He was never a chatty lover, but the utter silence of the office

241

made Emmie's soft breaths deafening, driving her temperature higher, her need greater.

Ox's mouth was deep red and a dark flush stained his cheek-bones. He reached for something in his back pocket, then grabbed a silver packet, tearing it with his teeth before he sheathed himself in the condom and then almost immediately in her.

The angle drove a soft cry from her mouth and Ox covered it with his kiss, pressing her to the door while he thrust forward. He held her so firmly the door didn't even creak. She ran her hands over his shoulders, played her fingers along the hard bands of muscle on his neck.

"So strong," she whispered, in awe of the mass of him and the effortless strength. He wasn't just an artist. He worked with his body on the ranch, and the evidence was burning her up.

"See," he whispered back. "You're good for my ego."

Emmie let the distant chatter of the shop fall away as he filled her senses. His hands. His flushed lips. The hard length of him. The massive strength he used so casually to bring her intense pleasure.

His brow furrowed as he locked eyes with her. "Are you close?"

She nodded. They were going to have to try this at home, because the angle was working in a big way. She fell into his chest, wrapping her arms around his neck as her focus narrowed on the building pressure and pleasure and the steady rhythm of his hips driving into her.

"Emmie," he groaned.

"There." She gasped and cried into his neck, the salt-and-cedar smell of his skin filling her senses as she came. Her mind went blank. Her skin was exquisitely sensitive to the feel of his flannel shirt against her belly and the denim against her thighs. She shook in his arms, the power of her release bringing tears to her eyes.

Ox lifted her higher, drove into her harder, and bit back a curse. Emmie held on with the last of her strength. He arched his hips up and slammed a hand into the wall when he came. Then he spun around and his knees buckled as he slid down the door, holding her close. She straddled him and swallowed his own deep groans in her mouth.

They sat on the floor, shaking and kissing softly. Ox framed her cheeks with his hands, brushing her hair back from her face.

"I fucking love the look on your face right now," he whispered. "I want to draw it, but I'm never going to. I'm the only lucky asshole who gets to see it, and I'm gonna keep it that way."

His rough words killed her. "Ox?"

"Yeah?"

She whispered, "Make-up sex is hot."

"Any sex with you is hot," he muttered back. He smiled. "But yeah, make-up sex is hot as hell."

"I want to do it again, but I really don't like fighting."

"I think that's what they call a paradox." He took a deep breath and drew her head forward until she was cuddled against him with her head lying over his heart. "Hey, Emmie?"

His voice rumbled against her ear and Emmie smiled. "I know. We need to get back to work."

"Yeah we do, but..."

"But?" She tried to pull back, but he kept her pressed close.

"It doesn't have anything to do with work," Ox said. "But I want you to stop freaking out every time something goes wrong, okay? Shit goes wrong in life. In relationships. You can't control everything, you just have to work on it."

She took a deep breath.

"Do you get what I'm saying?" Ox said quietly. "We have a fight and your eyes go straight to the door."

Emmie's first instinct had always been to run. Something not working? Cut ties and move on. And if you were really smart, you didn't get tangled up to begin with, because the first time you gave someone influence over your life, they'd drop the ball or disappoint you or decide you were too much work.

"I always hated group projects at school," she blurted.

Ox nudged her back and Emmie reluctantly sat up. His eyebrows were furrowed and his lips were quirked in amusement. "Group projects?"

She lifted her hands, then let them drop. "It's because… you'd get this assignment, right? And you want to get an A. But then you realize that not everyone wants to get an A. Some people don't care at all about an A. So you end up doing all the work because otherwise you hand part of the project over to someone who doesn't care. And everyone thinks you're a huge control freak, but mostly you just want everyone to do well."

"But you don't trust them to want the same things you do," Ox said.

Emmie forced her eyes to stay on his though she desperately wanted to look away. "Yeah."

"But what if you're with someone who wants that A just as much as you do? What then?"

Emmie frowned. "Did you want the A?"

"No. I didn't care about my grades. I usually tried to get in a group with someone like you who did want the A so they'd do the work for me."

Emmie narrowed her eyes. "I knew it."

"But I do want *you*. I want us. We're grown-ups now; no one is grading us. And if we both want the same thing, then we can work together and you can *trust me* to do my part."

Emmie nodded just as Tayla pounded on the door.

"Hey, you hussy, there are customers on both sides of the shop. Sexy times are over."

Ox said, "I told you stop calling me a hussy, Tayla."

"This time I was talking to Emmie. Get back to work."

Emmie looked at Ox. "You heard her—playtime is over."

"No," he said, patting her bottom. "We just have to press pause."

CHAPTER THIRTY-THREE

FOUR WEEKS LATER...

EMMIE HAD GONE to sleep with Ox beside her only to wake to an empty bed. For the past three weeks, that had been the pattern. He'd spend most nights with her, but would go out to the ranch in the mornings, come back to get in his hours at the shop, then collapse in bed at night. Sometimes he didn't even make it off the couch.

The times they could spend together were nearly blissful. They weren't fighting. They could talk about work, but they also talked about books and art they both liked. They teased each other about their taste in music, but most of the teases were laughing. One of Ox's favorite pastimes was drawing on Emmie when she was naked. He usually kept it under her clothes, like the line of buttons he'd drawn up the inside of her thigh or the burst of flowers he'd drawn to frame her small breasts.

They were planning a camping trip for the spring and talking about road-tripping so Ox could meet Emmie's mom.

They just didn't know when they'd have the time.

Tayla knocked on the door. "Em?"

She rubbed her eyes and sat up. "Yeah?"

"I have coffee."

"Come in." Emmie yanked up the covers and sat up. "You're a goddess of all things wonderful and caffeinated."

Tayla sat on the end of the bed and handed her a mug. "You're welcome. Ox is gone again?"

She nodded and drank.

"He's working crazy hours. Is his mom any better?"

"I think so? She didn't seem any different when we went out to dinner at the ranch last week, but his sister looks exhausted. They both do."

Emmie hadn't had much time to contemplate Ox's family problems when the holiday season was in full swing. Thanksgiving had been the week before, and while Black Friday had been pretty quiet, the Metlin Downtown Business Association did a huge Small Business Saturday event that Emmie and Ox had taken part in. The bookshop had seen gobs of business that weekend, and Ox had even sold gift cards for blocks of tattoo work as gifts, an idea that Emmie had offered as a holiday promotion.

Tattoos were a surprisingly popular Christmas present.

Tayla asked, "How long is this going to last? The double-job thing."

"I think the problem is his mom can't go back to her old schedule. They need another employee, and I don't know if they're not willing to hire someone or if they can't afford it. Maybe neither. I don't know. I don't know his sister well enough to ask. It's not really any of my business. Ox isn't missing hours anymore. In fact, he's been working more hours the past couple of weeks at the shop, not less."

"Which just makes him more tired."

Emmie nodded.

Tayla tapped her chin. "I wonder if they need someone to help with the books for the ranch."

"Probably. I think Ox said that Melissa does all that."

"I'll ask him."

Emmie stretched out her legs and smiled. "So you're doing more of that stuff now."

"The bookkeeping?"

Emmie nodded.

"It keeps me busy." Tayla swung her legs. "I don't know. I know you're all loved up with Ox, but I may ask to stay living here a little longer if that's cool."

"Totally cool." Inside, Emmie was dancing, but she had to play it casual.

"Yeah." Tayla sipped her coffee. "I'm kinda digging the fall colors and small-town vibe. Metlin has a Christmas parade. Who does that anymore?"

"Small towns everywhere? But in Metlin, Santa drives a tractor, so we do have that claim to fame."

"And the kid and dog costume float was just… ridiculous."

"Ridiculously adorable, you mean?"

"Did you see the little boy dressed as the Grinch who had the wiener dog with the antlers?"

"Yes. Maybe I should do a holiday costume contest or something."

"Might be too late for that this year, but it's a good idea for next. We could have a whole holiday schedule next year. Incorporate Hanukkah and Eid if the calendar is right."

"I'll start jotting down ideas and put them on the idea board in the office."

"Okay, cool."

Emmie finished her coffee and tried not to wiggle with glee. Her best friend was inching closer and closer to a permanent move to Metlin. Her shop was breaking even, which at this point was really all she could hope for. She had a boyfriend she was head over heels for. Emmie had all these future plans for the shop and for her life in Metlin, and Ox and Tayla were in all of them.

"Stop," Tayla said.

"Stop what?"

"I can practically hear you planning my life out for me in three-year increments for the next thirty years. Just stop. I'm young and flexible. I'm thinking of staying here for a while. Don't get ahead of yourself."

"Of course not."

"Bullshit. You already have me and Jeremy married with three brats."

Emmie groaned and fell toward her. "Come on. You know you'd be adorable together."

"Why don't you daydream about how you're going to get your boyfriend to not be exhausted all the time? He can't keep this schedule up, not that it seems to be putting a damper on your nocturnal activities."

Emmie blushed. "Sorry."

"No worries. Ox got me a very nice pair of noise-canceling headphones last week. I could live with him as a roommate."

"It's a little soon for that, don't you think?"

Tayla raised an eyebrow. "With his schedule, having him move in might be the only way to guarantee you have any time alone."

———

SHE COULDN'T HELP but think of Tayla's words the next day when noon rolled around and Ox still wasn't in the shop. Ginger came by again, and Emmie tried to pay as little attention as possible to the woman.

"Ox here?" she asked Emmie.

"Nope."

"Let me guess, out at the ranch?"

Her tone actually sounded commiserating rather than sneering. Emmie looked up. "Yeah. You heard about his mom?"

"Uh-huh." Ginger shrugged. "Trust me, it'll always be something." She put a piece of paper down on the counter. "Here's the info for the guy who wants the Celtic piece. Says he's been having trouble getting ahold of Ox. Might have to remind him to give the guy a call."

"I don't do his bookings for him."

"Good." Ginger gave her a wry smile. "I'd definitely try holding your ground on that one. Later."

And that was that. No profanity. No bitchy comments. Just a warning that echoed in her wake.

It'll always be something.

———

EMMIE WAS LYING next to Ox that night, stretched out on the couch with a car documentary on the television. She was reading. Ox was sleeping. He'd lasted all of five minutes before he nodded off.

"Ox." She nudged his foot. "Were you planning to stay here tonight?"

He snored. Emmie took that for a yes. She closed her book and set it on the coffee table before she crawled over to him and kissed his lips.

Ox started awake at the feel of her lips on his. "Hey." He rubbed his eyes. "Sorry."

"Don't be sorry. Let's go to bed."

He didn't get up. He reached for her and wrapped her in a hug, rolling her onto his chest as he took a deep breath and hooked a leg over hers, effectively trapping her.

"I hate them so much," he muttered drowsily.

Emmie frowned. "What?"

"Cows."

She smiled and rested her cheek on his chest. "So why are you spending so much time with them?"

"Can't let Melissa do it all," he muttered. "Not fair."

249

Isn't it her ranch?

Emmie didn't say anything. She didn't have any siblings, and most days she was jealous of Ox and Melissa's relationship. She'd love to have a brother who cared about her that much. She did feel like Melissa took Ox for granted though. It wasn't as if Ox was asking his sister to be an unpaid employee at his business. But Emmie didn't feel like she had a right to say anything about it. That was between Ox and Melissa.

She rested on his chest for a few more minutes but forced Ox awake before his breathing turned deep. He was way too big for Emmie to move, and he'd get a backache if he slept on the couch. They stumbled to Emmie's bedroom, and Ox fell into bed while Emmie got ready and turned off the lights in the living room. Tayla was still out, so Emmie left the kitchen lights on for her.

Sometime in the middle of the night, Ox sat upright in bed, jolting Emmie out of her sleep.

"Ox?"

"Did I close the gate before I left?"

It wasn't the first time he'd talked in his sleep. Emmie rubbed his arm. "I'm sure you did. You always do."

Ox blinked at her. He wasn't really awake, but the look he gave her was so painfully tender it nearly made Emmie cry.

"Don't drive in the fog."

Emmie pulled him down next to her. "I don't have a car, remember?"

"Don't drive in the fog, baby."

Emmie's heart turned over. "I won't."

Ox wrapped his arms around her in a nearly suffocating hold. "Love you. Can't lose you."

"I won't drive in the fog, Ox."

"She cries at night."

Emmie had to blink away tears. Then she started to feel guilty for ever resenting Melissa or the time Ox gave her and Abby.

"She'll be okay," Emmie whispered. "And I'll be okay. I won't drive in the fog."

"I love you."

"I love you too."

He was breathing deeply a few seconds later, but it took Emmie a lot longer to fall back asleep.

———

"WHY SO SERIOUS?" He bent down a grabbed a kiss as she poured a cup of coffee.

"I'm just glad you're taking the day off from the ranch."

He rubbed his lip and scratched his cheek. "Well..."

Emmie put her mug on the counter. "You're not taking the day off."

"I don't have any clients this afternoon. So I thought I'd spend the morning with you and then go to the ranch this afternoon. Stay the night out there and come back tomorrow."

Emmie nodded. "Okay."

"Are you mad?"

She turned to him. "I'm not mad. But I know when you stay out there you end up getting up at five in the morning to do chores. And then you work six plus hours before you come here and work another six hours."

"I know." He put his hands on her shoulders. "And I want to spend more time with you. I know we haven't gone out for weeks now. But Melissa has like a month before harvest starts and she's—"

"I'm worried about you. You're not sleeping enough. You're going to burn out with this schedule. And yeah, I'd like to see you more. All we do is work and sleep. And so far it seems like Melissa doesn't have a plan for getting more help. She's just relying on you and..." Emmie stopped and pressed her lips together. "Never mind. It's not my business."

His face was tight. "It's my family. I can't ignore them if they need help."

"But you have your own business now, and if you're always tired because you're helping out there—"

"The ranch comes first."

Emmie fell silent.

The ranch comes first.

His tone made it clear it wasn't open for debate.

"Right," she whispered. "Got it."

He'll always pick them over you.

Emmie's heart plummeted as Ox filled up a travel mug with coffee and kissed her on the head.

"I'll go out this morning," he said. "Try to finish so I can spend tonight with you."

"It's fine," she said. "I'm fine. Go do what you need to do."

Ox turned at the door. "I really hate it when you say fine."

Emmie shrugged. "I don't know what else you want me to say."

"Say that you understand how important my family is to me."

"I totally understand that. But is the ranch your family?"

"Kinda." He rubbed a hand over his face. "I don't know. I know you're right, okay? I can't keep up with this schedule."

"I'm not asking you to choose between your business and your family. That's a shitty thing to ask. I just..." Emmie took a deep breath. "I invested everything in this shop. I sold my car. I used my savings. And I need to know that it's important to you."

"I'm going to pay my rent this month, okay?" His jaw set in a stubborn line. "Don't worry about getting a check."

"I'm not asking about your rent! I'm asking if I can depend on you to be my partner like you said you'd be and..."

"And what?" His eyes burned her.

"I'm starting to think I can't. I'm starting to think that if it comes down to our business or your sister's ranch, then I'm going to be the loser."

He opened his mouth. Closed it. Then he shook his head and

walked out the door. When it slammed shut behind him, Emmie heard the echo of a hundred different doors.

It's an important gig, Marianne. You're thirteen now, not three.

I hope you're not too invested in this little business.

It's just not working with your mom and me. We'll still be friends. I promise.

I won't always be here to hold your hand, Emmie.

It's a spelling bee. What's the big deal?

Emmie took her coffee to her room and managed to set it down on the dresser before she started crying. This was why getting involved had been a bad idea. It had always been a bad idea. She'd just ignored her common sense. Ox leaving would have always hurt, but it wouldn't have hurt this badly. If she hadn't fallen in love with him, his abandoning her would have been a sting to her budget but not a rip to her heart.

Emmie gave herself approximately ten minutes to wallow before she cleaned up and got ready for work.

She had to get ready for work. No matter what else was happening in her life, the shop had to open. The coffee had to be made. The books wouldn't sell themselves. Ox might have been able to cancel on his customers and head back to the ranch, but Emmie's only backup plan was herself.

That's the way it was. That's the way it had always been.

CHAPTER THIRTY-FOUR

OX SLAMMED the posthole digger into the ground just as the steer butted into his hip, sending him into the barbed wire and tearing up his gloves. He kicked at the steer and yelled, "Fucking piece-of-shit bovine asshole!"

The steer snorted and turned, trotting off and leaving a trail of shit behind him.

Ox turned in place, surrounded by mud and new grass and fucking cows and rocks and broken fences, and wondered how the hell he'd come back to this place. How the hell was he still doing the shit that had brought him and his grandfather to blows when he was seventeen?

He dug the posthole digger into the ground again, tearing up his hands so badly he knew he'd be in pain when he went to work on the second half of Clyde's cover-up the next night.

Fucking cows.

Fucking mudslides.

Fucking ranch.

He heard the hoofbeats a moment before Melissa crested the hill. It was too muddy for the quad cab to make it up to the north pasture, so they were both riding that day.

"You need any help?" she called. "I'm done with the oranges for today."

"Good." He took a deep breath and tried to calm down. It wasn't Melissa's fault his life was shit. She didn't ask him to help. It was just something he had to do. "I'm almost done with this hole. Then I need to restring the wire."

"You don't have any clients today?"

"I told you it's been slow." It had been slow because he told his clients he needed to work less hours and he wasn't getting any walk-ins, but Melissa didn't know that.

"I'd really feel more comfortable with you working all these hours if you let me pay you," Melissa said. "I told you, we have the money—"

"It's not about the money, okay?" He wasn't going to take money from his sister that she needed for Abby. He threw the posthole digger to the side and went for the new post. "That's not why I'm doing this."

Melissa was silent as he fixed the new post in place and restrung the wire, looping it around the far fencepost and twisting it in place before he secured it with pliers. The fix hadn't taken as long as he'd feared, but he was still frustrated, angry, and in pain.

"Why *are* you doing this?" she asked.

"What?" He tore off his gloves once he was done and stuffed them in his jacket pockets. His hands stung in the cold, damp air.

"Why are you doing this, Ox?" She saw his hands. "You've torn up your hands."

"Yeah, one of your asshole steers shoved me into the fence."

She threw out her hands. "Why are you doing this?"

"Because I need to."

"Why? You're an artist and you're tearing up your hands? That's just stupid."

"Glad to know you think I'm stupid."

"Oh, shut up!" She slid off her mare. "You know that's not what

I'm saying. You couldn't wait to escape this place, so why are you doing this? You were finally going after what you wanted. What changed?"

"I'm the only one left!"

Melissa frowned. "What are you talking about?"

"First it was Grandpa and then Calvin. And now Mom's sick too. She's not gonna be around forever. If we hadn't gotten her to the hospital, then what would have happened? She could have died." His voice caught. "And then I'd be the only one left to take care of you and Abby. We're all we have left, Lissa. Of course I have to be here."

Melissa stood staring at him, not saying a word.

Ox cleared his throat and sniffed. "I'm the only one left. You won't ask for help from anyone else. Not when you really need it. So it's just me."

There were tears in Melissa's eyes. "You hate cows."

"But I love you and Abby." He shook his head. "I shouldn't have started my own business. It wasn't fair to Emmie. I worry every day I'm away from here. And I worry about Emmie taking care of everything in the shop when I'm away from there. But you're my family, and I have to take care of you. I hear you crying at night. I know I'm not Calvin, but I don't want you to be alone. I don't want you to have to do this by yourself."

Melissa walked toward him. "Because you are the biggest softie in the world regarding your niece—don't argue with me, hard-ass, you know you are—I will excuse your bullheaded macho assumption that I am not capable of running this ranch on my own. Of course I miss Calvin. I miss him every day. And every day I get up and I feed the goats and check the fences and order the parts for the tractor. Because the ranch is what I want. It's what Calvin wanted. It's what keeps me sane. That and Abby."

"I know."

"But this is not what you want. It never has been. And… you're right." She squeezed her eyes shut. "You and Cary are both right.

I'm too stubborn about accepting help. There are a dozen out-of-work cowboys who could be doing what you've been doing, but I've been too distracted to hire any. I've been using you here as a crutch, and that's not fair to you."

"I'm your brother. You can always ask me—"

"If it's an emergency, I will call. I promise you. But this isn't an emergency." She looked around the pasture. "This is a job. And it's not yours."

He crossed his arms. "So what are you saying?"

"I'm saying you're fired. And you should go get cleaned up and head back into town to your real job and apologize to your girlfriend for being an asshole for the past few weeks and probably take her out for a very nice dinner."

Ox's face fell. He couldn't stop thinking about his fight with Emmie that morning. She'd been right. The ranch was not his family. His mom, his sister, and Abby were his family. The ranch was a business, and he'd been putting his sister's business before the promises he'd made to Emmie. He'd told her she could depend on him, and then he'd failed.

He'd fought with her, *and then he'd walked out the door.*

Ox grabbed his head in his hands and cursed a blue streak.

"What did you do?" Melissa asked. "You idiot, what did you do?"

———

OX KNOCKED on Spider's door as soon as he made it into town. He'd called Daisy for the address and she'd told him, but she'd also told him not to bother calling because Spider was with a client until two and wouldn't pick up the phone even if she called. Ox also had to listen through an impassioned bitch session about the man refusing to get a cell phone. Since Ox had a sister, he knew when to make the right sympathetic noises and when to shut up.

He then managed to tease enough information out of Daisy to

confirm that a very grand gesture was called for. He'd fucked up big time. It wasn't so much the fighting, he realized now, it was the walking out.

That was the big mistake.

Ox heard movement in the house, then a rustle in the curtain beside the door. Multiple locks unlatched and Spider opened the door.

"Hey, man. What's up?"

Ox looked around. "Your house looks like *Leave It to Beaver*."

"'Cause my wife is a fucking goddess, so don't track mud on her carpet. Why are you here?"

"Because I finally figured out what I want. Then I really fucked up."

CHAPTER THIRTY-FIVE

EMMIE WAS GOING through the motions at the shop. Luckily it was a busy day. Like insanely busy. She was already considering another cookbook order and another big order of contemporary romances. Books were a very popular gift this year, but so were the notebook-and-pen sets Tayla had ordered and the selection of ironic book T-shirts Emmie had finally gotten in. She was wearing one of them this morning. BOYS IN BOOKS ARE BETTER.

It had seemed appropriate.

Tayla had been at her side all day, asking a few questions but mostly leaving her alone, which was highly appreciated. Daisy had walked in around two thirty to bring her a sandwich, glanced at her shirt, then winced before she walked out.

Ginger walked in around three, glanced over at Ox's empty chair, then she rolled her eyes and picked up the thriller Mr. Read Not Buy had left on the coffee table. She walked to the counter and set the book down.

"Hey," Emmie said.

"Hey." Ginger nodded at Ox's corner. "For what it's worth, I honestly hoped he was going to get his shit together, because everyone says you're a nice person."

Emmie blinked. "Thanks. Did you want to buy this one? I think that guy bent the pages and stuff. I can get you a new one."

"I heard this book is super generic and predictable even though the author's really famous."

"Honestly? Yeah. But like you said, the author is really popular, so I've been selling a lot of them. I have other copies."

"Nah. This is for my stepdad, who's the most generic and predictable person I know. So a used copy is fine."

Emmie nodded. "Fair enough. Would you like that gift wrapped? We can make it generic and predictable."

Ginger gave her a smirk. "Perfect."

Emmie went to the counter where they'd set up the wrapping station for the season. She glanced over her shoulder when the bell rang on the door. Adrian Saroyan walked into the shop carrying the umbrella she and Ox had both completely forgotten about. He caught her eye and waved.

"Hey, Emmie."

"Hey." Of course Adrian was here because the day could just not get any more wonderful. Perfect.

Emmie finished wrapping Ginger's book in plain red paper with a plain green bow placed exactly in the center of the book. She headed back to the counter to ring her up. She was scanning the credit card when she heard Adrian speak.

"Excuse me, but are you the owner of Bombshell Tattoos?"

Ginger glanced at Adrian. "Yeah."

"Would you be interested—"

"No."

Adrian nodded. "Okay then." He tapped on the counter. "I don't suppose you'd—"

"You wish, honey." Ginger signed the receipt Emmie handed her and reached for the book. "Merry Christmas and bah humbug and to all a good night."

"See you later, Ginger."

"Tell Ox I said hello and to call that fucking client back. I don't want to keep making excuses for his ass."

"Will do." Emmie tried to wipe even the hint of an expression off her face when she turned to Adrian. "That was Ginger."

"I figured. I hung your umbrella over on the stand."

"Thanks. I appreciate that." They'd gotten a little more rain since the storm when she and Ox... Better not to think about that. "So how've you been?"

"Good. I switched to historical fiction instead of more Jane Austen, but I've been reading more. My mom is very proud. And since I'm watching less news, my stress levels have probably gone down."

Emmie smiled. "I'm glad. I have a great biography of John Adams if you're looking for a new read."

"That sounds good, but how about I send my mom in for it since she's always asking me what I want for Christmas?"

"I'll set one aside."

Adrian turned away and turned back. "Are you okay?"

No, I'm not okay, but you're the last person I want to talk to about it.

"I'm fine," she said. "Just busy. Work."

Thank God for work.

"Okay. If you ever want to talk, you have my number."

"Thanks, Adrian. Merry Christmas."

"Merry Christmas."

———

IT WAS four o'clock and the shop was busier than ever. Someone down at Pacific Kitchen Supply had mentioned the ten percent-off-coupon for red enamelware they could grab if they bought a book at INK, so it seemed like most of Emmie's cookbook section was slowly being emptied out. Luckily, lots of avid cooks had decided that their friends and coworkers needed books for presents, so the shop was packed.

Both Tayla and Emmie were working the register, Tayla using her phone for mobile checkout around the shop. Daisy was at the wrapping station, and she'd brought her cook Eddie to work the complimentary holiday coffee and hot chocolate station. Of course, Eddie didn't work without his mini-television playing telenovelas. Emmie wasn't sure what he was watching, but it lent a dramatic and oddly appropriate backdrop to the overall cacophony of noise in the shop. Emmie was thinking about getting her own mini-television when Ox walked through the Main Street door.

She froze for a moment, then she put her brain on autopilot and got back to work. She saw Tayla walk over to Ox and say something, but Emmie wasn't thinking about Ox. She wasn't thinking about her trampled heart or the sick feeling in the pit of her stomach when he walked in the front door instead of his own shop door.

He wasn't here to work. He was here to talk to her.

And Emmie had a feeling she knew what it would be about.

She started mentally preparing a list of people who might be interested in the odd arrangement she and Ox had worked out.

Sure, you can do tattoos here, but only during these hours and oh, can you keep the language to a minimum while the bookshop is open?

I'd really prefer you leave the superviolent or dark flash off the walls please.

No, I pick the music and it's not classic rock. If I hear the Eagles played one more time—

"Emmie."

Fuck fuck fuck. She'd been checking out customers on autopilot and hadn't noticed he'd gotten in line.

"I'm really busy right now," she said. "So unless you want to buy something, we'll have to talk later." *How about never?*

Ox grabbed a pen-and-notebook set from the stand by the counter, ripped the outer wrapping off, and handed her the piece with the bar code on it. Emmie started to scan it while he opened the book and wrote.

"That'll be sixteen dollars and twenty-six cents," she said. "How would you like to pay today?"

He was still writing. "Which takes longer?"

"I don't... What are you doing?"

He'd flipped the notebook around and propped it in front of her register. It read:

I'm sorry.

I fucked up.

I love you.

Put this in your romance novel.

He pulled off his T-shirt, ignoring the gasps of the people around him, and tossed it over Emmie's head and onto the floor. Directly over his heart, he had a piece of white gauze secured with four strips of tape.

There were Spanish voices in the background and a dramatic orchestral swell. Eddie wasn't watching the telenovela anymore. No one was.

Ricardo! ¿Puedes ser tú?

Camila, ¿cómo pudiste hacerme esto?

The telenovela music dropped to a minor key, and Emmie's heart dropped to her feet. "What did you do?"

Ox walked around the counter. "Take off the bandage."

"Tell me you didn't put my name on your chest."

"I am committed to this. I am not walking out on you *or* the shop. I want you to know. I want the whole world to know."

Emmie's eyes went wide and a weeping violin played in the background.

¡Pensé que estabas muerto!

Ni siquiera la muerte podría alejarme de ti.

"You did not," she said. "You said yourself it's the kiss of death."

"Take off the bandage and find out."

"Ox, you better not have." Emmie stepped forward and started to peel off the bandage. Not a single person in the shop was talking. The only sound was Eddie's telenovela.

Emmie pulled back the gauze, but her name was nowhere in sight. Instead, on the grey-and-black expanse of Ox's chest, she saw a single butterfly resting on the anchor over his heart. The lines were delicate and strong, and the wings were inked in the vivid burgundy red Spider had used on her back.

"It's my butterfly."

"Spider helped me out."

Emmie looked up and couldn't fight the tears at the corner of her eyes. "You don't do color."

"Just once," he said quietly. "Just this."

She spread her hand over the anchor, carefully avoiding the newly tattooed skin. "It's beautiful."

Ox pressed his hand over hers as he bent down. "I'm sorry," he said. "I know I messed up, and I'm sorry. I didn't know what I wanted for a long time, but helping you here showed me. I know what I want now. I want to be your partner. Everything else comes second. Can you give me another chance?"

Emmie nodded. "I can do that. I love you."

The smile that spread over his face was brilliant. "I love you too." He kissed her, and every person in the shop applauded. Emmie was pretty sure she heard Eddie crying, but that may have been about the telenovela.

Ox whispered, "I walked out. I shouldn't have done that, and it won't happen again. I'm sure I'll fuck up in other ways, but I won't do that again, okay?"

Emmie nodded and pressed her face to his chest. "Everyone is looking at us, aren't they?"

"Fuck no, they all made a run for the romance section, Buttons. Best marketing ploy ever."

Emmie burst into laughter and felt Ox's arms come around her. She decided that for once, being the center of attention wasn't too bad.

And she was definitely putting this in her romance novel.

———

AT THE END of the night, it was the single busiest day they'd had at INK. Once Emmie wiped her eyes and took a moment to kiss Ox in private, they both got back to work. After all, it was the holiday season. No one had time to drag their feet.

Ox booked two walk-ins on the spot and sold six hours' worth of gift certificates. One of the walk-ins had the audacity to ask for Ox to keep his shirt off, but he gave her a half smile, pulled on his shirt, and told the girl he wouldn't want his girlfriend to beat her up.

Emmie changed her T-shirt after deciding that nonfictional boys were having a good night and I TRIED TO FORM A GANG BUT IT TURNED INTO A BOOK CLUB was a better choice for the evening. She also had several sign-ups for the romance book club, which probably wasn't a coincidence.

Spider dropped in to see Daisy and bring her a hamburger a little after seven. He sidled up to Emmie, who was wrapping books while Daisy took a turn on the register.

"Hey."

"Hey." She bumped his shoulder. "I like it."

"Yeah? Good. I'd hate to have to hold him down and cover that shit, because he's a big fucker."

"Was it your idea or his?"

"His. But he wanted the same style as yours and he doesn't know shit about color, so he was smart enough to come to me. Unlike somebody who didn't trust me enough for her first tattoo."

"I'm never going to hear the end of that, am I?"

"No." He turned and leaned against the counter. "I like him for you. I wasn't sure at first, but he figured it out."

She turned and kissed his cheek. "Thanks, Spider."

Emmie stared at him long enough that Spider frowned. "What?"

"Ox was having a hard time letting go of stuff with his sister and the ranch. And I was feeling jealous of that, but at the same time kind of not getting it. But I just realized that's bullshit, because if you needed anything from me, I'd give it to you. You never ask me for anything, but if you did, I'd give it without any conditions. And if I thought you needed something and you didn't ask for it, I might try to force it on you."

Spider smiled a little. "Same."

"You're the only person who never left, Spider."

"And I never will." His smile turned sad. "You know Betsy didn't want to."

"I know. Some things we don't choose."

"And some things we do." He leaned over and kissed her temple. "Love you, Mimi."

"Love you too."

EPILOGUE

Three months later

"HOW IS THERE STILL SNOW on the ground?" Emmie asked, panting. "It's already March. It's seventy degrees at home."

Ox looked up. "But it's not seventy in the mountains, and aren't you glad you get to see the trees with snow on them?"

"I'm a little afraid of that snow falling on us. One branch lets go and we're avalanche victims."

Ox stepped behind her and put his arms over her head. "I'll protect you."

"Whoo!" Jeremy ran up the trail ahead of them, nearly skipping. "Smell those trees!"

Emmie knew he was a climber, but she'd had no idea he was that fast. She turned to see Ethan and Tayla trudging behind them.

"You're doing great," Ethan said. "You've got this."

Tayla glared at them. "I blame you for this, nature boy."

Ox said, "It's okay, Tayla. I know you have to hide your love for me with aggression."

"Get bent!"

"Stop," Emmie said. "As soon as I told you it was an excuse to buy new shoes, you were in. Also, you look fabulous."

"Bet your butt I do." Tayla wasn't breathing all that heavily. She was way more proficient in yoga than Emmie was and had great breath control. She just liked to complain, and she was still a little freaked out by the vastness of the Sierras. Her best friend was a city girl even if she had decided to give Metlin a chance.

Ox put his arms over Emmie's shoulders and hugged her close as Ethan and Tayla walked past. "Was this a horrible mistake?"

He was still working his way back into Tayla's good graces. Spending more time at their apartment and installing shelves in Tayla's room had helped, but the newly dyed brunette still took more than the occasional jab.

"She'll be fine," Emmie said. "She'll do a photo shoot at the top of the hill with two handsome men wearing flannel and sporting facial hair. The likes and comments will assuage her."

"I'll have to trust you on that one."

Ox had social media accounts, but he didn't run any of them; Emmie did. INK: Books had social media streams and INK: Tattoo had separate ones. Ox already had a great following and was starting to sell some of his original sketches online through the website. Every little bit brought in a little bit more. The Main Street store. The online store. Books. Tattoos. T-shirts. Art.

They were making it. Personally *and* professionally.

"Hey, check this out." Ox grabbed her hand and dragged her off the trail, through the deeper snow that still blanketed the brush. "I want to show you something cool." She followed and watched as he seemed to disappear into the trunk of a fire-scarred sequoia.

"Ox?"

He peeked his head out and grinned. "It's hollow."

"Cool!" She ducked under the low entrance and inside the tree. The base had been burned out but the tree had grown past it, forming a large hollow that was still blanketed by damp pine needles.

"Come here." Ox pulled her into his arms and lifted her up for a kiss. Emmie wrapped her legs around his waist and held on while he kissed her silly.

Ox did a lot of things to make her silly. He coupled quiet, sardonic humor with teasing touches and an uncanny ability to read her moods. He'd taken to picking out books for her and hiding them around the house. An erotic romance hidden under her pillow. A Miss Marple mystery hidden in her underwear drawer after he'd teased her about her "granny panties." A book about stress and meditation techniques sticking out of his drawer in her bedroom, which was constantly overflowing and driving her crazy.

And what did she do for Ox? Sometimes Emmie wondered. She brought him a cup of coffee in the morning, and he smiled at her like she was the sun. She wasn't a natural with romantic gestures, but she was slowly figuring out that he loved it when she massaged his head at night, and giving him extra pillows would usually sooth any grumbling. If he was in a bad mood at work, she'd get him tacos, and he looked at her like she was a goddess.

Plus she made out with him in the forest.

Ox lingered at her mouth, tasting and teasing her lips with his own.

"You know," she said. "The first time I remember seeing you, you were standing on Main Street, kissing Ginger."

He hid his face in her shoulder. "Don't remind me."

"And I remember thinking: that man knows how to kiss a woman."

"Mmmm." He took her lips again, drawing out the kiss until Emmie's head was spinning. "I kiss you the best."

Emmie smiled. "I know."

"I everything you the best."

"Everything?"

"Of course. I'm the best me when I'm with you." He put her down and led her out of the hollow tree before he turned, letting Emmie climb on his back. "So everything is the best."

She hugged her arms around his shoulders as he hiked back through the snowy forest. "And I'm my best and happiest me when I'm with you."

"Yeah?" He looked over his shoulder and she kissed his cheek.

"Yeah."

"I guess you better keep me then. We should amend the employee manual."

"What should this rule be called?" Emmie asked. "The no-escape clause?"

"I'm in if you are, Buttons."

Emmie hugged his shoulders and smiled against Ox's shoulder. "I'm in."

THE END

Sign up for my newsletter and receive updates about the next *Love Story on 7th and Main* as well as other works of fiction.

ACKNOWLEDGMENTS

I love my hometown.

If you want to know the inspiration for this book and this series, look no further than the wonderfully diverse and dynamic small towns and cities in Central California.

I've traveled the world more than a bit, but nothing quite matches the vision of a fog-covered valley and rolling green foothills as you're driving down from the cold heights of the Sierra Nevada mountains. Nothing can compare to hundreds of acres of fruit trees flowering in the spring or the bone-dry heat of the long summer months. I've traveled many places, but the San Joaquin Valley will always be home.

I want to thank the many real people who inspired this book, the young entrepreneurs, passionate artists, farmers and ranchers, brewers and chefs, musicians and builders. Thanks for being the heart of this book and the fictional town of Metlin.

It might seem weird to center a romance series around a small-town business district and not a billionaire, but most of us aren't billionaires, and as my dad told me when I was young:

"It's a reality of life that you're going to spend more time at your job than you will at almost anything else. So just make sure you do something you love."

Here's to everyone hustling to pay the bills and finding passion in their work, whatever that might be.

———

To my readers, I hope you're not disappointed that I didn't kill any characters in this one and no one had any special powers. I did include a lot of book humor, so hopefully that will hold you until I can get back to the creatures who regularly bring humanity to the brink of supernatural war. Cheers!

———

Many thanks to those who worked to make this book happen. Jenn and Gen, the super-assistants. Emily at Social Butterfly PR. The passionate and hardworking admins in my reader group. You all are amazing and vital to everything I do. I am blessed by your dedication and professionalism.

Thanks to my wonderful editing team—Heather Monroe, Anne Victory, and Linda, proofreader extraordinaire. Thanks to Damonza, who captured exactly what I wanted for this cover.

A special thanks to wonderful author (and former bookstore owner) Mel Sterling for her beta expertise and hilarious notes.

Thanks to the extraordinary author community in both romance and fantasy who are supportive, encouraging, and more than a little hilarious. Thanks to Colleen Vanderlinden and Kendrai Meeks, Amy Cissell and Cat Bowen, April White, Penny Reid and all those who had to hear me being neurotic about this book for a few months.

Special thanks to my family for their constant and unwavering support. I love you guys. Mom, sorry about all the cussing in this one. Thanks to my friends who stick by me, especially when I'm being super-hermity.

And to David, for being himself.

ABOUT THE AUTHOR

ELIZABETH HUNTER is a *USA Today* and international best-selling author of romance, contemporary fantasy, and paranormal mystery. Based in Central California, she travels extensively to write fantasy fiction exploring world mythologies, history, and the universal bonds of love, friendship, and family. She has published over thirty works of fiction and sold over a million books worldwide. She is the author of Love Stories on 7th and Main, the Elemental Legacy series, the Irin Chronicles, the Cambio Springs Mysteries, and other works of fiction.

ElizabethHunterWrites.com

ALSO BY ELIZABETH HUNTER

The Bronze Blade

The Scarlet Deep

A Very Proper Monster

A Stone-Kissed Sea

The Elemental Legacy

Shadows and Gold

Imitation and Alchemy

Omens and Artifacts

Midnight Labyrinth

Blood Apprentice (Winter 2019)

The Cambio Springs Series

Long Ride Home (short story)

Shifting Dreams

Five Mornings (short story)

Desert Bound

Waking Hearts

CPSIA information can be obtained
at www.ICGtesting.com
Printed in the USA
LVHW041515191118
597647LV00012B/1439/P

9 781941 674284